The Esau Emergence

BOOK ONE of THE ESAU CONTINUUM

by

J. C. Lynne

Ngano Press
PO BOX 524
BERTHOUD CO 80513-0524
www.nganopress.com

Revision 3.4

Trade Paperback:
ISBN-10: 1940421004
ISBN-13: 978-1-940421-00-1

eBook:
ISBN-10: 1940421012
ISBN-13: 978-1-940421-01-8

Cover art by David Aimerito
Edited by Jennifer Top

NGANO
PRESS

PREFACE

Heigh Ho! Thanks so much for reading my book. It's always an honor and a risk when someone takes the time to read one of my novels, both for you and for me! I owe you one. Word of mouth is the key to my writing career and is the best way for me to reach a large audience. Thanks for telling a friend or two (or ten!) how much you loved the story! A word of praise on Amazon or Goodreads is also much appreciated. I'm humbled and beholden to you for the precious time you've spent with my book.

This new edition expands a few scenes and rearranges a few plot elements for, I hope, a more fluid and enjoyable read. I would like to thank Jennifer Top for her keen eye and help with the editing process. I'm sorely belated in thanking Sarah Jo Ahnstedt for her invaluable expertise in working out the science along with her irreplaceable humor and friendship. And I'm thankful daily for the love, support, and creative genius of my cousin and cover artist, David Aimerito.

I invite you to friend me on Facebook so we can chat about the stories and the characters. Follow me on twitter, or check out my website. I look for- ward to hearing from you and about your experience with my writing. I'm filled with gratitude and promise that this is the beginning of a long relationship with you, my reader!

http://jclynne.com
http://twitter.com/jclynnenow
http://facebook.com/jclynnenow

JC Lynne
November, 2015

And the LORD said unto Rebekah: Two nations are in thy womb, and two peoples shall be separated from thy bowels; and the one people shall be stronger than the other people; and the elder shall serve the younger.

And when her days to be delivered were fulfilled, behold, there were twins in her womb.

And the first came forth ruddy, all over like a hairy mantle; and they called his name Esau

— Genesis 23:25

PROLOGUE

He burned. His skin blistered and peeled away from the meat attached to his bones. His flesh melted; each nerve ending shrieked in agony as his throat constricted with thirst and heat. He clawed at his face. A crimson veil fell over his vision. The bones of his body no longer supported his weight; he fell to hands and knees unable to voice his torment. A rumble began deep in his belly, bursting through his throat. Snarling and snapping, he writhed on the ground, his nose flooded with stinging scents.

His teeth felt dagger-sharp against his ravaged and swollen tongue. He panted as his mind blazed with fury. Tissue containing the man he was oozed into the blast. Blind with rage and misery he imagined, with the last snippets of conscience, his soul wafting away. He lashed out with talons raking through the yielding flesh of another. The gaping wound quenched the hot torment where it splashed his skin. Craving deeper relief, he lashed out again. A cry of agony broke through the roar of his pulse. A new ache built in his throat. He coiled his strength and with a gnash of teeth he clamped onto the sweet flesh.

CHAPTER ONE

Afghanistan
2006

Sebastian Cole moved through the hollow shadows of bomb-wounded buildings. He kept clear of the walls where the rebar reached out from the plaster. Batawul hadn't fared any better than Kabul under the Taliban's rule. Bullet holes traced a dark, uneven staccato of injuries to the buildings along the alley. The darkness of the night did little to relieve the heat. Sweat slid along his hairline, continuing the length of his neck, sneaking under the black collar of his t-shirt. His boots sent up puffs of loamy dust that clung to pant legs. He fought the urge to clear his throat of scorching air.

Lieutenant Shaw walked rear guard ten feet behind as they approached their target. Sebastian flipped the cover off of his MTM Black Falcon to check the time, 0200 hours. He kept an eye on the east perimeter of the target for a quick, telltale flash of light indicating the sniper had eliminated the first guard.

Major Jeremy Hawthorne, the commanding officer of their Marine recon unit, would dress them down if they missed their timing. Almost overlooking the short burst of light from high in the blackness, Sebastian used his clicker and received a click from Shaw. *Get focused, Cole!* he admonished, mimicking

Hawthorne's gravel-throated voice. He and Shaw moved together in the dark. Two dancers who, from years of practice, knew their partner's steps.

Creeping along the western edge of the compound, Sebastian watched for any movement. A strand of low-lying olive trees overgrown and cracked in the summer heat provided cover. The cloying smell of dry olive leaves under his boots did nothing to relieve his urge to swallow. He focused on the dark hollow of space in front of him.

Reaching their entry point, Sebastian eased the door open with his foot. Training his weapon into the darkened corridor, he glanced in both directions. He shifted across the gap to take a position on the opposite side of the hall. Using his clicker, he signaled Shaw to advance. The school's ghost haunted the building anchored in the bones of the architecture. The long hallway mirrored the diagram they had studied.

He noted the doors at even intervals marking classrooms. Laughter had vacated the building long ago. The faint hum of a generator murmured from deeper in the building explaining the weak and flickering emergency lights. *Perfect slasher film setting.*

Ignoring a trickle of perspiration threatening the corner of his eye, he kept both hands on his weapon. Sebastian proceeded farther down the hallway toward the main courtyard. He raised his closed fist halting their movement as a guard crossed the opening ahead of them. Securing his M27 over his shoulder, he slipped behind the man. A powerful twist of the head left the guard crumpled on the floor. He motioned to Shaw to continue deeper into the building.

In the partial darkness, Sebastian and Shaw paused at the entry to the courtyard. Sebastian surveyed the space. The heavy steel doors gaped open. Moving catlike through the double doorway, he took point as Shaw moved forward to cover him. They waited for the signal to breach.

He caught a shade of movement across the quad. A whisper of footsteps on gravel traveled across the space. Sebastian looked at Shaw. His partner's closed fist indicated his inability to identify the movement. Silence returned, broken by the occasional sound of the night, a mewling cat, the distant cry of a baby unable to sleep in the heat. *It's never this hot at home. Maybe it's time to get out of this line of work. Nah, what else would I do?*

Sebastian held up two fingers then closed his fist. He waited for Shaw's nod and then moved with care keeping the north wall at his back. The change in vantage didn't reveal the shadow. Designed years ago as a play yard, the courtyard stood empty and black. Sebastian slowed his breath, waiting for Hawthorne's signal over the low-level hum of a refrigeration unit. Impatient, he gestured to Shaw then slithered further along the wall. A stark click echoed from the north side of the space, startling him. Shaw answered with his clicker.

Blinding light filled the courtyard. From another part of the building shots echoed over shouts of men. Explosions from flash grenades rumbled. Blinking his eyes, Sebastian saw Hawthorne and Orozco exposed on the east side of the yard. Standing unsheltered, midway on the north side of the space, Sebastian trained his M27 on two insurgents opposite him. Shaw took shelter behind the decrepit steel fire doors. Their adversaries aimed weapons on each team.

Marines and insurgents stood off amid the sound of scattered gunfire. One of the men had a canister in his left hand while he pointed an AK-47 pistol at Hawthorne with his right.

Shaw called out from his position at the door, "Opak de-par-mi-dzaka ki-xiz-de!" *Put your weapons down.*

The man holding the canister spit on the ground and replied in English. "You and your men will retreat."

Hawthorne answered, “We can’t. You need to put the canister down slowly.”

Sebastian calculated the distance between his position and the Talib holding the container. His suppressor might buy him two or three seconds before they heard a shot. He caught a glimpse of a fist from the second floor above the targets’ heads signaling their snipers had taken position.

Hawthorne, also noting the signal, eased further into the space. “We’ve contained the rest of the building. Let’s keep everyone safe.”

The second insurgent laughed. “You think we’re concerned about our safety. Our fate is in the hands of Allah, not you. We’ll die in glory.”

Sebastian groaned. *Believers.*

Hawthorne lowered his rifle and placed three fingers on top of his weapon. “We want everyone to walk out of here safely. Put the canister down.”

“Safety. Ha! We’ll never be safe until we’ve scoured your kind from our country. Move any further, and we will shoot.” Sweat dripped down the face of the insurgent holding the canister. Sebastian noticed the man’s hands trembling.

“We don’t want trouble.” Hawthorne removed one finger from the top of his weapon.

“Retreat or you’ll die.” The leader aimed at Hawthorne’s heart.

Hawthorne lifted a second finger from his weapon as he crept along the wall toward Sebastian.

The insurgent caught the movement. “Stop!”

Hawthorne removed his last finger. A sniper’s bullet hit the man in the shoulder as the report echoed through the courtyard. Time slowed as Sebastian watched each detail of movement. The shot to the insurgent’s shoulder threw off his aim. He fired his AK-47 into his companion with the canister. One of the bullets passed through his body rupturing the metal with a whoosh. A cloud of particles exploded into the air.

Sebastian heard Hawthorne shouting for them to clear out. Orozco fell to his knees disappearing into the dense cloud and sinking to the ground.

Shaw ran across the courtyard with an epinephrine cocktail in an auto-injector. Catching blurred movement from above him, Sebastian aimed his weapon up. Gellat drooped over the windowsill fighting for air as her weapon tumbled end over end to the ground. Sebastian raced by Shaw, grabbing two gas-fueled syringes. Hawthorne struggled with Orozco though he was breathing. Sebastian bounded up the stairwell. He burst into the room and saw Gellat hanging half in and half out of the window. Sebastian slammed the syringe into her thigh. He slid her down to the floor, left arm outstretched, on her side to ease her breathing. He took a brief glance across the space to see Haager draped over the opposite windowsill. He wasn't moving.

Gellat's pulse was faint, but the color returned to her face.

Sebastian spoke into the mic on his shoulder. "Shaw." There was a squawk of static.

"Yeah." Shaw sounded ragged.

"Gellat's up here. Weak pulse, shallow breath. I think Haager's dead. Is it clear to bring in the medics?"

"They're waiting for the yellow suits to give the okay."

Hawthorne's rumble broke in on the frequency. "Hang tight, Cole. The medics are moving as fast as they can. I'll send some of 'em up to check Haager."

"Yes, sir. The others?"

His pause stretched. "Just hang tight."

CHAPTER TWO

Washington, D.C.
2010

Sebastian Cole had just finished up the preliminary paperwork on the Serano case when his phone rang.

"We have a new lead," rumbled in Sebastian's ear.

"On my way." Sebastian secured his desk and headed for Jeremy Hawthorne's office.

He rapped on the door and received a gruff, "Enter." Director Jeremy Hawthorne spoke few words with little geniality. Sebastian respected him, trusted him, and liked him.

"Boss," Sebastian said, smiling at the irritation on the imposing man's face. Jeremy Hawthorne stood a mere 5'11" to Sebastian's towering 6'4" frame, but he was a block of granite. A variety of nicks and scars decorated his sturdy, bald head. His linebacker neck terminated in a juncture with a set of shoulders that could hold back the entire Redskin offensive line. The man was part of the earth beneath his feet.

Sebastian held a flood of memories in check. Both men shared the haunted look of tragedy. Working together dredged up those ghosts, but their bond made it impossible to work with anyone else. Somewhere deep down they both believed in saving the world.

Without ceremony, Hawthorne handed a file to Sebastian.

Sebastian flipped through the papers and whistled. He raised his eyebrow. “This looks similar.”

“I thought so.” Hawthorne, a stone, stared at Sebastian.

“I’m on it,” Sebastian said, sliding the file under his arm.

Hawthorne began dialing the phone. “Biogenesis Corporation?”

Sebastian’s determined tone matched the director’s. “First connection to the biotoxin we’ve had in four years.”

“You and Shaw head out to verify. I’ll have Gellat pull together dossiers on the players,” Hawthorne said.

“Yessir.” Sebastian nodded, eager to finish the hunt.

**** **Biogenesis Corp, Manhattan** ****

Neil Weber dialed the phone. He paced while he listened to the ring.

“Jesus, Neil,” the groggy voice moaned. “It’s seven. A.M. Don’t you ever sleep?” David Williams asked.

“We have another leak. The NSA contacted me about a biological agent released in Japan,” Neil hissed.

“Goddamn it, you’ve got to get this under control,” David said, sounding more alert. “You’re already at the office, aren’t you? Did you ever leave last night?”

Neil ground his teeth ignoring the question. “Baptiste knows more than he’s saying. I can’t move forward if I don’t have all of the information. Have you found out who brought his firm in to cover the breaches?”

“No, he must have someone by the shorthairs because whoever it is has broad access and is protecting his information. He may be working security, but I don’t think it’s for the company,” David said. “You might consider keeping your head down and letting it go.”

"I need this audit, David. The Slovenia project is moving forward. The FDA is breathing down my neck about the safety of the leukemia trials, and the Board keeps demanding a solution to these leaks." Neil ran a hand through his hair. He heard David sigh.

"Look, Neil, I know you brought me in to help you shore the company up, but I'm wondering if we both shouldn't start looking at other options."

"I didn't leave the Treasury Department to give up the opportunity of a lifetime. We're poised to become the front-runner in cancer research and treatment, not to mention Carlson's stem cell work. Our flu vaccine alone earns millions. I did that." The young CEO chewed his lip. "If the company's profits are undermined by these security breaches, my name won't make the shortlist for the fry cook job at Junior's Diner."

"You sound like your Bubbe. Remember her doom and gloom stories? The one from the Book of Isaiah? 'O Day Star, son of Dawn! How you are cut down to the ground, you who laid the nations low! I will ascend to the tops of the clouds, I will make myself like the Most High. But you are brought down to Sheol, to the depths of the Pit. Those who see you will stare at you, and ponder over you.'"

"You're not helping. I'm not being paranoid." Neil logged in to his computer and pulled up a list. "The flu mutation in China. The biotoxin exposure in Afghanistan."

"The government never linked those to Biogenesis," David reminded him.

Neil felt the throbbing knot at the base of his neck. "This new one was an exact match to a strain we patented for an E. coli trial. A group claiming to be Aleph weaponized it and aerosolized a passenger train. Ten more people are dead."

"Do you think Baptiste knows?" David asked.

Neil's stomach gurgled at the thought. "I don't know. The person who contacted me was adamant we keep it under the radar. Maybe not."

"Then we're golden. You meet with the NSA people and get the inside information on this leak. We finally track down someone and then feed Baptiste to the Board. They'll have to approve our audit. We'll be able to find every last person selling company secrets."

Neil thought a moment, fingers drumming a frantic rhythm on his desk. "You're right. If we handle this well, it strengthens our position."

"Now calm the fuck down and order some breakfast. I'll be in at nine. When is your meeting with the agency?" David asked.

"Tomorrow morning," Neil said, hearing his assistant arrive in the outer office.

He heard rustling on David's end of the line. "Okay, schedule lunch after your meeting. I'll have my staff draw up concrete plans for the audit and we'll go from there."

"I'm supposed to meet with Baptiste today." Neil brought up his calendar.

"Cancel it. And find out where the members of the Board are. We're going to win this one," David said firmly.

"You've always had my back," Neil said.

"Since the second grade and I won't stop now," David assured him.

Neil ended the call and punched a button. "Andre, are you ready to start?"

The crisp voice of his assistant carried through the intercom. "Yes, sir, I'll be right in."

Five minutes later, Andre entered the office with a cup of espresso.

Neil looked up from writing some notes on a legal pad. "Andre, I need to clear my morning schedule. Would you call and inform Mr. Baptiste I'll have to cancel?"

"You also have lunch scheduled with Branimir Cesnik from the Slovenian financial ministry. Would you like me to reschedule that?" Andre asked.

"No, but see if you can get us into Solo and make the arrangements with Cesnik. If the café is open will you order up breakfast?"

Andre set the coffee down so the cup wouldn't be upset by Neil's furious writing. "Yes, sir, the café is serving a lovely egg brioche with a fruit compote. Is there anything else while I'm here?"

"Huh?" Neil looked up at his assistant. "Oh yes, I have a morning meeting added to my schedule tomorrow and I'd like to meet with David Williams for lunch afterward. Will you find us a reservation?" He handed the yellow sticky note to his assistant. "Here's his number. Tell him to bring one of his auditors with him."

Andre nodded. "Sir, when would you like me to reschedule Mr. Baptiste?" His assistant raised an eyebrow with awareness of Neil's aversion to the security director.

Neil tapped his pencil against his chin. "You know? Tell him I'll have to let him know." He chuckled. "Thanks, Andre, and I've told you before—no need to 'sir' me. Please call me Neil."

Andre, eyes hooded, replied, "I'll take care of the arrangements. Neil."

Neil nodded with satisfaction at Andre's retreat and continued outlining his strategy with a quick sip of coffee. He stopped to savor the rich dark roast; it was exactly how he liked it. Andre never missed a beat. He would keep his assistant with him. He needed the best people around him and Andre fit the category. Oblivious to the quiet snip of the door closing and the immediate light on Andre's extension, Neil focused on saving his future with the company.

****

Andre Juricic placed the yellow sticky note on the desk with a cluck of distaste. He opened his agenda scanning for the numbers he needed. In his eloquent accented English, he made the reservations at Solo, spoke to Branimir Cesnik's embassy office. Next, he called Landmark to book tomorrow's lunch. He emailed David Williams's office in Finance with the time and restaurant details.

With all of the arrangements made, he contacted the café and ordered two breakfasts. The egg brioche sounded delightful to him as well. A slight twinge of regret flavored his next phone call. Neil Weber impressed him with a degree of respect with which no other superior had ever treated him. The young man recognized Neil Weber as a man who could go places and who might just make Biogenesis an internationally recognized corporation. It was understandable to feel some misgiving as he listened to the ringing at the other end of his call. Andre appreciated enterprise and loyalty when he saw it, and he saw it in Neil Weber. He'd given his allegiance to someone else, a sad circumstance for Neil.

"Živijo?" he queried into the receiver in his native Slovenian.

A cool and disciplined voice greeted him. "Živijo, Andre, how are you?"

"I'm well, thank you. There's been a change."

"Indeed, tell me?"

"I'm not certain, but I believe we have a problem with Mr. Weber."

"Ah, Mr. Weber. That's a shame. He has such potential."

"Dah, oprostite. I thought so as well."

"You've excellent discernment. I trust your inclinations about our potential difficulties with Mr. Weber. I will take care of it with haste."

"I will email you the particulars."

"Hvaležnost, Andre."

"Ni za kaj, svoj vodnik."

CHAPTER THREE

Washington, D.C.

"I stood at Westlove Gallery for forty minutes!" Deborah's voice rose. "You said you'd meet me at the opening at eight-thirty. It was humiliating." Sebastian watched the ice pick heel of the shoe fly at him. He'd already spent several days going over the agency's dossier on Biogenesis with Hawthorne. His research on biogenetics spread out over the king-sized bed, Deborah's high heel sent papers flying.

Sighing with acceptance of the inevitable, Sebastian said, "Deborah, I've apologized. This is the work. It's—"

She raised her hand up. "Important. I know. I also know that it'll always be more important." She kicked off her other shoe, flinging it into the bed. "I'll never be as important as your job."

Sebastian rubbed his eyes. This was a tired rehash of a conversation he had with every woman he dated. "Deb, you know my job's demanding. I don't keep regular office hours and sometimes I have to change our plans."

"Sometimes?" Her voice climbed another octave. "Sometimes! Try the last five times. At least tonight I wasn't stuck sitting alone at Chez Sere like last time." Her voice shifted to mocking. "Yes, your job's demanding, but Bob Reyes has plenty of time to make plans."

Sebastian's response was chill and low. "Reyes is an idiot. He runs sloppy surveillance, and if he's lucky he's only going to get himself killed one of these days."

Deborah's eyes narrowed. "You've nothing to say about my spending time with Bob except he's an idiot? I can't believe this. You wouldn't notice if I fell off of your balcony right in front of you."

"Oh, I think I'd notice." Sebastian couldn't keep the eye roll under control.

"Bastard!" Sebastian was glad she didn't have another shoe. "You take off whenever you want, disappear without a phone call and leave me stranded at an art opening."

Sebastian's eyes narrowed. "I went to a funeral. You knew that."

"Oh yes, I wonder if you were holding hands with Janice Davidson before her husband died!"

Icy cold radiated as Sebastian stood. "Stop talking now. We're done. I'm working, and I forgot the gallery opening."

Deborah took a step back from this side of Sebastian. Only a brief flash of doubt showed on her face. She pressed on. "You're not a superhero, Sebastian. Nothing you do makes any difference. You're wasting your time and I'm wasting my time with you."

Sebastian turned back to his research. "I'm leaving in the morning. You can clear your things out while I'm gone. I'll have Mr. Moore come in with you and you can leave the key with him."

Deborah stood gaping, fury and humiliation written all over her face.

He gathered up his papers and walked toward the door. "You know what? My bag's ready. I'll stay at a hotel near the airport." Sebastian heard the slightest swish behind him as the alarm clock flew past his ear, shattering against the doorjamb.

Deborah regained her momentum. A Serbian dish he used as a coin drop flew toward his face. He snatched it out of the air only to miss a whiskey glass. It crashed into the wall. *Zero strategic advantages and no good counterplan.* He made a tactical decision. Sebastian ducked his head to retreat.

Sebastian reviewed his notes in the cab on the ride from the apartment to his hotel. His flight from D.C. departed in the morning. After registering at the Washington Dulles Marriott, he checked the airline schedule to see it was departing on time. His cell phone chirped with a text message.

Left the key with your doorman.

He sighed thinking about the mess in the apartment. His apartment manager called him at the hotel to tell him Deborah had been escorted from the building, but unfortunately she'd left a wake. Sebastian mused. *Superhero. I'm comfortable with the idea. I draw the line at tights. No masks either. No matter what they say in the movies, I've never worn a balaclava without feeling claustrophobic.* His cell phone chirped again.

Cape is in the mail. Hope you trip on it.

He sighed. His commitment to his job meant everything else could be put on hold. True heroics had little to do with superpowers and everything to do with making the right choices when you were scared out of your wits. Death didn't frighten him. He settled back onto the hotel bed and thought about the past.

**** **London, 2006** ****

"You could have a common immunity to the pathogen, but it's more likely you're contaminated with the bacteria. Your bodies mutated the cells and adapted them into your own biology." Ian Cole, Sebastian's younger brother, ran tests on the Black Wolves survivors at his clinic in England.

Hawthorne grumbled, "We're mutants?"

Ian shook his head smiling and continued, his British accent stronger than Sebastian's, "If that's the case, we're all mutants. Every person has mutated cells and viruses in their bodies. For example, there are millions of versions of the virus for the common cold. Each time you catch one, you're immune to the particular strain. It doesn't prevent you from catching another version of the rhinovirus or coronavirus going around, but your body developed immunity to the first germ. Bacteria work similarly. Our bodies are full of bacteria and viruses. Some types of bacteria work with our bodies to maintain systems, like the bacteria in our intestinal tract. When the balance is disrupted by illness or medication, we become symptomatic. It's a symbiotic relationship. Viruses can also remain dormant and you might never know they're present. The chickenpox virus is one example. It remains in the body dormant but can later develop into shingles. The problem here is we've no idea what was in the canister."

"We're the lucky ones? Infected with some mystery bacteria that could do nothing or kill us?" Hawthorne said.

"We're not dead yet," Sebastian said.

Ian tapped his chin in thought. "You know, I think I've seen something similar to this resistance in Dad's old files."

Sebastian dug into his own memory. "The immunization trials with MI-6? I thought Dad said those experiments failed to produce any resilience to both pathogenic and non-pathogenic microbes."

"They did fail. Several men died and the rest suffered terrible side effects, but the antibodies remained in their systems. It's why Dad can't donate blood. The antibodies could cause a transfusion reaction severe enough to be fatal," Ian said, moving to his computer. "But a group of geneticists have started to study transgenerational epigenetics seriously. I swear I recently read an article in the *American Journal of Genetics* about the possible inheritance of environmentally acquired markers."

Hawthorne interrupted by raising his hand. "Non-science type here. How about dumbing it down?"

Pacing the floor, Sebastian voiced his thoughts out loud. "It means Ian and I could've inherited the inoculation antibodies from our father and despite the failure of resistance from the microbes tested, we may have developed immunity to other biotoxins."

Ian grew excited. "It would explain the lack of symptoms and I bet if I tested Shaw and you, Major Hawthorne, I would find similar antibodies. Sebastian's medical file indicates he's given blood to both of you."

"Gellat survived. Sebastian's never given her blood," the major pointed out, struggling to grasp the idea.

"Yes, but Sebastian administered the steroid cocktail shortly after her exposure and a couple of the others survived as well. Immunity is a complex concept." He looked up from his computer. "Dad will have to tap his MI-6 contacts to get the unredacted files and I'll put out feelers to some colleagues of mine. I'll run tests on you, Major, and on Thomas and I'm betting a case of Springbank single malt I find common antibodies," Ian said.

"Make it the twelve-year Campbeltown and I'll take that bet," Hawthorne said, sticking out his beefy hand.

CHAPTER FOUR

Manhattan
2010

Sebastian's cab driver laid on the horn and swore at a delivery truck cutting into the lane. *Afghanistan, Bosnia, Somalia. I'd take any of those over driving in Manhattan.* He reviewed the report on trace evidence of the pathogen used on the passenger train in Tokyo. The Japanese government recognized the dangers of biological weapons at once and requested any help the Americans could offer. It's no wonder this drew Hawthorne's attention at the NSA. Hawthorne's anxiety over finding an antidote or some counter to their exposure equaled Sebastian's.

Ian briefed all of them, including Thomas, before the trip to Manhattan.

Sebastian shook his head at his brother. "The sample of the bacteria isn't an exact match."

Ian reassured him. "No, but there's enough basic genetic structure in common to warrant another look at Biogenesis. Their genetic manipulation of diseases is our best lead. Even if they aren't the source, someone there should have insight as to who does this kind of work."

Sebastian, with his background in molecular biology, understood what Ian proposed. Understanding and accepting were two different things. All of the survivors struggled with the death of their comrades.

Jeffery Davidson survived the first encounter only to develop a disease linked with immune deficiency. The memorial plagued the remaining Black Wolves with thoughts of their own contamination. Their questionable future, as well as the loss of close comrades, fueled Ian's passion for his research institute. Sebastian focused on finding the source. Discovering some link to the creator of these mutated pathogens would be the first step to ensuring the survivors would live.

It's the tired debate over the boundaries of science. Sebastian ducked his head, stepping out of the cab onto the curb. The far-reaching consequences of altering things at the molecular level without true understanding were a game of chance. He paid the driver, musing on the philosophical struggle.

Sebastian stepped into the hotel with his satchel and laptop. He observed the people moving in and out of the lobby cocooned in the safety they perceived to be impenetrable. Sebastian knew scientists more concerned with the possibilities. He set his bag down on the counter to check in. The ends justified the means. That cliché peppered so many conversations both with his scientific colleagues and in his military dealings.

He worried his comrades' lives were lost in vain. Sebastian feared he and his friends were inconsequential to the larger rhetoric of Democracy, Freedom, and Security. He couldn't stomach the idea of acceptable loss. Signing the registration paperwork, he gave one final thought to Deborah's accusation. *Cape or no cape, Superman didn't believe in collateral damage.*

After a quiet night, Sebastian arrived in front of the Biogenesis Corporation Building at 8:00 a.m. Sebastian didn't meet with Neil Weber until 8:30. He arrived early to reconnoiter the building. Observing his surroundings beforehand had always been a sound and often life-saving practice. He took care to choose his attire to avoid government stereotypes. Epitomizing the slick Manhattan corporate animal, he grabbed a coffee from a street cart.

Over his *New York Times*, the corporate juggernaut staggered into motion. People went into the Biogenesis building while Sebastian filed bits of information away for later.

The woman seems a bit harried.

That gentleman's arguing on the phone.

The gentleman's worried he's late.

He would go over employee files later with Shaw, putting thoughts to people's faces and names. They would double-check the list for anyone with the opportunity to access the biochemical labs. The hunt would begin.

Gellat had sifted through the minutiae of these people's lives. Her report waited for him at the hotel. Sebastian would comb through the details in the hope of discovering a potential suspect.

Recognizing Neil Weber from his file, Sebastian watched the man exit a black Mercedes with his Gucci briefcase in one hand, coffee in the other, and a *New York Times* folded under his arm. Sebastian noted how he strode into the atrium. This positive, jovial man didn't match the nervous and disillusioned voice from their earlier phone conversation. Something transpired in the last seventy-two hours to render change in the man.

Looking at his watch, Sebastian pushed back the memory of the chaotic night in Afghanistan. Shaking himself free of the echoes of gunshots, he rose from his perch. Most people didn't wear watches anymore. Cell phones and PDAs kept the time for them. He rubbed the watch, reminded of people he'd lost. A sleek gray Audi S8 sedan slowed and parked in front of the building. Sebastian moved behind a water feature taking shelter from a direct line of sight. The driver exited and came around to open the rear passenger door. A polished black sling back emerged from the car and stepped gingerly onto the concrete. It was attached to a slim and well-shaped leg that supported the slender, diminutive frame of a woman in her forties. A black wool crepe suit hugged her slight, lithe figure.

This woman, Deborah would have commented, compensated for her lack of physical beauty. The tailored clothes, the elegant style, and the fit physique all distracted from indistinct features. This icy blonde was Dr. Vivienne Carlson. She preferred to stay out of the scientific limelight. Her contemporary, Junying Yu, made a name for herself in the field of cellular reprogramming as an alternative to embryonic stem cells. Dr. Carlson devoted her time without fanfare to subculturing embryonic stem cells. Both women were on the crest of the fastest growing and most controversial scientific research since the early beginnings of the field. In a profession dependent on big publicity, her reticence troubled him.

Sebastian thought she'd be the best source of information about the pathogen. Part of her research involved genetically altering the DNA of viruses and other chemical pathogens. The dossier on Carlson mentioned her involvement in Biogenesis' recent bid for human trials on an immunization for the most common form of childhood leukemia.

After contact with the altered pathogen, Davidson contracted leukemia.

Sebastian walked to the other side of the fountain. Dr. Carlson waited on the curb while her driver, a man who appeared to be in his early fifties, reached into the car and retrieved her briefcase. The driver tipped his hat. The scientist took a cool sweeping glance around the courtyard of the building. She scanned for an ambush. Sebastian had seen the same look on Hawthorne's face right before penetration. *Battle readiness.*

Carlson dipped her head in a pleasant greeting to the doorman, who treated her with deference. She carried herself with a singular, polished grace. He understood her notice flattered the doorman and her driver. Her carriage radiated regal bearing and gestures reminded him of a benevolent monarch bestowing blessings on her loyal subjects.

Sweeping past security, she entered the bank of elevators beyond the desk. The guards beeped her through with an efficient dignity she returned with another one of those icy little nods. Sebastian hung back as the other crowding bodies parted, allowing Dr. Carlson unfettered access to the next available car.

No one joined her on the ride up, and it wasn't until the doors slid shut that the noise and bustle of the lobby returned to a much higher pitch. Using his physicality and body language to manipulate people's impressions improved his chances of finding information. He recognized the self-possession and confidence Vivienne Carlson exuded from that 5'1" frame. *I won't underestimate her.*

Sebastian approached the security desk placing a bright smile on his face.

A stern-looking, close-cut security guard with a pugilist's nose blustered, "Can I help you, sir?"

"I have an appointment with Neil Weber at eight-thirty." Sebastian suppressed his Oxford accent. People would notice an Englishman in New York.

"I need your name and your identification, please," the guard said.

Sebastian gave a smile as he handed over his identification. "Robert Miller."

The guard handed him back his credentials. "Mr. Weber's expecting you. Take car number three to the eighty-fifth floor."

"Thank you. Have a nice day."

****

Neil Weber met the NSA agent at the door to his office. "Mr. Miller." He offered his hand. "I'm Neil Weber."

The towering man shook his hand. "Robert Miller. I'm pleased to meet you."

Motioning toward Andre, Neil asked, “Could we offer you something?”

“I’d appreciate some coffee,” Sebastian said.

Andre nodded. “I’ll order it up. Some for you as well, Mr. Weber?”

Neil shot a reproving glance at his assistant. “Yes, thank you.”

Closing his door, Neil gestured to a large wingback chair. “Please sit, Mr. Miller. I have to say hearing from you has me frustrated.”

“I understand. My supervisor told me you would keep our visit here confidential.”

“Yes, as he stipulated you’re Robert Miller with Control Robotics. You specialize in biomechanical applications for prosthetic limbs. We’re at the end stages of the acquisition of the company. It would be appropriate for you to come see what to expect in the way of merging departments. I’ve had Andre arrange a brief meeting with Dr. Carlson. She’s our leading researcher in biogenetic engineering.” Neil Weber scanned the file on the Aleph attack. “She’s also arranged a more in-depth tour of her labs for you tomorrow.”

A discreet knock announced Andre leading a cart pushed by a young-faced woman. “Your coffee, Mr. Web—Neil.

“Thank you, Andre.” He turned to Sebastian. “How would you like it?”

“Light cream and one sugar, please,” Sebastian said.

Andre quietly directed the coffee preparation and delivered the mugs.

Sebastian took his cup. “Thank you.”

Andre tipped his head and shooed the woman out of the room, leaving the cart.

“Now, where were we?” Neil asked.

Sebastian said, “The Aleph attack.”

Neil cleared his throat. “A complete in-house audit is necessary. Records, staff, security. I could get a team together to comb over every department. I can find where these things are coming from. I'm not confident the security here is effective. I'd like to see change. This new case will allow me to do that."

"We want to see results in this investigation as well. You can understand our concerns about bioterrorism," Sebastian said.

"My concerns mirror yours. In addition, thinking our technology has been used as a weapon makes me sick." Neil assured him. "I've discussed your visit with Dr. Carlson under the auspice of merging some of her stem cell research to the biomechanics in prosthetic limbs. It's my understanding from your supervisor you've done research on the topic," Neil said.

"I'd appreciate whatever time she's able to fit into her schedule." Sebastian smiled.

"Organics often reject the mechanical components. Dr. Carlson works with similar types of rejection in DNA manipulation. Chimeras contain the complete genetic structure of different donors. The genetics can be inherited and she has fine-tuned her process of transfusion. She's using this to perfect the nuclear transfer process hopefully allowing us to clone embryonic stem cells.

"Dr. Carlson's use of genetically modified bacteria and viruses as delivery systems is what brought me to you. She'll have the knowledge to help us trace the source of the pathogen released in Tokyo," the tall man explained.

Neil nodded. "DNA transfer is a crucial step in our attempt to render successful acceptance of biotech implants. It also helps with immunization testing. Some animals share a common biology with humans, and if we can narrow down the genetic differences, we can produce formulas safe for human trial. That's a critical factor in FDA approval. We are close to what may be a formula to prevent the mutation of white blood cells in the bone marrow. Can you imagine a world without the fastest growing childhood disease?" He stood up. "I'll take you to Dr. Carlson's office. I have to warn you, she's a bit reserved."

Sebastian rose. "I understand. I won't take it personally. I'm looking forward to seeing the nuts and bolts of Dr. Carlson's research."

Neil smiled. "I have lunch scheduled tomorrow with David Williams, one of our accountants. We're planning our audit. I'd love for you to join us and perhaps you can help us tighten up our strategy."

"Thank you. I'd be happy to offer you some tips on how to focus your efforts. If the government knows anything, it's audits." Sebastian grinned.

Neil held the door for him and chuckled. "Yes, I know too well."

The two men stepped into the waiting elevator car, and Neil gestured a good-bye to Andre as the doors slid shut.

****

After the elevator doors closed, Andre pulled a cell phone out of his leather satchel and hit speed dial. "They're on their way."

"Hvala Andre. Opinion?"

Andre thought about the imposing visitor who charmed Neil Weber. "Whoever he is, he's certainly made Weber happy."

"Noted. Let's keep on our toes, shall we?"

"Dah, Mr. Weber has lunch with David Williams tomorrow after the tour. Weber's very excited about the meeting. Any close look at finances and an anomaly could be discovered."

"Very well. I'll take care of it on this end. Do slej."

CHAPTER FIVE

"I can't tell you how much your involvement in our internal investigation will help," Neil said.

In Sebastian's estimation, the CEO seemed honest in his desire to find the corporate leaks. He said, "It must be difficult to know whom to trust."

The elevator opened up to an organized laboratory space taking up the entire floor. A bank of offices with frosted glass doors and walls sat to the right of the elevator, allowing the light without losing privacy. The lab spread out across the floor of the building with widely spaced aisles allowing unhindered movement from one area to another. The space was divided into stations outfitted with individual refrigeration units, stainless steel countertops, and state-of-the-art electronics. Vivienne Carlson's hand shone in every detail. Sleek, high-tech efficiency met with ergonomic flow and greeted visitors with bright, sunny light. For a genetic laboratory, any hints of Frankenstein's dank lab didn't exist.

Researchers and technicians moved about with purpose. Animals were located in small pods or islands spaced around the lab. Sebastian deduced they were placed depending on the research. Animal rights activists would be hard-pressed to convince the average person there was animal cruelty taking place in this lab. The spacious Lucite cages looked cleaned and freshly bedded. Each animal had a companion. He guessed the researchers wanted their subjects both physically and emotionally healthy.

Dr. Carlson stepped out of her office. Her crisp, white lab coat complimented the black Manolos. She approached them, a keen look of interest on her face. "Neil," she said, her tone reproachful, her hand extended. "To what do I owe this honor?"

Neil fidgeted, looking torn between feeling pleasure at her notice and being nervous about incurring her wrath. "Vivienne, I'm glad you could make time today to meet us. This is Robert Miller from Control Robotics."

Vivienne craned her neck to take in Sebastian's height. Sebastian stood under her keen gaze. To his amusement, she didn't hide her frank appraisal. Her regency impressed him.

"Mr. Miller." A statement of acknowledgement rather than greeting.

"Dr. Carlson. Thank you for taking the time," Sebastian said.

Neil withdrew to the elevator. "Vivienne, will I hear from you later?"

Sebastian watched her dismiss Neil with a distant glance. "If I have time." She turned back with a predatory gleam.

"You're a scientist?" she asked, head tilted.

Sebastian avoided lying outright. "I dabbled in college. Currently, it isn't my primary focus."

"You're not ignorant of the work," she stated with a hint of condescension.

Sebastian couldn't help a low chuckle. "No."

She waved her arm across her fiefdom. "Well then, Mr. Miller, shall we?"

Vivienne's perfunctory explanations illuminated her work and fascinated Sebastian. He interjected with questions when he deemed it appropriate or found it necessary. Sebastian remembered being lectured by his brother Ian, though he had earned his own degrees in chemistry and molecular biology. Ian's strength in biogenetics spurred good-natured competition, and he never missed an opportunity to inspire feelings of numb confusion.

Sebastian spent time brushing up on genetic engineering over the last couple of weeks. Between his theoretical knowledge and what he put together from Vivienne's tour, he didn't stumble with the research. The surprise evident on her face, Sebastian suspected she didn't often come across the surprising. During their movement around her lab, her interactions with her staff and her apparent affection for the creatures she genetically engineered impressed him.

"I realize we scheduled a short visit, Mr. Miller, but I'd like to continue our conversation. Would you join me for lunch?" she asked.

Sebastian didn't have a schedule. Shaw arrived from Washington later in the evening. Vivienne's work with viral vectors and recombinant DNA fascinated him. Something else pricked the back of Sebastian's thoughts, but each time he reached, it skittered out of his grasp. Lunch might provide information to help clarify his thinking.

"I'd enjoy that," Sebastian replied.

"I could have my assistant order from the company's café. There's a good chef on staff."

"Whatever is most convenient," he said.

"Good." Vivienne waved down an assistant. "Have the chef prepare my usual order and bring it up, please." The young woman glanced shyly at Sebastian as she passed him. He offered her an appealing smile and appreciated her blush.

"You realize she may forget her errand?" Vivienne smirked.

Sebastian chuckled, mock chagrin on his face. "I'm quite sure, Dr. Carlson, I don't have any idea what you're talking about."

Vivienne led him into her office with a puff of feigned exasperation and offered him an easy chair. "Would you like something to drink while we wait?"

The space he thought to be one office was two combined. One side contained her desk while the adjoining space, where they sat, was a casual boardroom. A clutch of chairs surrounded a white board with a pull-down screen allowing for brainstorming and collaborative computer work. As sterile and spare as her laboratory, the space utilized bright, clean lines.

"Thank you, no. I'm more interested in clarifying some questions I have about your research," he said.

"Of course." Vivienne settled in a chair to his right.

"Your focus on nuclear transfer to create human embryonic stem cells—why not use the pluripotent cells Junying Yu uses?" he asked.

Vivienne sighed. "There's no discounting the advances Junying is making. The induced pluripotent cells they create from adult shed cells can be specialized for tissue regeneration, but the struggle is to prove consistent results. The research must continue from both directions in order to gain any concrete application. My research also focuses on using inert viruses to carry engineered genome sequences. This would allow for more dramatic tissue regeneration. I believe the embryonic stem cells will allow for more effective tissue growth." The energy in her voice contrasted with the cool and reserved air she'd shown.

"I've read some scientists have made advances in nuclear transfer," he said.

She waved her hand in the air. "We can replicate the embryonic stem cells in several different species, but we can't seem to decipher the process in human cells. Part of the difficulty in the research is the limited availability of embryos. We need to have a supply of embryos to work with in order to perfect the process of generating more stem cells from one source. Of course, there's opposition, in addition to concerns about degrading the cells."

"As I understand it, you could harvest a large number of stem cells from just one embryo if you could use the transfer. Wouldn't you only need a limited number of embryos in that case?" Sebastian asked.

"But then you have the cloning argument. Many people are proposing the idea human dignity is inherent to each and every embryo, cloned or not. In my opinion, if even the Hasidics can't theologically argue against cloning, how can anyone else? Of course, the argument's moot at this point because the president has cut off our embryo supply source and prevented any serious research from taking place by vetoing the Stem Cell Research Enhancement Act. As I mentioned, with any cell replication, there's the possibility of error in the sequence during the replication. It happens in living creatures all of the time. Take cancer for instance: it's just a matter of a glitch in the cell replication; something in the DNA strand is interpreted incorrectly and suddenly your body is producing deadly cells."

"I know there are embryos in cryogenic storage left from fertility clinics." Sebastian couldn't remember the numbers. "Is there a way for you to access those embryos?"

Vivienne walked over to her computer and entered a few strokes. "There are over 400,000 embryos in frozen storage in the United States alone. Infertile couples typically inseminate up to twelve eggs because success rates are unpredictable. For every woman who delivers one or two of those embryos to term, there can be up to eight embryos left."

"What happens to those embryos?" Sebastian asked.

Vivienne gestured toward the large flat screen on the wall across the room. She clicked a few more keys. The screen lit up with a website. "Welcome to Snowflake," she snorted, "the embryo adoption site that's being awarded the research funds we're being denied. They specialize in matching infertile couples with frozen embryos."

Sebastian tapped his fingers together. "Isn't that a good thing?"

"Oh, Mr. Miller!" Vivienne laughed. "On paper, I'm sure it seems like a noble enterprise. In almost ten years of adoptive services, they have completed only one hundred adoptions. There are no statistical reports of those embryos carried to term, though I doubt the number is high."

"Why?"

"Infertility doctors inseminate twelve or more eggs in the hopes of ending up with four to six viable candidates for implantation. That means the other eight or so eggs are not the healthiest embryos in the first place." She paused. "Cryogenic storage can be damaging, so embryos stored for any length of time will begin to degenerate on their own. Not to mention their low adoption numbers in the first place, infertile couples who don't adopt typically prefer their own genetic line. We can't find homes for all of the unwanted children delivered to term, let alone cast-off embryos."

"Encourage couples to donate their embryos to science?" Sebastian suggested.

Vivienne gave a short bark of derision. "The ban on embryonic stem cell research prevents couples from donating their embryos, but they can opt to have them destroyed. It's illogical, but that's the mind-set of the current administration. Never mind we might be able to find the technology to grow internal organs or limbs for amputee patients. Oops, that would put you out of business."

Sebastian smiled. "I'd find another line of work if I could see a soldier walk on his own leg rather than one of our titanium prosthetics. Take a pill and grow a kidney, huh?"

Vivienne smiled at the *Star Trek* reference. "Yes, it might not be that simple, but imagine growing a new spinal cord for paraplegics or finding a safe way to splice out Down syndrome in vitro? We can eliminate flaws in the species preventing basic diseases."

"You can make those changes? You'd have to trigger a mutation, wouldn't you?"

"Mr. Miller, mutation of cells happens all of the time. Not just in the case with cancer. You're sitting here replacing cells as we speak. If I could perfect the genome sequence, I could deliver the sequence into a developing fetus so those inherent weaknesses would be removed from the cellular process. We could, for lack of a better word, immunize in utero so a baby would be born with an immune system a hundred times more effective. Think of it: you sneeze, you had a cold. Rather than spending days in bed a victim of some new flu virus, you could have a low-grade fever for a day or two and then be done."

"You're skirting close to made-to-order human beings. Want some fries with that baby?"

Vivienne rolled her eyes and quoted, "And that after this is accomplished, and the brave new world begins when all men are paid for existing and no man must pay for his sins."

Sebastian recognized it. "Rudyard Kipling a la Huxley. Talk about my lack of creativity. You're confident our complacency and self-indulgence won't win out? Who will regulate all of this altruistic correction of birth defects and organ replacement? The government? The FDA? You?"

"That, Mr. Miller, is the billion-dollar question."

A knock on the door announced the arrival of their lunch.

CHAPTER SIX

Manhattan
Sebastian's Hotel Suite

Thomas Shaw arrived at the hotel around eleven p.m. and dove into Sebastian's notes with enthusiasm.

"There's some pretty intriguing stuff here." Thomas raised his shaggy golden head from the files. "Carlson's manipulation of DNA strands in bacteria means she or someone in her lab could've modified the Afghanistan pathogen."

"Right?" Sebastian agreed. "She's used multiple strands of DNA introduced via infectious vectors to genetically engineer her chimeras. Ian will have to confirm, but I think her expertise moves her to the top of our suspect list."

"We finally have a concrete lead after chasing ghosts and shadows." Thomas took his steaming cup of tea from the desk. "I'll spend some time on the phone and computer shoring up information. I can scan these files and send them to Ian. Lorena can help me cross-reference Carlson's personnel lists to research dates. See if any match up between those dates and the different exposure events."

Sebastian leaned back in his chair and nodded. "I'll come back here after lunch. Helping Weber prove the link between Carlson's lab and his tech leaks will help him move forward with the audit. Weber might provide a direct link between our exposure and Biogenesis Corporation."

"We have a plan," Thomas said.

"Finally," Sebastian agreed.

****

Sebastian arrived for his second tour of Carlson's lab. The grand dame pleaded too much work to escort him personally, so he spent two hours talking to Carlson's team. He focused on the work involving the use of viruses and bacteria as a delivery vector for new genome sequences. *Ian would be drooling.*

At the end of the morning's tour, Vivienne appeared from her office to accompany Sebastian to the elevator. She hesitated for a moment. "Mr. Miller … Robert, I spent several years working with the Human Genome project mapping out DNA. I'm interested in samples of DNA that may offer insight into the causes of diseases. Healthy samples help me map out how people use their immune systems. I think you'd make a fine specimen for my research."

The question blindsided him. He stood awkwardly silent, thoughts swirling. The antibodies present in his blood would be evident. There was no telling if they contained specific genetic markers familiar to the person who constructed the pathogen. Carlson, while brilliant, remained high on their list of suspects. If she were the source of the pathogen, she'd recognize it in his blood, exposing their investigation. The NSA would have to vet any geneticist before he could risk exposing his identity with DNA samples. Record of his DNA had been wiped from the system because the world believed the entire Black Wolves unit dead.

"Dr. Carlson, I recognize the compliment, but understand I'd have to think about it at length."

Sebastian noticed her stiffen and doubted refusal was common for her. She acknowledged his initial refusal with a slight incline of her head. "Don't think I'll let this go. You'll be hearing from me again."

The doors opened to the lobby and Sebastian spotted Neil Weber standing near the security desk. He offered his hand to Vivienne in parting. "It was fascinating, Dr. Carlson. Thank you."

Taking his hand in a forceful grip, looking him directly in the eye with her expression declaring their business wasn't over, she said, "Likewise, Mr. Miller."

****

Sebastian mused on her DNA request as he crossed the atrium to meet Neil.

"How did it go?" Neil asked.

"It was informative," he answered.

The two men stepped out into the bustling Manhattan lunch hour. His DNA, Ian assured him, absorbed the pathogen as it would any virus and developed antibodies with possible danger to others. Like his father, Sebastian couldn't donate blood to anyone but Hawthorne and Thomas.

His brother's work focused on distinctions at the molecular level, but with Carlson's unique expertise, she might see something new. He imagined the collaborative power between Carlson and Ian.

"We're headed to Landmark. It's over there opposite our building." Neil pointed.

Thoughts swirled around Sebastian's head. He nodded, distracted by possibility. Traffic bustled with the downtown lunch crowd. Vaguely aware of the press of bodies around him, the idea of harnessing one of the most brilliant scientific minds in the United States to his own brother's work wormed around in his brain. Their collaboration could create a cure.

The traffic light turned red. Aggressive Manhattan pedestrians surged out across the intersection. Sebastian followed Neil at the tail end of the group. The light turned green. Sebastian, intrigued by Carlson's help with their situation, trailed Weber into traffic. Cars honked. Drivers shouted.

An engine gunned with a growl and tires squealed, gaining momentum on the pavement. A white-paneled van accelerated. Sebastian's shoulder rebounded with the unforgiving impact of the front grill. His head snapped down as he flew sideways, making agonizing contact with the tarmac. He lay stunned trying to focus on the screams and shouts around him. His vision blurred, but he struggled to scan the scene. A short distance to his right, Neil Weber sprawled motionless, his neck at an awkward angle. Pain surged in his head as blackness tunneled his vision.

****

A soft, rhythmic beep persisted in the thick fog of Sebastian's awareness. Murkiness pressed upon him and prevented him from opening his eyes. *Medicated.* Feeling only a little pain, he remembered the squeal of tires and the strike of the vehicle hurtling him through the air. His thoughts floated through a black cloud. *A concussion at least, probably a hematoma. Ian would be proud I remembered a bit of medical terminology.* Sebastian knew more than a bit. *I can put a knife into a man's body forty different ways with fatal results.*

Heaviness pressed upon his chest making it difficult to breathe. He couldn't reach deeper into the chasm cleaving his thoughts. *This is your brain; this is your brain on drugs.* The rhythmic beep kept him floating in miasmic limbo rather than letting him sink into full unconsciousness. Through the haze,

Sebastian became aware of the presence of another person. He tried to speak, to raise his hand. *Nothing*. Everything felt heavy.

"Is he stable?" A familiar and measured voice floated to him through the fog.

"Yes, we've taped his rib and splinted his arm. No cast as you requested. I don't believe we'll have to evacuate the hematoma. It's dispersing without treatment. Overall he's in pretty good shape for someone run down by a truck."

Sebastian put meaning to the words despite the drugs in his system. *I'll be fine. That's a relief.* It wouldn't take Hawthorne long to get the flag on an injured Robert Miller. They wouldn't quit looking for him. If he could wiggle a finger, he might be able to pull himself out of this floating pool. *Nope, no finger wiggling.*

The cool voice poured through the darkness like water. "Watch his sedation, Rihard; I don't want anything to go wrong at this point. It'll take a few days to stabilize his injuries so we can move forward with the procedure. His blood work is perfect." Sebastian heard a hungry edge in her voice.

What procedure? Ian would be furious. Sebastian wished he could tell them to wait; his blood wasn't perfect. His brother would be on his way as soon as Hawthorne found out Sebastian was injured. He needed them to let up on this medication so he could think.

"We don't want to get ahead of ourselves. We've had other strong candidates. Let's get him healed up." Another cautious voice made it clear he would need to tread lightly.

"I'm telling you this is it. Two days, Benko. I'm giving you two days. He'll be stabilized; and we'll proceed. Reduce the sedation and make certain the restraints are placed. It wouldn't do to get lazy, and I don't want him damaged any further." Icy disapproval hung in the room as footsteps retreated.

Sebastian disliked drugs. *Something's not right.* He couldn't wrap his mind around it doused in painkillers. Sebastian tried to fight the weight of the narcotics.

"He could be the one or not. I wouldn't want to be him, whoever he is," the voice named Benko said.

"She doesn't like to be disappointed, but there's no sense in rushing things. I'll turn down the drip. Don't think it's a good idea," the voice named Rihard said.

Relief filled Sebastian. A lower IV drip meant less medication. *I can clear my mind and let these people know who I am.* A quick phone call to Thomas would do it. *Is my cell phone with me or in the street, a pile of broken components?* Thomas wouldn't be able to get a GPS location without his phone. Something tugged at his thoughts, but he couldn't remember. Something important. Directing his focus along his body, he tried to take stock. A broken arm and some ribs he could handle. The drugs would work their way out of his system and things would be fine. Behind schedule, but he could pick up the pace. *Biogenesis Corporation.*

"Course, he may not want the meds turned down. Not with what he has coming. He may be a perfect specimen, but the odds don't increase," the weak Benko said.

"I am laying five-to-one odds against successful insertion, old chap. Nothing personal. No one has survived. This one won't either," Rihard said cooly.

Sebastian lay there as his brain struggled against the drugs to comprehend. *Not in a hospital. A deliberate trap.* Neither Thomas Shaw nor Jeremy Hawthorne knew where he was. Help wouldn't come right away. Thomas would have to do some recon, and with Weber dead his contacts at Biogenesis would have no idea where to look. The drugs would wear off in a few hours, depending on dosage. *Two days.* Sebastian railed as the drugs came sweeping over him in a warm and seductive wave. He needed to stay awake. Thoughts slowed as the fog grew thicker until it wrapped itself around his consciousness, pulling him down into the dark depths of sleep.

"One last dose to make certain you get a good night's rest, then it'll be rise and shine, my lad." Sebastian sensed rather than felt Benko pat his hand.

****

Sebastian struggled through the grainy sludge of his consciousness. With no sense of time or direction, he wrestled with awareness. Something tugged on the edge of his obsidian prison. His eyes glued shut and useless, he could almost see a brightness glowing on the horizon of his mind's eye, faint at first, then a glimmer. With growing apprehension, Sebastian felt the jet of flame flow down his spinal chord and radiate in bright, scorching licks through his veins. Time and pain blended together beyond his counting. Sebastian floated on a sea of fire. His eyes flew open against the brief, icy kiss of morphine and he screamed, but made no sound.

Two men in lab coats stood with heads together studying the monitors. Electric nodes placed at various locations along his body transmitted information into the computers. A younger man in a white lab coat swabbed the sutures at the base of Sebastian's neck with an antibiotic solution.

"Look at the tissue regeneration." Benko's voice now had a face. The short man gestured with enthusiasm. "The virus is replicating at an even rate. He should be developing the correct antibodies allowing for normal mutation into inert cells."

The other man, Rihard, scanned the bank of monitors. "I'm worried about his temperature. He's getting close to one hundred and four. I'm not sure his cortex could survive any higher without damage, no matter what the cellular regeneration looks like. The goal is to keep his mind intact."

Benko gestured to a lab assistant near his office. "Bring a cooling blanket. Let's see if we can manage his temperature without interfering with the chemical process. I'm uncomfortable with the use of the morphine, though it appears to be burning off in the regeneration process."

The two men disappeared into one of the offices bordering one side of the laboratory leaving Sebastian to his torment.

CHAPTER SEVEN

Benko took out a handkerchief and mopped his sweaty brow.

Rihard glared at him. “Get ahold of yourself. She’ll hear the slightest hesitation.”

Benko cleared his throat and pocketed the handkerchief. “You realize our danger. That isn’t some homeless indigent we picked up. He’s a corporate officer. We snatched him off of the street in front of witnesses. They’re looking for him. It’s made the papers.”

Rihard sneered. “Baptiste is good at what he does. The trail won’t lead here. It’s been two weeks; if they haven’t figured it out by now it’s unlikely they will. We had to use this candidate. Do you want to risk a minor investigation or would you rather face her?”

Benko winced, the sweat dripping down his back. “No, you’re right. This does seem to be working. Go ahead, make a call.”

Rihard hit the speed dial and pressed the speaker button. Both men stood in silence listening to it ring.

“Gentlemen,” a smooth voice crooned out into the office. “I hope you’re calling with good results.”

Before Henrik Benko could open his mouth, an explosion jarred the building from an upper level.

“What’s going on?” the voice on the other end demanded, then the line went dead.

Benko pulled a .38-caliber revolver out of his drawer before both men rushed into the lab. The lab filled with smoke, and several people hurried out the rear emergency exit. Rihard rushed to the computer monitors to check on the state of the mutation sequence. He signaled to Benko with a shake of his head. The explosion upstairs disrupted power. The scientist pulled together as many papers as he could and made his way to the rear exit. He hoped enough information made it to the remote server.

Benko took position near the door to the laboratory. He grasped the small revolver in his shaking, sweaty hands and crouched behind the steel fire doors. A powerful crack sent the doors flying open, slamming one of them into Benko, knocking him flat. Four armed, uniformed commandos strode into the room, each one outfitted in deep navy blue from head to toe: rip-stop cargo pants belted with utility webbing that carried extra clips of ammunition, a knife, and weighty Maglite flashlights. Smooth, tight-fitted, long-sleeve shirts highlighted the strong, muscled arms of trained fighters. They led their confident entrance with Heckler and Koch UMPs strapped onto their arms. Each one topped their uniform with a lightweight Kevlar vest.

After a cursory scan of the laboratory, one of them rushed to Sebastian and pulled off his cap to examine the incision at the base of Sebastian's neck. He gestured to another of his compatriots. A figure slighter than the rest approached the equipment. Side strapping the submachine pistol, the smaller soldier removed cap and gloves. She inspected the hard drives.

He asked, "Well?"

She shrugged. "Our flash grenade knocked their systems offline. He doesn't need life support. I think I can jump this terminal so I can transfer files."

The man gave a sigh of relief. A bull figure of a man came striding into the lab as the two other commandos divided their positions to take the front and rear guard.

"Ian's on his way down with a medical team," the mountain growled. "We picked up a few of the stragglers, but I think most of the big fish managed to slip out."

"Lorena's going to download files. That'll help Ian figure out what happened here. Good thing someone neglected to check his cell phone." The first man shrugged at their enemies' oversight.

A third man rushed through the gaping doors leading a small medical team with a gurney. He gazed around at the laboratory through the residual smoke. Without a word, he examined Sebastian.

"We'll have to leave him in this contraption until I get him to my clinic. I need to get a CAT scan and an MRI before I can determine anything. His fever's too high. They tried a cooling blanket." He gestured to the water-cooled blanket that slipped to the floor. He turned to his team. "We'll continue that treatment. I don't want to administer anything without a complete blood panel." He looked around at the various cages and files. "We'll need this entire laboratory transferred. It'll take us a while to piece together what's going on here."

The mop-headed man looked at Sebastian. "Can you keep him stable?"

The man examining Sebastian responded grimly, "I'll have to."

Through the sinking layer of smoke, Henrik Benko thought frantically. Blood dripped from his temple where the door met his head. Several people gathered cages and files to carry out. Obscured by the door, Benko looked around, careful not to move his pounding head. He saw his revolver near his outstretched hand. He inched his hand to close over the handle of the gun. He had to protect his work. More importantly, he had to protect her work.

Benko accepted his death. He had to do what he could to minimize the damage. He aimed for the patient, hands shaking. They couldn't take him alive—bad enough they'd have the corpse for an autopsy. Noting a swish in the layer of smoke near the door, the large bald man turned to see him aiming a .38-caliber Smith and Wesson at Sebastian's head.

One of the men, following the movement, shouted out loud, "NO!"

The first man brought his pistol to bear on Benko, but didn't have a clean shot. The huge man jumped in front of Sebastian as Benko fired in panic.

A rear guard fired at the gun flash through the smoke, throwing Benko back against the wall with a shot to the chest.

Everyone froze.

The black-haired man rushed to the injured man as he slid to the floor. "Major!"

The burly man grasped out for his hand and the ashen-faced doctor clasped the thick, beefy hand in his own.

"Sir!" The first intruder with the shaggy blonde hair rushed around Sebastian's feet to fall with a strangled cry.

The laboratory went silent aside from Sebastian's labored breathing and the soft gurgling of blood escaping from the hole in the wounded man's throat. Benko's vision dimmed as he heard the boulder of a man expel his last breath.

**** **Cole Estate, Norwich, England** ****

"Christ, Sebastian! Someone get him off of me!" Crashing to the floor with the weight of his friend, Thomas struggled in pain.

"Don't move! I'll tranq him!" Ian shouted.

Lithe and undaunted, Lorena raised a weighted, leather sap. "No time!"

"Lorena, look out!" Ian cried.

The man they knew as Sebastian turned with crimson eyes ablaze and leapt at Lorena. He sank razor-edged canines into her shoulder as she brought the sap down with powerful aim into his temple. She slammed into an examination table, the breath knocked out of her.

The din of the struggle over, silence loomed. Ian snapped back to rational thought. He shot two tranquilizer darts into his brother and winced as each struck his target.

Lorena, unable to move her left arm, used her legs to push up the wall and gain her feet.

Thomas grabbed hold of his arm to stem the flow of blood.

All three friends stood hushed, staring at the body lying prone on the floor.

The exterior door to the lab boomed open and broke the heavy silence. Sir Gerald Cole stood haloed by the weak English sunshine, rifle aimed and ready to fire. He took in the bizarre scene. No longer organized, the lab looked tumbled and topsy-turvy as though the planet, rampaging and furious, hurled the building in an attempt to shake it off. Glass was shattered out of cabinets, an examination table was turned on its side, and blood was spread around the room. His gaze trailed the path of mayhem landing on the creature in the middle of the floor.

"Bloody hell, what've they done to him?"

CHAPTER EIGHT

London 2014

The fountain at 25 Canada Square bubbled in the cheery London sunlight. From his offices on the thirtieth floor, Sebastian watched the early lunch crowd trickle into the pedestrian mall. He turned away from the view with a glance at his watch. "She's late!" he shouted toward the open door.

Thomas poked his head in unfazed. "She's on her way up. You don't need any more coffee."

"We're closing in on Carlson," he growled. "This might be the only chance we have."

His friend plopped down in one of the overstuffed chairs. "Not the only chance, just the best chance."

Sebastian leaned on his desk. "Are you always going to be the silver-lining guy?"

"Someone has to balance out your doom and gloom." His messy-headed friend shrugged. "It's a heavy burden, my friend."

"Oh ho, a burden? Really?" Sebastian snorted. "And how do you think I tolerate your constant good humor?"

A grin broke out on Thomas's face. "With the deep affection one has for a comrade in arms and brother, of course."

Sebastian shook his head at the familiar grin. "Incorrigible."

"Who is?" Lorena walked into the office with Alonzo trailing her.

Without answering the question, Sebastian pounced on her delay. "What took so long?"

"Well," Lorena started, inserting a flash drive into a terminal near the wall. "If someone had agreed to do this in Vancouver, I wouldn't have had to travel to England where the goddamn London traffic is nuts."

He glowered at her sweet smile.

Alonzo waved his hands. "Come, come, we have some decisions to make."

One of Sebastian's office staff knocked at the open door. "Sir?"

Whirling in irritation, Sebastian spat out a response. "What now?"

"The food has arrived." The mid-twenties man winced.

"Who ordered food?" Sebastian all but bellowed.

"I did. Hello?" Lorena raised her hand. "Three countries, six days. Can you say jet lag?" She breezed by him. "Bring it in, Andy."

"You heard her." Thomas interceded. "Bring it in."

Three other staffers brought in a cart with a large carafe and baskets laden with fruits, cheeses, and pastries. Sebastian didn't care if his annoyed pacing sent them scurrying.

Alonzo said, shaking his head, "You know, if you keep terrifying the staff I'll have to give them raises or hire new people."

"Bah!" The tall Englishman replied. "How often am I here? They'll live." He turned to Lorena, who was pouring coffee into her mug. "Can we get started now?" His hostility hissed out through his clenched teeth.

She grabbed a tablet. Dragging her finger across the screen, she brought up the digital files on the flat screen above the conference table. Lorena took a bite of a croissant and shifted to business.

Sebastian waved off Alonzo's offer of coffee and sat at the conference table. Thomas took a plate of cheese and fruit to the seat left of Sebastian. Alonzo leaned against the wall with his mug.

Sebastian gestured to Lorena to begin.

She nodded. "Out of the list of six you gave me, I culled it down to two. Knowing David Williams worked as a low-level accountant at Biogenesis Corp. with Neil Weber cut my target choice to one." She tapped the tablet. "Cordelia Fiore, thirty years old. Working as a freelance appraiser and broker on some art pieces belonging to one Senator Jonathan Matthews." Tapping the tablet again, Lorena brought up a photo along with several documents. "Fiore holds degrees in law, art history, and business. She's fluent in Italian, German, and French and speaks passable Spanish. She built a reputation working at Vancouver Art Gallery valuing and authenticating historical masters." Pausing for a sip of coffee, Lorena scanned the group. Sweeping the documents off the screen, she opened several more photographs. "Fiore's the daughter of Enzo Fiore and Keelin McShane. Mother died 1988 of a diabetes-related stroke. Fiore was raised by her father and grandmother, Lucia Rosalina Fiore. Both Enzo and Lucia are living. Enzo Fiore owns a popular bookstore/coffee shop near the University of British Columbia. He has an older brother, Carlo, who owns a butcher shop in the same neighborhood. Carlo has a daughter two years older than Cordelia. Adrianna Fiore recently moved from Los Angeles to work for Kickfuse, a marketing company. Interestingly enough, we employ Kickfuse at the Vancouver office."

Sebastian studied the photos of the Fiore woman's apartment. The decor showed a tasteful blend of modern elements blended with classic pieces. The building housing the bookstore and their apartments was a talented restoration of 1930s brick boom architecture. His eyes traveled back to her photograph.

Lorena continued. "Fiore travels frequently, but keeps close contact with her family. Finances are clean. So that's a dead end. She pulls in six figures a year and has zero money problems. She even bankrolled the building restoration." She sat down opposite Sebastian. "She's clean. I dug pretty deep. She has a reputation as a ball breaker. Even the people who dislike her, and there are plenty, conceded she worked hard and reluctantly respected her."

Thomas spoke up. "So she's legitimate. How do we approach her?"

"I'd recommend the straightforward approach. She's on the up and up. If she knew Matthews was dirty, I think she'd help us," Lorena said.

"Clean or not, I'd prefer not to reveal too much. We can't afford to allow Dr. Carlson the tiniest of suspicions we're this close." Sebastian steepled his fingers under his chin. "What about Seamus?"

Lorena snorted. "She'd cut him off at the knees. Three lovers in ten years. She's careful and locked down. Seamus wouldn't get past hello." She added another tidbit. "She's a Krav Maga Black Belt Third Dan. So she could literally cut him off at the knees."

Thomas sat back in his chair. "Thoughts?"

Sebastian remained silent for a minute. "Cordelia Fiore could provide access to David Williams's computer and many of Senator Matthews' financial records. Even limited access would allow Jarske an opportunity to hack into the rest."

"Yep, but how do we recruit her?" Alonzo asked.

"I'm telling you, ask her," Lorena urged. "She'll help."

"You like her," Thomas said, smiling.

"I think she can handle her shit," Lorena said bluntly. "People say she's tough. She cares about her family, which says a lot about her character. I couldn't find a single scratch-my-back-and-I'll-scratch-yours deal in which she participated. I did find plenty of people she's pissed off because she's a by-the-book player." She looked at Sebastian. "Ask her."

Sebastian stood abruptly. He reeled in his ill temper. "No." He turned to look out into the London sunshine. "I've already damaged your lives. I'm not bringing anyone else inside." He turned and scanned them all. "We'll tap her in Rome and get a feel for the situation. Maybe we can use her to plant a transmitter to allow Jarske remote access."

Thomas chortled. "You're going to maneuver her?"

Alonzo looked into his mug while Lorena grinned outright.

Sebastian glared at his partners. "I'm an expert operative."

"You remember she's a woman?" Lorena asked eyes twinkling.

Thinking for a minute to the last woman he'd dealt with and the carnage left in the wake of her anger, Sebastian shrugged. "Thomas will go with me." He glanced at Thomas. "You're engaging."

Thomas threw his hands back. "Yeah, because my appeal will conceal your … " He paused.

"Reticence?" Alonzo offered.

"This is going be good." Lorena cracked up. "Should we start a pool?"

CHAPTER NINE

Rome
2014

"She's on the street," Sebastian said, linked by comm with Thomas.

Cordelia Fiore stepped out of the lobby and bent to adjust her shoe. Her left hand on one of the hotel's pillars, she tilted her head to the left to tug on the strap of her sandal. Dark tumbles of waves framed her face, shown in clear profile as she began to straighten back up. Her foot poised in the air spreading the light cotton skirt. She looked like a tourist advertisement or a photo from a catalog. His retinas burned with the image.

He wasn't prepared for her in person. Devoid of make-up, the creamy olive tone of her skin complimented not quite black hair. Almond eyes and full mouth balanced a straight Roman nose some might consider too big. He felt a tug deep in his belly and took a harsh breath.

"Roger," Thomas said. "Concierge says she's headed to the Colosseum. I'll move ahead."

I've seen women before.

"Sebastian?" Thomas asked. "You copy?"

"Yeah, I copy," he snapped. "Rendezvous at the Colosseum." *Focus.* That moment Cordelia stopped to look toward him, cocking her head as if she heard something. Remaining calm, Sebastian continued forward for fear of giving away his presence. He relaxed the moment she shook her head. A quick breeze and her sudden launch forward propelled the air swirling backwards in her wake and into his face.

Sebastian's pupils dilated as the hair on the nape of his neck rose. He inhaled, drawing the scent of her deep into his sensitive nose. Cordelia Fiore smelled fantastic. A perfume of vanilla, amber, and something else he couldn't name. Sebastian stopped in midstep squelching the urge to bury his face in her hair, into the crease of her neck to … taste her. Making a sound close to growl, he forced himself to move after her as the plaza began to fill with people.

"I didn't get that, Sebastian," Thomas piped into his ear. "Say again?"

"Nothing," the tall Englishman said.

The sun climbed up into its midmorning position in the sky by the time Fiore arrived at the Colosseum. The stony surface of the ancient steps began to radiate heat upward. Sebastian trailed her at a discreet distance. His keen eyes picked up a slight tickle of sweat that trailed its way down the back of her neck.

****

Thomas watched Cordelia enter from across the Colosseum platform. He looked the proper English tourist with a camera around his neck, a wide-brimmed straw hat and Keen sandals peeking out from under his khaki rip-stop trousers. She strolled along the perimeter of the main floor stopping to stare down into the gaping space of the holding pens. He made his way closer to Cordelia in a serpentine meander while keeping her in his sight.

Spotting Sebastian's entrance, Thomas offered a brief touch of his hat. "She's approaching my twelve o'clock." He stopped to take a photo, lining the woman up in his lens. Between the magnification and his sharp eyesight, he noticed her brow wrinkle as though she smelled something rotten. Before he could blink, her knees gave way and she tumbled face forward to the ground. The camera fell to his chest as he moved in a blur. He met Sebastian at her side.

"What happened?" Sebastian demanded.

Thomas answered kneeling down to touch the woman's throat. "I don't know. One minute she strolled along. She made a face and collapsed." He gently rolled her to her side. "Ouch, her knees will be purple tomorrow."

****

Cordelia blinked her eyes open. She reached up to brush a loose strand of hair out of her face. *I should've worn my hair up today.* She gazed up at two men—one kneeling at her side, the other shading her from the sun.

"Oh ho, she's back." The golden, mop-headed man kneeling at her side chuckled. She tried to sit up, but the cheery blonde placed his hand on her shoulder. "I'd take it slow."

His chipper English accent made it hard to resist. She simply propped up on her elbow. "Thank you. I'm so embarrassed."

"Don't trouble yourself." He turned to his companion. "Sebastian, can I have your water?"

Still without saying a word, the swarthy-haired man handed a water bottle to his friend.

"My name is Thomas Shaw and this effusive man is my friend and partner, Sebastian Cole." He opened the water bottle and helped ease her up to sitting. "Sip some water, Miss…"

Cordelia took a sharp breath. "I'm so sorry. I'm Cordelia Fiore. Thank you for your help." She sipped the water.

A Colosseum docent approached, concern on her face. In broken English she asked, "Is all okay?"

The man named Sebastian turned to respond. "Yes, Signora, we're fine. Thank you for your concern." The tone in his voice brooked no argument.

"Oh buono, Signore. Ciao." She moved on with a brief glance at Cordelia.

Thomas stood and brushed off his knees. "You ready to stand?" He held out a hand to her.

Squinting against the sunlight, Cordelia nodded. "Yes, I think so." She took his hand, feeling firm strength in his grip. Slowly standing, she touched a hand to her forehead.

"Still a bit woozy?" Thomas moved his grip to her elbow, taking her hand in his other one. "We'll go slow. Are you ill?"

The question surprised Cordelia. "No, uh, I felt a bit unsteady."

"You dropped like a stone," Thomas remarked in a sunny tone. "I hope you're feeling better."

After a brief glance at the stone-faced Sebastian, Cordelia smiled weakly at Thomas. "I am. Maybe a little fresh air."

A snort from Sebastian mingled with a chuckle from Thomas. He waved a hand at the open space. "We're outside my dear."

Chagrined, Cordelia blushed. "Perhaps some air outside of the Colosseum." Shaking off her fog to more closely evaluate the two men, she encountered a strange hum of energy. She spent her days surrounded by the static electric sound of people's presence. Call it aura or magnetic field. It didn't matter. It buzzed, a dentist's drill in her head. *They hum.* A vibration emanated from her rescuers that traveled deep into her chest.

The tall, dark man took her comment as an opportunity. "There's a little outdoor café a short way from here. You could thank us with a cool limonata? A bite of something to eat couldn't hurt either." The suggestion from the somber, dark fellow sounded as if he'd take a bite out of her. A deep, predatory menace exuded from his sizable frame.

The sun climbed high only to drill down on her head. The thought of the shade of a café appealed to her. Sitting with a cool drink sounded refreshing. She pushed out with her mind to scan the two men. No immediate hints of a threat caught her attention. "I think I'd like something cool to drink." She turned to the fellow still holding his arm around her shoulder. The more affable of the two, she asked him, "Would you mind if I kept your arm? I am a bit wobbly."

"Not to worry, luv, I'm all yours to command." Thomas stood straight, taking the weight of her lean easily.

The brooding Sebastian nodded and made room for them to pass.

Thomas, leading her out of the Colosseum, reminded Cordelia of a big golden retriever with his shaggy blonde hair and open, amiable brown eyes. Slighter than his friend Sebastian, Thomas charmed with an outgoing and cheerful face. His jovial demeanor asked for a good scratch behind the ear. Cordelia imagined his tail wagging with a lolling grin.

By contrast, his friend reminded her of a dark, predatory cat. She resisted the urge to stand taller under his impassive measurement. Potential energy kindled under his calm facade. Reaching toward Sebastian with her thoughts, she felt the smolder of banked coals bound up and ready for a blaze. From both men the deep, resonating hum pushed back the annoying rasp of static coming from the people in the city. She puzzled around it the way one would worry a loose tooth. She'd never experienced the sensation before.

"You're quiet," Thomas remarked, helping her into a taxi. "Are you certain you're feeling better?"

Startled out of her thoughts, Cordelia shook her head. “Really, I’m fine. Just thinking.” She glanced out of the corner of her eye at Sebastian sliding in from the other side. “Just thinking.”

CHAPTER TEN

"How about this lovely table in the shade? I'll go find a waiter." With a cavalier toss of his hand, Thomas disappeared inside the little café. Sebastian kept his face composed as Cordelia took a seat opposite him.

"You've known Thomas a long time?" she asked.

Sebastian measured her through hooded eyes. "A very long time."

He heard her small sigh. His mind revisited her dossier. Cordelia shunned most social company. He guessed small talk irritated her. His reluctance to chitchat wouldn't make this easy. Neither of them had a talent for engaging strangers.

She tried again. "How long are you in Italy?"

He settled back into his chair. "Our plans are open-ended."

"I'm traveling for work and decided to take a break. My father grew up outside of Rome," she offered.

Sebastian gave no response; he sensed her heart rate increase and smelled her irritation, a tingling snap of fresh rosemary among the vanilla and amber scent. *Nervous or frustrated? Where the hell is Thomas?*

The waiter approached them, saving him from more meaningless banter. "Per favore, da bere?"

"Si, Vorrei un limonata e …" turning to Sebastian, Cordelia asked in English, "What would you have?"

Sebastian, slowly translating what the waiter said, stared at Cordelia. "An espresso's fine."

The waiter, appearing to understand the word espresso, nodded, saying, "Si Signora, uno momento."

Though he hated to admit weakness, he acknowledged her skill. "My Italian's … slow."

Thomas returned to the table bright and cheerful. "I spoke to the office and cleared our afternoon. We can make sure Miss Fiore returns to her hotel." Meaning Sebastian and Thomas would switch surveillance shifts with their men, MacColgan and Jackson.

Cordelia tilted her head and said, "We ordered drinks. I didn't know what you'd prefer." As if on command the waiter brought out her limonata, crisp over ice with a straw, and Sebastian's espresso.

A glistening bead of sweat trailed down Cordelia's collarbone, drawing Sebastian's attention. He forced his attention to his espresso.

The waiter asked Thomas what he would have.

With cheerful flare, Thomas answered in Italian, "Una limonata anche e vorremmo ordinare pranzo. Potreiamo avere un menu, per favore."

The waiter exited with several sis and in frettas.

"You should improve your Italian while we're here, Sebastian," Thomas said.

With a slight rise of his eyebrow, Sebastian replied. "I leave the romantic languages to you. I prefer the gutturals—fewer vowels, and more substance." Neither man had won any advantage in this long-standing debate.

Cordelia's eyes rested on Sebastian; he met her gaze resolute. He brushed his thick, black hair back, annoyed at its length. His ease toward Thomas slipped from his face as he turned his scrutiny back to her.

Thomas continued, "Remember when you thought that fellow in Belgrade could speak German and Anton misinterpreted it as Serbian?" He chuckled, remembering. "We almost boiled our own kettle of fish before Lorena realized it was Czech and stepped in to save our ahh .... " With an apologetic look at Cordelia he corrected, "butts!"

Sebastian looked at Thomas with wry humor. "As I remember, you forgot the contact and put us into that kettle in the first place."

Thomas laughed. "Sorry, Cordelia, you have to forgive a couple of soldiers. All of our stories seem to revolve around freezing weather and terrible food!"

"Which branch?" she asked Thomas.

They paused conversation when the waiter brought out menus and offered to freshen their drinks.

Smiling at Cordelia, Thomas said, "Marines. You spend a lot of time in strange places with strange people in strange situations hoping you won't be shot."

"And for what?" Sebastian added a slight bite to his tone. "Home and Country?" His snort finished his thought.

"Ah, now you sound like Rachna." Thomas turned to Cordelia. "My wife. She spent her fair share of long nights alone waiting for the phone to ring. We work for ourselves now." He wagged his eyebrows at Sebastian. "Don't sound above it all."

Sebastian looked out into the plaza where the tourists and the pigeons maneuvered for space, dismissing another well-worn conversation.

"I suppose the motives are clearer working for yourselves," Cordelia said. "Political reasons are vague and wrapped in propaganda. Now you're free to follow your sense of honor."

Sebastian startled back to Cordelia, echoes of his own thoughts spoken out loud. He bore his eyes into her. How could she know?

Thomas handed her a business card. “Global Sureties. Our security company.”

She read the list of offices. “Vancouver. I live there, though I’ve been traveling for work.” Thomas nodded congenially. “Business takes us far and wide as well.”

Sebastian remained inscrutable. *He likes her, but our plans have to move forward.*

“I brought my wife with me on this trip but she’s not staying in the city,” Thomas said.

“Some of us have to work,” Sebastian said wryly.

“The rest of us enjoy living a little.” Thomas winked at Cordelia. “We’re staying in Sperlonga on the coast.”

“It sounds lovely.” Cordelia glanced at the sun. “You know, it’s getting late. I think I’ll head back to my hotel. Clean up a bit.” She gestured to her scraped knees.

Sebastian caught the change in her mood. “Thomas, why don’t you head back to the office and I’ll see Miss Fiore back in one piece, bumps and bruises aside, to her hotel.” He gave Thomas a look.

Thomas returned a brief nod and dropped some money for the bill. “Cordelia, why don’t we meet for breakfast? That way I’d be satisfied you wouldn’t have any more accidents.”

“I have your card. Can I call you tonight and let you know? I think I’d like a bath and some down time before I decide my plans for tomorrow.”

“Of course, of course. We have a late dinner meeting, so don’t worry about the time. We’ll look forward to hearing from you and I hope we’ll meet again.” Thomas walked to the curb to wave down a taxi.

Sebastian stood and held her chair. “Shall we?”

****

Cordelia played the afternoon over in her mind. She eased into the steaming water of the large, claw-footed tub. Wincing as she lowered her battered knees into the water, Cordelia thought about the two men and the rich thrum of their minds. Vapor rose from the surface of the water while she sipped a glass of crisp Soave.

She rubbed down with a thick towel and belted the soft, light cashmere robe at the waist. Taking her phone off the charger, Cordelia dialed her cousin, Adrianna. It wasn't until the phone began to ring she calculated the time difference. "Oh shit," she said.

"Way to greet me at this ungodly hour," her cousin's groggy voice rasped.

Cordelia winced. "Sorry, I didn't think about the time difference. I can call you later."

"Damage is done." Cordelia heard her rustling around. "I'm already awake. You talk while I make coffee."

"You're connected to the city scene, right?" she asked her cousin.

"Of course, it's kind of my job. What's this to do with you in Italy?"

Cordelia poured more wine. "I ran into some people today I think you may know. Sebastian Cole and Thomas Shaw? They own a security company—"

Adrianna cut her off. "Global Sureties. Yeah, we just picked up their account. It's a subtle gig, not media ads or anything, but events, dinners, that kind of thing."

"Have you met either of them?" Cordelia asked.

"Not really, they deal directly with top management, but I've seen Cole. He's a tall hunk of repressed sex if I've ever seen it." Adrianna sighed. "Some kind of Jason Bourne type. Retired Marine, worked for the NSA, can kill a man with his thumb. I'd jump on that in a heartbeat."

Cordelia laughed. Adrianna had zero inhibitions. "He is handsome, but he isn't too talkative."

"Who needs to talk? Just looking at him made my knees wobble." Cordelia heard her blowing her coffee. "So you just bumped into him?"

"No, I sort of fainted," Cordelia admitted.

"Hot damn! How perfect is that? Damsel in distress shit should be right up his alley." Adrianna laughed. "Ouch, I spilled my coffee." The sound of rustling fabric carried over the line. "Why'd you pass out?"

"Remember the field trip to the missile silo in eighth grade?" Cordelia asked, swirling her wine glass.

"No shit? Ha ha ha! You went to the Colosseum, didn't you?" Adrianna laughed more. "I told you not to try it."

"How could I visit Rome and not see the Colosseum? It's like going to Hawaii and not hitting the beach." Cordelia snorted. "I didn't expect to find any time remnants. The last spectacles took place in the sixth century."

"And then they turned it into a cemetery. How could you not pick up a vibe or twenty? You full-on fainted?" she asked, her amusement clear.

Cordelia puffed out her breath. "Yeah, total face plant. You should see my knees."

"Oh, I wish I'd been there. In front of the Global Sureties guys?" She couldn't control her giggle.

"You know you're enjoying this a little too much," Cordelia snapped.

"Not even close, prima. It could only get better if there were pictures," Adrianna said. "You can Google Cole. He has a general bio on his website, but he keeps a low profile. You have wi-fi?"

"Yeah, I looked already. Cornell University grad, top honors in biology and chemistry. A Princeton doctorate in molecular biology. Nothing impressive." She snorted.

Cordelia heard Adrianna trying not to laugh. "Cor, seriously, this guy is better than James Bond. If he's interested, snap that shit up."

"Interested? He might as well have been talking to a brick as a woman. I don't think he said more than five sentences. He's far from interested. His friend is nice."

"Married too, I'll bet," Adrianna said.

"Of course," Cordelia said.

"Your track record sucks in the sex department anyway. Your brain doesn't always shut off when you like," Adrianna offered.

"Funny thing, I can't read them. They don't have the same energy as most people. One of the reasons I enjoyed lunch was zero overflow," Cordelia told her, still baffled by the soft thrum both men transmitted.

"Well damn, Cor, talker or no, hop that train." Adrianna cackled. "Think about it: blissful, non-psychic sex."

It was Cordelia's turn to cackle. "You're suggesting I attack him? Jeez, Adrianna, I like to think I have some dignity."

"Okay, okay. At the very least, if they invite you to do something enjoy the company. These guys are upstanding hero types. You don't have to worry about Nonna's white slavers." Her cousin twittered.

"I'll think about it. Thanks, cousin," Cordelia said.

"Oh Ducky, anytime," Adrianna said. "And I expect tawdry details if he does show interest," she added in a wicked tone.

"Love you," Cordelia said.

"Bacios, prima," she said hanging up.

"The hum," she said out loud. Her curiosity, intrigued by the difference, wouldn't let it go. The military? That kind of training changed a person. Both men showed mastery of the Tell. The minute physical gestures that give away what people are thinking. Cordelia could read a lie in people's minds.

After a lifetime, she recognized the Tells accompanying the lies without even scanning folks.

Not that she tried; she went out of her way to avoid it. The Knowing reached out and grabbed her without warning. She knew things about people or events past, present, or future. She learned the hard way people didn't want to know. They would rather believe in what could happen. Cordelia couldn't tell much about Sebastian. His impassive demeanor hid all clues to his thoughts.

"Not one twitch from the elusive Mr. Cole," Cordelia mused aloud. She poured another glass of wine. Her neck might've broken when she fell and he could've complained about the dust she stirred for all of his concern.

Thomas seemed different. She couldn't read him any more than his stoic friend, but he appreciated her looks as he appreciated a fine painting. His wife had stolen his heart. That was apparent in the way he talked about her, but he found Cordelia attractive. His body language spoke volumes. Thomas's easygoing nature appealed in a friendly way. He leaned in when speaking to her, and even touched her arm once. She developed the strange impression he leaned close at least once to inhale her scent.

Despite Adrianna's enthusiasm, she didn't know where this acquaintance with Sebastian Cole could go. Waves of déjà vu tumbled over her with sudden force. She tried to concentrate on it, but the specifics eluded her. Every ounce of his body language reinforced dispassion. People suck.

Cordelia returned to her wine lamenting the scraped and bruising ache in her knees. She opened the cover of a new novel but couldn't get those dark and menacing eyes out of her thoughts. Or the hum. *What does that friggin' hum mean?*

CHAPTER ELEVEN

Sebastian radiated a foul mood. "Dinner was a waste of time."

"You don't like southern Italian. I enjoyed my meal," Thomas said.

"They're not going to use us. Did you see their faces?" he grumbled.

"I did. They have a decision to make." He tried to buoy the evening. "They may come around. We are expensive."

Sebastian growled, "It culls out the stupid duffers. I hate dealing with idiots."

"Didn't you enjoy Cordelia Fiore today? She smelled fantastic." He switched topics. "I liked her. Maybe we should think about Lorena's suggestion."

Thomas's unfailing good humor and bright side thinking grated Sebastian. He didn't want to think about Cordelia Fiore or her scent. His mood grew darker. Some people might ask if Sebastian's mood ever cheered. "Let's see if she takes you up on your offer."

"Our offer. You were there." Thomas grinned.

"I'll talk to you in the morning," Sebastian said getting out of the car. "Try to keep focused on the job."

"Aye aye, Captain," Thomas said with a cheeky grin. He waved as he pulled into traffic.

Sebastian strode to his hotel room, a big predatory cat. He poured himself a scotch and went to take a hot shower. Stepping into the scalding water, he leaned his forehead against his arm and relaxed into the steaming mist.

He worked up a thick lather using the sandalwood soap Rachna made and tried to ease the spring-tight tension gripping his body. The fragrance of the sandalwood drifted up with the steam creating an earthy-scented fog. He sucked deep into his olfactory glands. The sandalwood mixed with the last residue of vanilla and amber plaguing him all evening. The heady cocktail of aromas pinned down the source of his frustration: Cordelia Fiore.

Her scent had lingered in his nose since he opened the door to her hotel and said a curt good evening. The cool afternoon breeze sifted through her hair and delivered the last rich taste of Cordelia Fiore. Not what he expected, she tangled his thoughts like a cobweb. *Clear her out.* The steam in the shower swirled to match his thoughts about the day. Sebastian stepped out of the shower and gave a shake to his hair. He stalked out of the bathroom.

His phone vibrated on the night table. "Cole."

"Hey, brother, how's it going?" Ian Cole's sharp London accent cut into his brooding.

"Fine. Everyone all right there?" He didn't want to discuss the job.

"Lorena says the Canadian is a stunner." Sebastian couldn't miss the puckish tone.

He grumbled, "I suppose you've taken a bet in the pool."

Ian chuckled. "Me? Never, but Lindsay's placed a hundred in your favor. I'm less optimistic."

"Very funny." He tipped the bottle of Glendronach eighteen-year single malt over his glass. "It's a job. We need access to Matthews' books. If we can connect him to Carlson, we have her."

"Yes, yes, I know. Some research files would be nice." Ian's frustration showed. "Are you sure you want it to play like this?"

"I can't remember the last time I was sure of anything." He held the sip of scotch on his tongue.

"Of course you can. You take on too much." His brother's voice softened. "You've got this, brother, and we're with you."

"Tell Dad and Lindsay hello. I'll be in touch." He had his moments. He swirled the deep amber liquid around in his glass.

He used to believe in the greater good. Hell, he still believed in the greater good. He simply understood some people worked toward it and some didn't. Rachna called him disillusioned. She said he needed to reaffirm his faith in the world. He downed the warm, astringent scotch in one last gulp. *I have faith in what I can control. That leaves the world out.*

The fragrant moisture from the shower hung over his disgruntled mood. The trip to Italy brought Matthews into close range of one of his biggest investments, Biogenesis Corporation. Sebastian sipped his single malt and brooded. He needed proof Dr. Carlson was funneling money to support illegal experimentation. Senator Matthews was a thread in that funding stream.

His frustration swelled and he wanted to take a bite out of somebody. He flipped through the Fiore file looking for something he missed. Something to explain the tenacious hold this woman had on his brain.

A knock on the door broke his concentration, and he remembered room service. Cordelia Fiore whirling through his mind, he flung the door open to food service. The waiter struggled to ignore Sebastian as he pushed the cart into the room. He lifted the food covers to display the selections and offered Sebastian the ticket to sign. The waiter backed out of the room without making eye contact. Sebastian turned a hungry eye on his steak and caught a glimpse of himself in the steel framed mirror on the wall. He raised his eyebrow in amusement. No wonder that poor waiter choked on his tongue. Sebastian looked at his naked reflection.

****

Thomas Shaw returned from the meeting with a bounce in his step and a whistle on his lips. He didn't mind the hour drive south to Sperlonga. Light traffic made the drive easy. The Fiat flew on the autostrada. Cordelia called to confirm their breakfast. He whistled along with the radio. Tempted to douse his headlights, he didn't want to cross with the Polizia di Stato. Rachna waited for him. He whipped the little Fiat up the hill banking it into the short driveway to the villa: the little white stucco box perched on a hill with twenty other little white boxes, the only difference being the colors of the roof tiles. Rachna fell in love with this little box because of the bright green roof. It also had two balconies looking out over the marina at the base of the hill. Rachna had tidied up the sad little villa.

Thomas put the top up on the Fiat and reined in his desire to hop two flights of stairs to the main door in one leap. Nosey neighbors. The lights glowed though it was almost ten; sometimes Rachna turned in early after a full day. Originally a hobby, using essential oils and herbs to create skin products flourished into a full-time business. With a generous seed investment from Sebastian, Rachna had now leased a small warehouse space in Sperlonga to create and house her products. She hired local women, a lot of them grand-mothers, to mix and test her creations then she shipped them off all over the world. *I don't mind.* Rachna's business approached the point when she could give a return on Sebastian's investment. Not that the man cared if it made any money. *If it makes Rachna happy, Sebastian is happy.*

He knew Sebastian felt responsible for his situation. No matter both Thomas and Rachna assured Sebastian they didn't blame him, he wouldn't let go an opportunity to make it up to them. Thomas didn't complain. His work with Global Sureties paid more than enough. Rachna loved traveling and with her new business taking off, their hope to have a baby would become a reality.

Ian Cole, Global's resident physician, ran a battery of tests on both Thomas and Rachna. He pronounced no obstacle to having a happy, healthy baby. His friends always had his back. Thomas wanted nothing more.

He had sensed Sebastian's distraction during the entire meeting. The sixth sense they shared carried the tension and befuddlement like little electrical impulses. Sebastian's pulse racing; he had radiated so much heat one of the clients asked if he was ill. *Oh, Sebastian had it bad. He couldn't see it. Better ignorance; give things a chance to settle.* The minute Thomas met Cordelia Fiore, he knew his friend needed her.

"You're singing a happy tune," Rachna called in her singsong English from a chair on the balcony, a glass of wine in her hand.

Thomas swept a dashing kiss on his wife's luscious, berry-colored lips. "That's because Sebastian Cole has met his match."

Rachna stood up with knowing eyes; he loved the way they communicated without words. Rachna knew the import of the situation without any explanation. "Tell me more."

Thomas took the glass of wine out of his wife's hand and led her into their bedroom. "We hit one of our targets today. Her name's Cordelia Fiore."

Rachna murmured over the sensation of his lips and teeth on her fingertips. "Oh, I can't wait to see how he handles this."

CHAPTER TWELVE

Research Laboratory
Location: Classified

Dimmed overhead lighting allowed the denizens of the lab the opportunity for some rest. In the morning, the lab would stir back to life as the larger complement of the staff came in to work. Viktor Rihard liked the nighttime. The soft, muted glow soothed his nerves. The daylight hours bogged down his clarity of thinking: his brain would scramble around for a term or formula that should be readily accessible.

Viral vectors allowed for the transmission of DNA into an embryonic cell. Gene splicing perfected by the creation of chimeras. The laboratory housed such creatures. Beyond the chimeras containing the intact genetic material from both a pocket mouse and a kangaroo mouse, the scientists worked with much larger and more complex animals. The certainty of being able to manipulate human DNA in such a way continued to befuddle the researchers.

Advances made in gene splicing and gene therapy had been reached in the public sector. The leader of the research team fed bits and pieces to a variety of other scientists so that they too made progress. In return, those labs provided insights and improvements to inform and strengthen their own research. Dr. Rihard thought it a beneficial and efficient system. The chimeras that were capable of breeding provided the first clue to the successful insertion of genetic material in the big cats.

After some stumbles, the process of using embryonic stem cells to source the genetic mutations allowed the team to create a healthy, stable chimera from two species of primates. The chimera, named Elsa, slept in her place of honor. Using embryonic stem cells from Elsa to host a new genetic combination provided even further progress. The team provided Elsa with a more efficient immunity: though she couldn't regenerate—her little finger never grew back—she could heal wounds at a much more rapid pace. The addition of the nanomites as the delivery system to the spinal fluid generated real breakthroughs.

The nanomites helped control the spacing of the insertions and allowed precise control. They learned if they timed each new DNA code right, the transformation process, the reproduction and assimilation of the new cells, caused little or no permanent damage in the primates. Each one of the team members pushed their experiments further. In seven attempts, they couldn't recreate the conditions that allowed the one complete insertion. Each time resulted in clumsy, shambling creatures with none of their original species' intelligence, coordination, or spark. Members of the staff began to despair of recreating the anomaly. Failure paralyzed them with worry over the director's response.

Dr. Rihard strode into the workspace, his vibrant silver hair dull and lank from tension. "Chart," he clipped, his voice belying the foreboding that fed the ulcer in his stomach.

A young researcher spoke reluctantly. "Though stable, the subject exhibits cellular degeneration. The rate has slowed with chromosomal injections, but stabilization seems unlikely. Also, the subject is suffering from severe cortex damage. CAT scans show limited cognitive function."

"The subject still has simple cognition?" Rihard's brow furrowed.

"On a limited basis and not with any consistency." The young researcher winced.

"Continue the chromosome treatments as well as maintaining adrenaline levels. These are the best results we've had since—"

The creature lying on the table groaned in misery. The inexperienced scientist failed to keep the grimace from her features.

Dr. Rihard turned his back and removed himself without expression. "You may turn up the morphine drip as long as it doesn't affect the subject's stability."

Returning to his office, Dr. Rihard logged into his computer and reviewed his notes from the day's rounds. His growing stress took its toll. His head pounded after reviewing the test results. Each step had been recreated from the successful experiment, yet something key eluded them. He cross-checked each notation, each formula, and the timing of the release. Nothing changed. The thought of the displeasure and censure the staff faced caused the ache in his head to grow. Dr. Rihard turned from his desk and unlocked the glass cabinet set into the wall. He perused the labels affixed to the bottles neatly ordered in rows and chose one. Two little blue pills would set him to rights.

He poured a short level of amber whiskey into a clean blood beaker. He popped the two lovely gems into his mouth and followed them with the liquor. Dr. Rihard turned the ringer off on his phone then laid his head on his folded arms. The whiskey and chemicals would ease his headache and offer him a few hours of freedom from his woes.

****

Outside of his door, the young researcher monitored the subjects of their testing. She approached Elsa's space and noticed the liquid-eyed chimera awake and restless. Looking over her shoulder, the mousy-haired woman signed with her hands, "Elsa, you okay?"

The researcher hid the fact that the chimera had learned sign language from the rest of the staff and the creature never seemed to let anyone else know. The large, russet creature gave a low grunt to accompany her gestures. "Bad animal. Elsa no like."

The milky-skinned researcher looked over at their most recent subject lying prone and restrained on the large examination table in the center of the lab. "He won't hurt Elsa. He's sleeping," she gestured, trying to soothe the chimera.

Elsa gave a deep, rattling snort. "Bad animal. Elsa no like."

The scientist sighed. The gentle primate didn't approve of the newest addition to the lab. It upset her Elsa felt threatened. An IV with a morphine-benzo combination kept it unconscious and alleviated some of the painful side effects of the treatment. The woman couldn't explain all of this to the genetically engineered creature in front of her. She just repeated herself. "He's sleeping. He won't hurt Elsa."

Elsa didn't like the response, and waved her blanket. The primate shifted her weight and clutched at a stuffed rabbit the staff had given to her for comfort. Elsa's large hands cuddled the bunny. The research assistant avoided looking at Elsa's missing finger.

Nothing more to say, the woman turned her back on the cage and continued with her rounds. Dr. Rihard wouldn't be out of his office for hours. Everyone knew the lead scientist had a penchant for whiskey and his little blue pills. She didn't blame him. A nice bottle of red wine waited for her at the end of the shift in an hour. Each member of the research team found his or her own way of blowing off steam with the continued failures. She would sink into a bath so hot that it scalded and drink the bottle of wine and then drift off into her own oblivion.

The subject on the table stirred with a small groan. The woman moved to the IV and adjusted the dosage to make certain that the test subject settled down. Now that Elsa had put it in her mind, she worried the sedation wouldn't hold. She turned the dosage up a tiny bit more for her own piece of mind.

CHAPTER THIRTEEN

Rome

Sebastian harbored serious doubts about Thomas's change in plans. His phone rang at five a.m. He wanted to slam it into the wall across the room, but he couldn't keep writing cell phones off on his taxes as business losses if he destroyed them. At least that's what his accountant explained. He took a deep, lung-biting breath and answered his phone. "Better be important, Shaw."

Thomas chuckled. Sebastian called him by his surname when annoyed. "Rough night?"

"Get on with it," Sebastian snarled.

"Rachna had an idea. Why don't you have Alonzo bring you a car so you can drive Cordelia down here to Sperlonga? We can grab a late lunch on the beach and it's market day in the piazza. The ladies can do a bit of shopping. Rachna wants to make a great dinner. You can drive Cordelia back into the city after that. You know how much you love Rachna's cooking." Thomas dangled that tidbit as a lure.

"Humph," Sebastian grunted. "I need coffee and food."

"I'll call Alonzo. He'll pack up some coffee and some bomboloni con la crema from Tazza d'Oro for your drive. What do you say?"

"I say I need a quad shot!"

Thomas took this as a concession. "Great, the car'll be ready at seven. I told Cordelia to be out at seven-thirty. You can be in front of the hotel, coffee and all!"

"You had an idea, eh?" Sebastian remarked dryly.

He heard the smile in Thomas' voice. "Yeah, well, I didn't want you to have to arrange things so early in the morning."

Sebastian had spent a miserable night tossing and turning on the thousand-count hotel sheets. Cordelia's potent fragrance haunted him. Every nerve in his body blazed with tension. Each time he dozed off, he jerked back to consciousness. In his feverish dreams, he loped around, nose to the ground and panting with the effort to pin down the shimmering, elusive blooms. He scented, bundled his muscles in a coil to strike, and then dove into the tangle of sheets wrapped around his legs. He controlled situations. It irked him to be out of control. He took another shower to rinse off the acrid muskiness his fitful dreaming generated.

He gave his unruly hair a shake and perused his wardrobe choices. He hadn't planned on making contact yesterday, so his nondescript t-shirt and sports jacket both sported a shade of gray, his jeans black. It made an effective and versatile uniform. It also simplified his wardrobe choices. People found his tall, dark frame intimidating in those colors, so he used it to tactical advantage. Intimidation might not be the best strategy for today. Feeling stonewalled, he picked up his phone to call Rachna.

A couple of hours later, he leaned against his car waiting for Cordelia, an unfamiliar tension deep in his stomach. *Nervous? No, that's stupid. This is just a job. Just a lead. Don't get ahead of it, idiot.*

****

Cordelia spent a poor night trying to sleep. She tossed and turned, becoming tangled in her sheets. She threw off her cotton chemise and lay in the middle of the bed with the night's breeze on her naked skin. She felt cooler and yet no closer to sleeping. For the brief intervals, she did doze off, she awoke with a start from dreams she couldn't recall. She felt on the brink of combustion from a ball of molten within her. She couldn't distinguish between the visions and the nightmares.

When morning arrived, she clambered out of bed to take a quick shower. She pulled on a breezy, cotton camisole and some slouchy slacks in eggplant, regretting the entire time her decision to meet Thomas Shaw and Sebastian Cole for breakfast. She didn't care if she stayed in her hotel room and read the entire day into oblivion. The thought of going another round with Sebastian Cole in this state of cranky exhaustion set her teeth on edge.

Cordelia grabbed an oversized bag and stuffed a lightweight cardigan into it, along with a pair of casual ballerina flats as backups. She learned the hard way to be prepared. She tied her hair back into a loose and floppy ponytail at the base of her neck; light tendrils of loose waves broke free and framed her face. She tilted her head in the mirror. "Screw it," she grumbled. "Who do I need to impress?"

She stumbled out of the room in desperate need of espresso. As she entered the old-fashioned cage elevator, her cell rang.

"This is Cordelia Fiore."

"Cordelia, David here. I'm sorry to bother you, but I can't find the Di Volo file."

Cordelia resisted the urge to stick her tongue out at the phone. Not new for David, who couldn't find his shoe lace if he had to bend down to reach it. *Funny, he always seemed to find her breast to brush up against.* "David, the

Di Volo file isn't with that information packet. I didn't know you needed it this week."

She could hear David rummaging around in the file. She would need at least a day to reorganize it. "Oh, you're right. I mistook the Di Volo piece for that sculpture in Milan. Sorry."

"If you need the file on the Di Volo piece, I can have my office fax it to you later today." She sighed.

"Oh, no. I'm looking at our schedule and I won't need the Di Volo piece evaluated until next week. It's safe in your warehouse. What're you up to today? Enjoying Rome?"

She debated how much to tell him. "Of course, Rome is Rome. I'm having breakfast with a friend and then he's taking me out to tour the city." She could hear the pause as David absorbed the masculine pronoun in that sentence. Her conscience pinched her a bit, but between his accidental brushes against her arm and the lascivious thoughts she could see in his eyes, he deserved to be taken down.

"I didn't know you knew anyone in Italy." A note of jealousy crept into his tone.

"I don't. He's a friend from Vancouver in Rome on business. It just worked out that we arranged things to fit his schedule." She enjoyed the way her light and breezy attitude with David improved her overall grouchiness.

"Do I know this friend of yours?"

The punch line for this joke made yesterday's gauntlet worth it. Innocence dripped from her words. "I think you've mentioned his company in the past, Global Sureties?"

She heard him gulp. "Sebastian Cole?" Of course, David would have heard of Sebastian Cole.

She heard recovery in David's voice. "I think the name sounds familiar. I'm sure I've met him." She wasn't fooled by his laissez-faire tone. "Hey; you have a great time and I'll see you when you get back to work."

Cordelia ended the call with nostalgia for the days when hanging up on someone had more punch.

Cordelia floated through the hotel weightless and sparkling. David overreached their relationship. Rumors were constantly flying around about his inappropriate relationships with underlings. David got off on being in charge. It felt great to show him that he didn't have any power over her. She hoped the idea would end his endless plays for her attention. She had a slight twinge at the implication of something significant with Sebastian. She stepped out onto the sidewalk with a cheerful ciao for everyone.

Sebastian leaned against an elegant little convertible, sporty and beguiling. The pleasing car gleamed white and complemented his choice of clothes. His 6'4" frame improved a simple white cotton shirt, a classic wardrobe staple given a little more flair with a wider collar that opened low on his throat. Its sleeves ended in broad cuffs and he chose to leave it out rather than tucked. He topped it with a navy blue vest with narrow pinstripes. His stonewashed straight-leg jeans left no doubt as to the length of his legs. The kicked back, devil-may-care look was completed with a pair of Naot sandals that displayed handsome, well-shaped feet.

Damn, even his toes are attractive. Not letting that tiny bitter thought ruin the overall effect of his transformation, she breezed up to him with a cheerful and impish, "Ciao, we've met before? You look familiar, but I can't quite place you."

Sebastian raised his eyebrow, a sign Cordelia decided meant amusement. "It's possible, Signora. Would you be the graceful Cordelia Fiore?" The brusque tone in his voice tempered a bit.

Cordelia, taking Adrianna's advice, tossed her head back and chimed her delight at this poke at yesterday's tumble. "Si, di sicuro. The one and only." She took in the car and his clothes without bothering to contain her grin. "We'd better get you off of the street before you cause a riot." She swept her hand to indicate the serious cases of whiplash the poor women along the sidewalk suffered taking in a second and sometimes a third glance his way.

Sebastian glanced around with little interest. "What about you, Sophia Loren?"

Cordelia had her own admirers. She stepped up beside him, calling his attention to their reflection in the hotel's glass doors. "We look like we stepped off of an Agenzia Nazionale per il Turismo poster."

He muttered, "Italia, where the beautiful people play." Cordelia thought there might be a compliment hidden there, but he turned and opened the passenger door. "Signora?"

Cordelia moved to step into the low-profile car and Sebastian cupped his hand around her elbow to assist her. The moment he closed contact with the skin of her arm he felt something akin to a high-voltage shock. At the sound of a crackle, they both recoiled. Sebastian rubbed his hand and Cordelia rubbed her elbow.

"What happened?" Cordelia asked in amazement at the shock's intensity.

"I've no bloody idea, but I seem to recall being zapped with a taser that felt a little like that once." He walked around to the driver side door. "Could be a static discharge from the car." He touched the handle. She smiled at his readiness to leap back. Nothing. "You all right?"

Cordelia wiggled her fingers. "Lucky for you, I won't be throwing any hard right uppercuts today."

Surprise lit up his face, but he smothered it. She wanted to crow at her small triumph.

****

His voice neutral, he inquired, “Where’d you learn to throw a punch?”

Cordelia laughed. “Enzo fought amateur featherweight in his day. Taught me everything he knows.” She sized him up. “I think I could give you a run for your money despite your reach.” She nodded, reading the tiny glimmer of incredulity in his eyes. “Yep, I bet you have a glass jaw.” Cordelia two, Sebastian zero. She managed to get a raised eyebrow for the second time in less than fifteen minutes. The day could shape up in her favor. “You’re feeding me, right? I’m famished.”

“Change of plans. There are two thermal cups loaded with caffeine and some bombolini in a basket on the backseat.” The engine purred to life. “Thomas, well maybe more Rachna thought it would be a good idea to drive you south to Sperlonga. Rachna wanted to meet you and there’s a market in the piazza today. She thought you might like that. I also looked up a couple of things on the Internet and Sperlonga has a bookshop that specializes in antique editions.”

For a moment Cordelia stayed quiet; she glanced at him before facing forward. He found a bookstore that she would love. She paused. “Southward we go then, but I’ve got to have some of that caffeine. Please tell me it’s turbocharged.”

“It is or I’m giving Alonzo the ax.” He didn’t soften the menacing undertone in his voice. She didn’t know Alonzo, but she hoped for his sake the coffee met expectations.

CHAPTER FOURTEEN

Ljubljana, Slovenia
Biogenesis Corporation Headquarters

Vivienne sat in her sleek uber-modern office of white leather and stainless steel at the top of a classical Slovenian building in Prešeren Square. The two great windows looked out over a view of the statue of the Slovene national poet France Prešeren with his muse at the center of the square. Beyond the statue of Prešeren, the Ljubljanica River flowed, traversed by the city's best-known bridge, Tromostovje.

"Prime Minister, Biogenesis Exploration Corporation had several prospective cities in which to house their main corporate offices, but Ljubljana offered a growing economy founded in part by research and scientific institutions. I know you appreciate our financial investment." She spoke pleasantly into the speaker.

"Of course, Dr. Carlson, understand I value your contribution to our economic stability and growth. I'm hearing rumblings from some of your fellow technology companies about underbidding and shortcuts."

Vivienne loved thinking about the symbolism of pursuing her research in a city where according to Greek legend, the hero Jason and his Argonauts found and struck down a monster. The dragon took its place on the city's coat of arms and flag. Vivienne believed in the symmetry between the ideas of Jason discovering a monster and her own quest for new discoveries. "Prime Minister, how can I respond to rumblings? Perhaps it is merely the sound of envy. You understand, I need concrete evidence to address any of these rumors."

The prime minister coughed. "Until I have documentation I will put these whispers to rest. Please believe we have the highest regard for your work. We look forward to seeing the technological repute of our country grow. Will you be attending the orchestra next week?"

"Oh yes, my New York friends always question my decision to settle here. The orchestra is one reason I give them. None other can surpass it. Tell Brina I look forward to seeing her." She rested her chin on her fingertips.

"My wife loves your addition to our company," he said. "Until then, poslovite."

"Poslovite, sir." Vivienne ended the call. Walking over to her espresso machine, Vivienne smiled with anticipation for the performance. She wanted for nothing in Ljubljana. Tamping the grind into the portafilter, she gazed out the window again. *Well, almost nothing.* Successful insertion and the creation of super immunity was within her grasp.

She would surpass her family's ignominious background and do what her grandfather couldn't.

****** Tennessee 1987 ******

"Vivienne, you have to listen to me." Benjamin Carlson looked rumpled and baggy, a shell of a man on her grandfather's porch.

"Why should I? How do I know you're Benjamin? You could be anybody." She had returned home from university on holiday break.

"I have identification. I can tell you about your childhood."

She cut him off with a sharp wave of her hand. "You've nothing to tell me. If you're Benjamin, you left. Abandoned us to live in a home you couldn't. You killed her."

The man claiming to be her father drew himself up. "She killed herself."

"Keep telling yourself that." She moved past him to go into the house.

"Minns Solagget, lite tra tomte?" *Remember the Sun Egg, little wood elf?*

She stopped in her tracks. "Jag minns. Det betyder ingenting." *I remember. It means nothing.* She moved to open the door without looking at him.

He followed on her heels. "I know where his lab is."

Vivienne snorted. "I know where his lab is. I live here, remember?"

"He has another lab. I can show you. I can prove it."

The Sun Egg hovered in her memory. In spite of her loathing, she swept her arm across the threshold. "Show me."

Her grandfather kept his basement lab tidy. He didn't allow the housekeeper down here. Vivienne looked around at the basic lab unimpressed.

Benjamin—she refused to think of him as her father—scuttled around the far corner of the room. The basement didn't extend under the garage. She watched him running his hand along the walls as if caressing a lover. "We're done—" Just as she turned to head up the stairs, she heard the click. Its loud, mechanical echo seemed to fill the room.

A harsh rattle sounded as the wall slid open along a cogged track revealing another section of the lab.

"I told you," Benjamin crowed, rushing into the new aperture.

Vivienne paused a moment, one foot hanging above the last step. She hardened her resolve and moved to follow.

Benjamin flipped pages in a journal. "It's all here. He's continued his eugenics studies. Useless of course, but he wouldn't ever see it that way."

Vivienne moved to the journal, her eyes roving over the cages of small animals, eyes blinking against the light that disturbed their sleep.

Benjamin gave way, allowing her to examine the pages. "All of the past is here. He'd never get rid of it. The only way I can live with myself is to turn him over to the authorities. He's a war criminal, you know."

Vivienne remained silent. She scanned the journal, then turned her eyes to the rest of the room. Photos of her grandfather with des führers, with Himmler, with Mengele and with Aribert Heim decorated the right wall of the room. One photo of her grandfather, at the time a very young man, under the gates of Ravensbruck Concentration Camp set her mind moving in fast forward. His work in Sweden with the People's Democratic Party. Her grandmother's constant fear or panic when the phone rang or a knock on the door startled her. Pieces of conversations fell into place. She stood thinking for a moment of the ramifications.

"I've tried to alert the authorities, but I needed the proof. I knew he'd never lower himself to get rid of these things. He always loved the work more than he loved any of us."

Benjamin's rant broke through her deliberation. "He never loved any of us," she said. "You're a fool if you didn't know that from the beginning." She strode toward the stairs. "Stay here, I'll go make sure he's not home yet. It's about that time."

"I'll need all of this for documentation." Benjamin indicated the files and photos with his hand.

"It's yours," she said with a remote tone to her voice.

Vivienne climbed the stairs. She closed the basement door and turned the deadbolt into place. She moved toward the front door where the sound of her grandfather's tires on the gravel drive alerted her to his arrival. Vivienne smoothed her hair in the mirror in the entryway. Her grandfather insisted she look neat and presentable. She stood in the entryway as he opened the front door.

"Vivienne, you're home." He dropped his keys in the bowl on the table to the right of the door. "How did your classes finish?" He hung his coat in the closet on the left without looking at her.

She stood with her hands behind her back. "Well, I think."

"Excellent. You'll be in a research lab soon." His pride wasn't for her, rather for his influence on her. He noticed something missing from the table. "Did something happen to the candlestick?"

"No, grossvater," Vivienne answered, swinging the silver candlestick into his temple.

The old man crumpled into a heap at her feet. She watched a thin trickle of blood slide toward the floor from the gash in his scalp. Nudging him with her foot, she knew he was unconscious. A pounding from the kitchen revealed Benjamin discovered the door locked. The candlestick had traveled with them through the years; so had the memorabilia in the basement. Those images, those files, would make headlines. Her medical career would be over. It would be a freak show.

She returned to the kitchen placing the candlestick on the table. Vivienne thought it fortunate he insisted on a gas stove. You needed control, he said.

Vivienne turned the gas on in each burner, took her coat and purse from the table, and headed for the front door. Benjamin shouted and pounded on the door to the basement. Solid oak because Grandfather wanted complete silence while he worked. It would hold. She opened a drawer on the entryway table and took out a small silver lighter. Stepping over her grandfather's body, she smelled the gas spreading through the house. Vivienne cracked the door as the smell of sulfur intensified. She ignited the lighter and tossed it into the house. She fell backwards into the driveway as the house whooshed into flames.

The ringing of her office phone shook Vivienne free of the memory. "Yes?" she answered.

"The subject is stable, Dr. Carlson," Viktor informed her.

She smoothed a strand of hair behind her ear. "Very well Dr. Rihard. Keep me informed."

CHAPTER FIFTEEN

Ancient history. Brittle family skeletons crumbled to dust and char. The sharp, business-minded ring of her phone stopped her before she became mired in the past again. No nonsense in her tone, she poked the speaker button. "Dr. Carlson."

An oil slick of a voice caressed the air of her office. "He's in Rome. I've emailed your photos as requested."

"Alone?" The hair on Vivienne's neck tingled a bit.

"No, he's doing business, but he's also seeing someone." The speaker hesitated as if she might reach through the airwaves and wrap her fingers around his throat.

"Seeing someone." The fact needled the pit of her stomach.

"Yes. They're traveling in Rome. Separate hotels, but they drove to the coast together today. I have a local on them. Sperlonga. I don't dare get too close. He missed my man in Rome this morning, but he won't miss a shadow in such a small town."

"Very well, you sent photos." Her throat constricted with a feeling unfamiliar to her. "Stay on him the best you can. I want to know everything."

"I'll email you updates. I thought his presence in Rome warranted a call."

"Yes, he's close." She punctuated her desire for Sebastian Cole with a jab to disconnect the phone. Vivienne sat, both hands clutching at the mahogany of her desk. She let the swift twist of hunger in her stomach pinch, and then with precise surgical control she cut off the need. She logged into her computer. Her breath catching in her chest, she sat looking face-to-face with a man she needed to complete her research. The key to everything she worked toward lay somewhere in his DNA. A man she might, her mind tripped over the unfamiliar thought … love?

Vivienne composed her thoughts and evened out her breathing. She sniffed at her reaction to the surveillance photos of Robert Smith aka Sebastian Cole. *Love.* She sneered into the empty office. Arthur Carlson had pounded the ideologies of rational thought and good genetics into her head.

"Andre!" Her voice sounded shrill.

Sebastian declined to participate in the human genome program at their first meeting. It fueled her desire to get a DNA sample from him.

"Svoj podložen?" The polished young man dipped his head through the door with a slight incline.

Vivienne thought back to the day she lost Sebastian. He refused any contact with her and it galled her how much she needed him to further her research.

Andre repeated, "Madam?"

Vivienne snapped back to the present. "I need to speak to Rihard again and then would you order some breakfast?"

Andre retreated with a bow, keeping the surprise at her emotional outburst guarded.

She dialed a number on her phone.

"Živijo?" A gruff and abrasive voice answered.

Vivienne modulated any tension out of her voice. "Živijo, Viktor."

The hoarse voice of Dr. Rihard softened. "Vivienne, I reported the subject stable. I thought we were done for the night."

"There's been a change of plans. I know things aren't quite settled, but I've decided it might be time for a test." She lightened her voice with a touch of honey. It wouldn't do to alienate the good doctor.

The pause on the other end of the line stretched. "This has been the most promising candidate yet. A field test could cost us. We might have the link we've tried for with a little more time and continued stabilization." Rihard's voice remained neutral.

"Viktor," she spoke with more honey, "I've every confidence in your assessment at this point. The test results I looked at last night show the most stabilized insertions to date. Taking the subject into the field will either speed up improvements or show us gaps in our process."

Rihard resigned. "Karkoli vi biti brez. *You know best.*"

Vivienne smiled in her victory. "Thank you, Viktor. I'll send you the details. Contact Baptiste. He'll make sure that you have the support you need."

"Yes. It'll be done."

"We'll discuss the results tomorrow when I drop by, srečno."

****

"Enzo says, if she says she can do it, she can do it. Jack Mullens stepped forward thinking he's going to teach me a lesson about where girls belong. Jaimie is sitting off to the side nursing his fat lip. I started bobbing and weaving. Jack had a good six-inch reach on me, but Enzo taught me how to compensate for that."

Sebastian liked the way Cordelia spoke with her hands, holding them up illustrating her boxing form. He watched her in his peripheral vision, listening to her story and driving close to breakneck speed. "He expected you to fight." He shook his head admiring the moxie of Enzo Fiore, who had enough confidence in his eleven-year-old daughter to allow her to fight a middle-aged man.

Cordelia snorted. "Why bother teaching me to box if I wasn't going to use it? Jack started moving. He threw the first punch, a quick right jab; he thought he would pop me and I'd go off crying. I could tell he didn't consider me a threat." Cordelia shook her head. "I dodged it, and his punch swished through the air near my left ear. Before he could reset his feet, I came around on his weak side with a sharp uppercut and knocked him on his butt." Her laugh tumbled up from her diaphragm.

Cordelia didn't strike him as the type of woman who would hire her business out. The idea pleased him with a twinge of guilt. *Maybe Lorena was right.* He pushed the thought down remembering the job.

Cordelia reached back for a water bottle from the food basket. "Water?"

Sebastian nodded and pulled a deep drink from the bottle. He noticed she took a sip of water from the bottle without wiping it off. *Focus.*

He enjoyed the drive. The autostrada took them through the countryside, and whenever ruins appeared, Sebastian took a moment to give her a brief history or explanation. In between these short informative lectures, they fell into a companionable silence. He liked her comfort with the quiet. By necessity of the work, he didn't chitchat.

Sebastian pointed ahead of them showing her the sign for Sperlonga. "The town's ten minutes from the turnoff. We'll arrive at Thomas and Rachna's place in a tick." Sebastian pushed a nondescript button on the dashboard, dialing Thomas with his hands-free device. "All right, you bulldog devil, we're here."

"Great! Is everything fine? You haven't eaten her or anything?" Thomas inquired, his good humor pouring out of the speaker.

"No, she's still alive." He turned to Cordelia. "Say something so he'll believe you're whole and in good health."

Cordelia laughed. "I'm whole and in good health," she called into the microphone on the dash.

"You old goat." He clicked off and made a left turn that brought the town, spread out along the coastline, into view.

Sperlonga served as the ancient coastal retreat of Emperor Tiberius. Tiberius built his villa and a series of grottos to serve as his own private resort. The town earned its name from the Latin word for grotto, speluncae. Sperlonga popped onto the tourist radar after construction of the Via Flacca.

"Getting around the town's much easier by foot if you don't mind walking up and down stairs. Most of the old streets are too narrow for cars," Sebastian told her.

Sebastian drove away from the main square. A few streets into the building block tumble of villas, he made a quick right turn pulling into the driveway behind Thomas's bright green Fiat.

****

Cordelia smiled at the affection and camaraderie on Thomas's face. She snuck a glance at Sebastian. The affection for Thomas shone on his face for a moment. *See,* her imp said, *he can't be all bad. He loves his friends. Whatever,* she told the imp. T*his isn't anything. I'm on vacation. This is just a moment, a blink.* The imp didn't answer. Cordelia leaned against the car, hesitant to break the spell. He looked … good, walking with a hand out to take Thomas's. She reached out to the two men with her talent.

For a moment, standing in the airy blue sunlight of the Italian coast, hefting a picnic basket out of the backseat of his bright little sports car, Sebastian Cole looked human. Cordelia frowned a bit as a double image of

Sebastian floated into her consciousness. Like the double exposure of film, each image ghosted over the other. She blinked her eyes, nauseated. It looked as though someone smudged a damp photograph. The two distinct images became overwhelmed by a third image that bloomed to take over the other two—a darker shadow. It brushed at the edge of her mind. If she reached for a bit more energy, she could feel pieces of a tumbler spinning to click into place. She couldn't tell if she reached into the future or the past, but something pushed back against her.

Placing a hand on the car and rubbing her eyes with the other, she tried to release the dizzying visions. She worked to focus her eyes on the real Sebastian in the white shirt who strode toward Thomas. Thomas stared at her face. Sebastian turned back to her. In Cordelia's mind, the concrete vision she had in the present blurred. Losing her tenuous hold on reality, her head swam with visions that seemed to be a mix of past, present, and something else she couldn't define. A pair of liquid jet black eyes burning with flame filled her head. She succumbed to vertigo and the ground slammed up to meet her.

CHAPTER SIXTEEN

"I'm an idiot," Cordelia muttered, adjusting the ice pack to look at the beautiful woman. Slender with creamy caramel skin, Rachna Singh wore her hair pulled into a waist-length ponytail. Her rich almond-shaped eyes glistened with humor. The ankle-length silk skirt swished around her legs when she moved. A light rose-colored camisole displayed her shoulders and a tattoo of the goddess Kali at the center of her spine starting at the base of her neck.

"This is stupid," Cordelia said, touching her forehead.

Rachna smiled and handed Cordelia a cup of hot tea. "Are you saying that for my benefit or yours?"

Cordelia smelled the Oolong wafting up from her cup. She set the ice pack down and took a sip of tea. She wondered where Sebastian disappeared.

The elegant Indian woman sat in an overstuffed chair covered in curry-colored paisley. She picked up her own cup of tea and blew to cool it. "He's at the café with Thomas buying bread, meat, and cheese, probably the entire deli counter. Thomas is berating himself for depriving you of a real breakfast." Her laugh punctuated the humor in her eyes.

Cordelia sipped her tea, surprised Rachna read her thoughts.

Rachna gave a throaty chuckle. "I'm not a mind reader. It's not a gift that runs in my family, but I'm good at reading people. You might take a while, but I'll get the hang of you. What happened out there?"

Cordelia didn't know. It would be awkward and embarrassing to try to explain to a complete stranger, no matter how kind.

"Look, you aren't dying are you?"

Cordelia shook her head. "I hope not."

"You aren't narcoleptic or schizophrenic?"

"Not diagnosed." Both women laughed.

"You like Sebastian." No question, just a statement.

Cordelia thought about it for a moment. "I haven't decided."

Rachna chortled. "You'll be fine. Just so you know, I'm a good listener."

Cordelia gazed at the unusual woman sitting across from her. She couldn't think with her head throbbing to the rhythm of her pulse. To her credit, Rachna waited, allowing Cordelia time. A few silent moments stretched out between the two women without tension or discomfort. She struggled with self-doubt. Trusting people had never played out well.

Rachna, to her credit, settled into the cushions of the chair without any impatience. Cordelia had never met such a serene woman. The absence of friends didn't bother her. Rachna's poise and deportment tugged at a small space where Cordelia had tucked her loneliness. Her suspicious nature and keen judge of character worked overtime trying to pinpoint any dissembling on Rachna's part. Stepping out on a ledge she had been pushed off made her wary. Cordelia reached out with her senses and found nothing but open warmth in the woman. *Here we go.*

"I'm a freak. I know things no one possibly could."

Rachna's serene and patient countenance didn't waver. She absorbed Cordelia's serious admission.

"I like the kitchen for serious conversation. Everything's better when food is involved." She motioned Cordelia to follow her through an arch. "Come on, let's freshen our tea."

Cordelia didn't offer an argument. Rachna sounded like her nonna. She followed the graceful woman into the kitchen. The comfort and light in the kitchen soothed her nerves. Warmed by the colors of the Mediterranean, the kitchen's high ceiling allowed the flow of fresh air from the wide open doors on the balcony. Hand-painted ceramic tiles wrapped around the walls above the counters. Handwoven rugs broke up the cool, stone floor with coarse, natural fibers dipped in vegetable dyes.

Outside of the kitchen, the balcony wrapped around the entire upper floor of the villa. The bright open arch offered a view of the town and the bay below the hill. A cool ocean breeze danced its way through the sunny kitchen to the rest of the rooms in the villa. Filled with a familiar feeling of light and love, Cordelia relaxed. Rachna indicated a stool for Cordelia near a countertop on the stovetop island.

The Oolong tea went a long way to restoring her calm and now her stomach growled. Glad there wasn't a mirror in the room, she touched her forehead.

Rachna peered at her injury and took the ice. She emptied melted ice into the sink with a light laugh. "You'll live; I think. The skin isn't broken. You're lucky to have missed the car. Sebastian wouldn't forgive you for denting it. So you're the mind reader." Rachna commented while she removed things from the refrigerator. She brought out a head of lettuce, tomatoes, and several other vegetables to put on a sandwich. To answer Cordelia's quizzical gaze, she shrugged. "We're going to have sandwiches for lunch. I like more than meat and bread." She placed a fresh red onion in front of Cordelia then handed her a knife and a cutting board. "You can slice an onion?"

Cordelia rolled her eyes. "Please, I have an Italian nonna."

Rachna nodded, slicing a tomato, and coaxed, "Explain. You're psychic."

Discussing the topic would be a relief, freeing her from isolation and secrecy. Her stomach roiled with nausea. "Psychic may not be exactly correct."

Rachna thought for a minute. "Do you know what I'm thinking?"

"Not right this minute, my head is throbbing. Sometimes I can pick up a person's thoughts. Most often I know someone's intentions. I can tell if someone is lying or dangerous. I know things happened in the past, particularly if the past is violent."

Rachna sighed. "So you don't know exactly what I'm thinking, more what I'm feeling."

Cordelia nodded. "If I push, I can see your thoughts and if a person's a strong transmitter then I might see into his or her mind, but I usually see the future or the past."

Rachna waved her knife in the air. "Transmit?" She slid the tomatoes onto a platter and moved on to banana peppers. She shook her head, distracted by a random thought. "Do you like banana peppers? Thomas loves banana peppers. I just don't understand it. They're not sweet, they're not spicy. I don't get it." She looked up at Cordelia. "How long have you been doing this? This picking up transmissions."

Cordelia slid her own stack of paper-thin slices of red onion to the plate, resting them next to the tomatoes. She remained silent for a minute.

Rachna clucked approval at Cordelia's knife skills.

"If I'm picking up signals then I'm that piece of tinfoil you have to hold in just the right position to get a station."

Rachna laughed.

"All my life, no one paid much attention until I turned four. My nonna claims I've always been a step ahead of people. Once, my father loves this story, at two years old I wanted to play with keys. Not his keys, not my mother's keys. I wanted a set of keys from a hook in our kitchen. I screamed and screamed until I had my hands on those keys. I refused to go anywhere without those keys for days. On a grocery trip in the Vancouver winter, my father locked the keys in the car. He said I held out the key ring without a noise. I had the spare set of keys."

Rachna sipped the last of her tea without a sound.

Cordelia took a soft breath. "I anticipated my mother's death. I didn't know how to articulate it. I followed her everywhere worried."

Rachna took the water kettle from the stove and poured the steaming liquid over the Oolong leaves in the teapot. After rinsing Cordelia's cup, she refilled it.

Cordelia shook her head at the past. "I carried a toy doctor's bag demanding to give her medicine."

Rachna nodded.

"I wore the stethoscope and would take her blood pressure then give her a shot. Without warning, she began to get tired. Her legs would give out on her. Sometimes her hands would quit working, and she would drop things. Insulin-resistant type 2 diabetes. Back in the '80s, treatment took a lot of time. Not like now, with portable pocket-sized blood monitors and insulin pens." Cordelia moved to the sink to wash the lettuce. She peeled the leaves and stacked them on a paper towel. "She tried to keep up with it. She had a hundred little reasons why she neglected to get checked."

Rachna handed her a cucumber to peel.

"She slipped into a coma and died a few days later." Cordelia's memory of the antiseptic smell of the hospital room came back with sharp clarity. She remembered the sound of the nurses and patients in the hospital. Cordelia recalled the exhaustion and anxiety as they watched her mother struggle with each breath, the moments of apnea when it seemed as if each gasp would be her last. Sometimes the pause between her breaths would be as long as ninety seconds; she held her breath with her mother.

She stared at the cucumber and shook her head clear of the memories. "That's one of the few times I could tune into someone's mind. I think she had abilities of her own and it strengthened our connection." Cordelia reached back into time. "I could hear my mother. She couldn't talk, but I could hear her thoughts. She recited lists of things in the house she didn't want my aunt Rita to have after she passed. She shouted with frustration at her inability to make us hear her. I told Nonna, and she started writing things down." Cordelia looked up to see Rachna nod, a sad look on her face. "She commanded me to tell her everything I heard. I did, and Nonna wrote." Cordelia could see her worn and gnarled hands fly over the paper frenzied with purpose. "Do you want this cucumber in slices or spears?"

Rachna looked up from the counter. "Oh, I could whip up a little tzatziki to dip them in, yes? Spears." She moved to the refrigerator. "Go on."

Cordelia sliced the cucumbers into spears. "Nonna kept it to herself for a while, but soon she called my father into the room and showed him what we had been doing. He crouched down to look me in the eye with his hands on my shoulders and asked what Momma said. I told him about her love for us. I couldn't explain it all. I've only seen him cry one time." Cordelia took a deep breath, clearing her lungs of the choking, threatening tears.

"I climbed up on the hospital bed to whisper in Momma's ear I loved her. That's when she spoke directly to me. I almost fell off the bed. She sent a flood of images I still think about. She told me how much she loved me.

"She said good-bye, then went silent. I told them Momma left. Enzo and Nonna looked defeated. The doctor took my mother off of the machines." She looked up resolved. "That's when I accepted my ability. It helped Enzo and Nonna deal with my mother's death. It helped me. I haven't missed her as much because I said good-bye."

Both Rachna and Cordelia had stopped working on the food, caught up in the story. Rachna shook herself, wiping a stray tear from her cheek, and put on the kettle for more tea. "A gift. Not many of us experience that. Does it work like that always?"

She shook her head. "No, but, in general, men are the easiest to read, and I can hear them because they're loud thinkers. Most of the time, I know when something's going to happen. It's déjà vu only stronger."

"Oh, you poor thing!" Rachna blurted. "Imagine, being able to hear what men are thinking! I love Thomas, and he's not a stupid man, but to hear his every thought? I'd go mad!"

For a moment, Cordelia sat a little confused at the sudden change in tone, but as the comic look of horror on Rachna's face sank in, she started laughing.

Rachna joined her. The two were bent over in tear-stained mirth by the time Sebastian and Thomas walked in with brown paper sacks under their arms.

Sebastian set his burdens down on the counter and shot Thomas a look. He popped open a bottle of beer then stomped out of the kitchen. His exit sent Rachna and Cordelia into another wave of laughter causing more tears down their cheeks. Thomas beat a quick retreat to join him.

Rachna managed to catch her breath long enough to mutter, "Laughter through tears, what a relief."

Cordelia, gasping for air and wiping her eyes, nodded with a chuckle.

"Hearing people all of the time must get tiresome."

"Yes, it does." Cordelia sighed. "But I can turn the volume down to a buzz. It's like static. Otherwise, I know sometimes it's useful, but often it's terrible."

Rachna gave her an understanding look. "Too much information!"

"Exactly. You'd think tapping into the future would be an advantage, but not everyone has a bright future. Sometimes I see things I don't want to know. Imagine meeting a man you're interested in and knowing he'll cheat on you or steal something. Or picking up random thoughts from the minds around you … it's great when you're doing business and you know the price that'll close the deal. Knowing a person's stealing from their parents or is going to walk in front of a bus tomorrow?" She shuddered.

"You could save people."

"People don't believe me. They call psychic hotlines or have their palms read, but they don't want to know the future if it's terrible. The future isn't written in stone either. I've been sure of something and it played out differently because someone made a different choice. Choices alter our paths. Some people are locked into their destiny and it frightens me. I developed a filter. People on the street, people in restaurants, those people are white noise. What can I say? It sounds nuts."

"What about me? Want to look into my future?" Rachna smiled at her.

"Nope. First off, it doesn't always work and I never look at family," she paused, "or friends."

Rachna placed her warm caramel hand over Cordelia's own olive one. "Have you peeked at Thomas and Sebastian?"

"A little. When we first met, I looked to see any threat, but they're unusual. I can't get more than a rough impression of their mood. Also," she thought about it, "they don't buzz. They hum. I think they filter their thoughts on their own."

"Filtering on their own?" Rachna frowned.

"The hum I detect. I think over time, they've learned not to transmit. I would never admit it to them, but it's more pleasant than the normal buzz. Military training's my theory. Eighty percent of human communication is non-verbal. I think they've been trained to prevent information from slipping and it's shaped their conscious and unconscious communication. At least that's what I'm going with at this point." Cordelia worried about the mood on the terrace. "I'd better go explain. What am I going to say?" She pushed up off of the stool.

Rachna stopped her with a gentle squeeze of her hand. "What happened in the driveway? At the Colosseum?"

Cordelia stopped. "I can tell you what happened at the Colosseum. When I visit places, I pick up strong emotional …echoes. That's the best way to describe them. The strongest echoes are linked to violence, pain, or fear. They are powerful and they make me ill. At the Colosseum I wasn't expecting any echoes. One hit me and I wasn't prepared."

"And the driveway?" Rachna prodded.

"No clue. Not the falling part." She smiled. "I'm kind of a klutz. I had a clear vision of Thomas's image of Sebastian. Happy to see him, Thomas transmitted a wave of joy and pleasure. Those are also forceful. Good job helping Sebastian with his clothes, by the way, I'm impressed."

Rachna shook her head smiling. "I don't know what you're implying. Sebastian is a big boy."

Cordelia rolled her eyes. "It's like I stepped into his mind and saw through Thomas's eyes. Sebastian walking toward him looking fabulous in his shirt and vest, the present. The image contrasted with a recent memory of Sebastian, dour and menacing. On top of those thoughts, another indistinct image, powerful but smudged, overlay the two images." She stopped in frustration.

Rachna looked at Cordelia with a measuring gaze. "Are you afraid of what's going to happen? Afraid of Sebastian or something he's going to do?"

Cordelia shook her head, then put a hand to her bruised forehead. "No. Don't get me wrong; Sebastian's dangerous. He exudes power though I don't feel threatened. It doesn't matter …" she trailed off closing her eyes.

"What?" Rachna leaned in waiting.

"This is crazy, but right before I fell before things went dark, Sebastian's eyes glowed with flames. I don't know what that means, but Rachna ..." Cordelia looked at the gracious woman across from her before closing her eyes to remember. "Yesterday morning leaving the hotel, I thought I heard something or maybe remembered something. It felt like snatches of a dream." Cordelia opened her eyes looking for a response from Rachna.

"Cordelia, Sebastian's a good man. He's been hurt and changed in a way that can't be fixed, ever. That said, there's so much inside the man, deep inside, so deep I don't think he knows it. Believe me when I say Sebastian's the last man you'll ever meet who would hurt you." She cocked her head to the side, a naughty gleam in her eye. "Of course, he might do many stupid and hurtful things without thinking. He's a man, after all."

CHAPTER SEVENTEEN

Sebastian sipped his beer brooding over the marina. “Women are crazy. Well, Rachna isn’t completely round the bend. Cordelia clocked in the head with a rock and they’re in there giggling. That makes no sense.”

“Look, Cordelia’s fine and they‘re getting to know each other. Rachna likes her. I can tell.” Sebastian noted a strange look on Thomas’s face, but it passed. “I’m famished, and I don’t dare go back in there until Rachna gives the go-ahead.”

Sebastian’s stomach growled in agreement. Cordelia and Rachna stepped out into the fresh air on the balcony.

“Shaw, come help me slice up the bread you bought. We’ll have sandwiches out here.” She had a knowing look in her eye. Sebastian appreciated the room to talk.

“Sebastian …another beer?”

“Not right now, thanks,” Sebastian said, eyes evaluating Cordelia. A bit of prey to be snatched up for a meal. Sebastian gestured to her battered forehead. “How’s that feel?”

Grimacing, she admitted, “Like someone coldcocked me in the head with a bat. I‘m all right.”

Sebastian doubted it. “If you’re fine, why do you spend so much time falling down in a faint?”

Offense to his sardonic tone bloomed on her face. “Twice, okay. I’ve fainted twice, and I didn’t faint the first time, I swooned. No, I didn’t swoon. I hate that word. I stumbled.” She took a breath and cut off his attempt to make a comment. “And you’ve only known me for two days, that doesn’t qualify you to judge whether I spend most of my time fainting. In fact, after all of the sugar and caffeine you supplied on the drive, it isn’t any wonder I became lightheaded. You promised me breakfast, well, Thomas did and I’m not a chic Italian mantenuta who breezes through the day on an espresso and a sweet cake. I’m from North America. I need sustenance in the morning. I may be a klutz,” she frowned. He felt his eyebrow rising on its own. “I admit that I’m a little prone to trip or bump into things, but I’m not a helpless, swooning—god, I hate that word—female.”

“You finished?” he asked.

He thought she might stick out her tongue at him. “I think so,” she replied. Reluctance radiated from her body.

“First, I don’t think you’re a …kept woman, isn’t that what mantenuta means?” His eyebrow rose a little higher, and he suppressed a chuckle. “Nor do I consider you a swooning female. I don’t bother with swooning females. Do women even swoon these days?” He proffered the question with real wonder in his voice. He put his finger up when she opened her mouth to respond. “Rhetorical question. I’m bothered you fell face forward into the driveway, and you’ve no good explanation for it. I don’t think you could injure yourself more without the local polizia thinking I’m the one beating you.”

Her puff of frustration amused him. “When I figure out what happened then I’ll be happy to fill you in. Until then, I promise I won’t trip, bump, stumble, burn, or otherwise injure myself for the duration of your company. Acceptable?” She frowned.

He tried to maintain a serious mien. “If you promise, I suppose I must take you at your word.” Sebastian allowed the corner of his mouth turn up.

Thomas, carrying a tray of cold cuts out to place on the table, stopped in his tracks. The pair turned toward Thomas, the moment over. Thomas blinked. “I thought I saw you smile. I couldn’t have seen you smile. Did you smile?”

Sebastian’s eyebrow rose again. “Very funny. Is that lunch?”

Thomas chuckled, and he shouted over his shoulder, “Rachna, aliens have replaced Sebastian. He attempted a smile.”

Rachna clucked her tongue as she sashayed onto the balcony with thick slices of fresh bread and the vegetables she and Cordelia prepared. “You could hurt yourself if you’re not careful. You might strain something.”

“Cordelia, I give you my best friends. People never skittish about drawing a little blood.” Sebastian gestured to the couple.

Cordelia admonished, “You afraid of bloodshed? I doubt it.”

“Right you are, Cordelia, right you are,” he replied. He shot a look at Thomas and Rachna.

Rachna passed out plates and shifted the conversation. “Why don’t we eat so we can head down to the market? There are some artists there I’d like Cordelia to see.”

Sebastian received her silent command to lighten up and pulled out Cordelia’s chair. “I’m ready to eat. Cordelia?”

“I’m ravenous.” She took a plate from Rachna as Sebastian slid into his own chair. Sebastian avoided looking at Thomas, who grinned, and Rachna cleared her throat.

“Thomas, I forgot the limonata. Be a dear and go get it for me?”

Looking chagrined, Thomas retreated for the drinks.

After lunch, the small company walked down the hill to the center of the old town and the market square. The piazza overflowed with a variety of vendors and artists beneath colorful awnings and canopies, each one with something to sell. Organic farmers, several bakeries with all sorts of breads and rolls, painters, weavers, potters, and jewelry makers. Cordelia clapped her hands with pleasure at each new turn.

Rachna strolled under a Chinese parasol shading her head from the bright sun. Several people greeted the Shaws. The couple made their mark in the short time they lived in Sperlonga. Cordelia hung back a bit, Sebastian a polite distance at her side. She purchased a straw hat from the vendor Thomas said made his hat. Sebastian thought Cordelia, cosmopolitan and jaunty, as she strolled through the piazza with her Audrey Hepburn-style chapeau and an oversized bag. *All she needs is a scoop of gelato dripping down her chin like a Fellini movie.*

Sebastian enjoyed Cordelia's delight. He swept his eyes over the buffalo cheese and cotton rugs while keeping pace with her. He gave a cordial nod to several people he knew. Though fewer people offered convivial greetings, people showed their amicable respect.

Catching Cordelia in a sideways glance, he remarked, "You're surprised the people here like me."

"That isn't fair to you. Not every impression I have of you is negative."

He challenged her. "Really? Tell me something pleasant that you've thought about me today."

She drummed her fingers on her chin pretending to think hard. "Okay, you look very Italian today."

"Oh, that's rich. That's supposed to be a compliment?" He snorted.

Cordelia paused to look at some jewelry. "I suppose I mean that you fit in today. You look affable, not as if you're going to pounce any minute for a fresh jugular." She fingered a ring with a cabochon of green amber as big as her thumb. The plump vendor encouraged her to try it on.

Sebastian noted her pleasure in the large ring and queried, "Do I usually look like I'm going to snack on the nearest warm-blooded creature?"

To which Thomas, eavesdropping from the neighboring candy vendor, called out, "YES!"

Cordelia laughed, and Sebastian scowled. "Mind your own business, Shaw."

Thomas turned away, popping a caramel he'd just purchased into his mouth. Sebastian could tell by his shaking shoulders that he still chuckled.

"Need I say more?" She turned to the portly jewelry maker. "Quanto per l'anello?"

"Tre cento cinquanta euro, signora."

Sebastian stood off to the side as Cordelia felt the weight of the ring and scrutinized the green amber. "Duo cento euro."

The woman knew a tourista when she saw one, but didn't know Cordelia's skill. She scoffed at the offer. "Tre cento, signora."

The bright Canadian countered, "Duo venti euro." The artisan rolled her eyes.

"You think I'll pounce on you?" Sebastian interrupted into dicey territory. His brain shied from the silly line of inquiry, but somewhere in the pit of his stomach he waited for an answer.

"Me? No, I don't think you'd gobble me up big bad wolf style." She turned the ring in the sunlight. "I think you view people as … oh, I don't know, but not as equals, not in general at any rate. There are people you like and respect, Thomas and Rachna. I imagine the people who work for you."

"That's all, I have a general disdain for the human race outside of myself and a few select souls?" He knew his face looked stony.

"You don't have to make it sound like that. It sounds mean that way. Let's just say I wouldn't ever want to cross you."

"Duo settantcinque euro," the jolly woman countered.

Sebastian gave a disgruntled huff, pulled out a handful of euros, and paid the woman 275 euros. The woman smiled jabbering about his good sense and value.

She took Cordelia's hand and slid the ring onto her right index finger.

He walked away into the square, hearing her move to catch up.

Reaching his side she complained, "Haven't you dickered? I'd have bargained her down to a better price."

"We would've stood there the rest of the day while you two haggled like a couple of old hens."

"Well ..." she stopped. "Thank you." She extended her right hand admiring the green amber. "Amber's one of my favorites."

Her quick cool down took Sebastian aback. "You're welcome."

Sebastian saw Rachna and Thomas chatting with an organic fruit farmer. Rachna smelled and poked the plums.

"I have a confession to make," she said.

Sebastian gave a slight turn of his head to listen.

"I'm afraid I dropped your name this morning to shut down a co-worker."

"You dropped my name?" He kept his voice neutral.

She kept her eyes straight ahead. "I may've alluded I knew you .... better."

He looked at her with the corner of his mouth turned up. "Did it work?"

Cordelia pointed to him. "You're making a habit of that, you know." He dropped his mouth to a stern line. She sighed. "Yes. David's good at what he does, but he's an ass. He called me this morning looking for some information. He assumed I'd be alone and pining. It ticked me off so I dropped your name."

"Did it dampen his spirit?"

Cordelia gave a light laugh. "It certainly did. I may've implied we arranged to meet. I shouldn't have, but it felt good to squash him."

"We're intimately acquainted?" He stopped to regard her.

Cordelia cleared her throat a little. "Yep."

"Okay," he stated and swept his arm out for her to lead the way.

Mid-step she grabbed his arm. He looked into her eyes surprised at the physical contact. A sharp addition of citrus to her earthy, floral scent filled his nostrils.

Her pupils dilated, focusing on the invisible. In a formal, ceremonial tone, words spilled out of her mouth. "Hunger. Turmoil. The painful taste of desire unsatisfied. There's no changing the past. That created can't be unmade. The hunter approaches."

CHAPTER EIGHTEEN

Sebastian frowned at her. "What?"

Mute for a moment in concentration, she startled back to the piazza, to her hand on his arm. She shook her head as her vision cleared. "I . . . I'm not sure." Cordelia looked around at the hustle and bustle of the piazza market struggling to recall her words. "Hunger, desire, and creation?" Her mind regained focus. The spinning tumbler in her mind clicked into place. "I think you're being followed."

Without a word, Sebastian gave a short two-toned whistle. Thomas, out of sight around a booth, appeared with an expression of watchfulness.

Cordelia detected a slight ripple in the air, but as she tried to focus it disappeared.

Sebastian signed something to Thomas. Thomas whispered to Rachna then vanished between two vendor stalls. Rachna came to stand near Cordelia.

"Sebastian?" she asked in a low voice.

"Take Cordelia back to the villa. Wander, meander, but make sure you're not followed. It's a small town. A tail will be easy to spot. As quickly as you can without appearing suspicious." Sebastian gave a brief glance toward Cordelia, chilling her, and then strode off determined.

Confused, Cordelia allowed Rachna to take her arm. They stopped at several vendors though Rachna headed them back with a purpose.

"What's going on?" Cordelia managed to squeak out.

"Look at that rug! Isn't it lovely?" Rachna exclaimed, and then under her breath she added, "I'm not sure. Sebastian believes we're being followed. He and Thomas are going to look for whoever it is."

Cordelia groaned.

"What? What is it?" Rachna looked over her shoulder.

"I said something. I had a vision …it just poured out. I told Sebastian someone hunted for him."

"A premonition?"

"More a prophecy. I just know someone's looking for him. It might not mean right this minute."

Rachna gave a thoughtful nod. "Okay, but Sebastian and Thomas haven't remained alive this long without taking precautions. It's good to be alert." She pointed to a side stairway that led up to the next street. "Let's turn up here. They'll get us back to the villa faster than going through the piazza. No one will follow because there's no cover. Besides, if there's someone watching, they know where we live."

The two women hurried back to the villa and flew into the safety of the door. Rachna took her purchases into the kitchen.

Cordelia slumped onto a stool. "Whew. Fear and paranoia are exhausting."

"Three flights of stairs and two miles don't help," Rachna quipped. Being followed didn't ruffle her. "I don't know about you, but I think a light Prosecco might be in order." Just as she opened the wine, Thomas and Sebastian arrived with grim expressions.

Pouring two glasses, Rachna asked, "Well?"

Thomas pulled down another glass. "Someone's in town asking questions about Sebastian."

Sebastian grumbled. “I don’t think anyone tailed us in the piazza. There’s just not enough room, but there’s a presence here and that means there’s a presence in Rome.” He slammed his hand on the counter.

Rachna handed him a glass. “Sebastian, darling, please don’t damage my new kitchen.”

Sebastian looked up. “Sorry. I missed it. I didn’t notice anything in the city.” He glanced at Cordelia.

Thomas said, “It isn’t a problem. Thanks to Cordelia we know someone’s shadowing our movements.”

Cordelia watched Sebastian thinking about his distraction. He shook his head. Indecision flitted across his face; strange or not, the warning helped.

“I didn’t mean to cause a problem.” Cordelia saw the look on Sebastian’s face. She didn’t need to read the thoughts in his head because they appeared on his face.

Thomas sat down at the table near Cordelia. “Someone’s poking around. I’ll call into the office. Tulane and Jackson can track these people. We’ll be on top of this in no time.”

“We’re going back.”

They all looked at Sebastian. He stared with an inscrutable face at Cordelia. “Now.”

Sebastian loaded Cordelia into the car to return to Rome after a brief good-bye and exchange of numbers.

In the silence on the ride back to Rome, Cordelia thought about the piazza. That kind of divination hadn’t happened in a long time. She wondered what Sebastian thought. Irritated that it mattered to her, Cordelia played through each and every nuance of their conversation. She sensed Sebastian casting glances at her as she dozed.

The twinkling lights of the city began to dance in the distance. "Are you hungry?" His deep, growling voice cut the silence.

Cordelia roused back to consciousness. "Yes. A little."

"I know of a place, kind of a hole near your hotel," he said, his tone brusque.

"Okay," she said.

"Okay." Sebastian settled, a little less on edge.

They lapsed into silence until they reached the restaurant. The valet jumped out into the street and waited while Sebastian helped her out of the car.

Entering the little place, a short, round Italian man approached them beaming. "Signore Cole, so good to see you." He pumped Sebastian's hand forcefully. "Come, come, I have a quiet table in the back for you and the bella signorina."

"Thanks, Lucca. Can we have a bottle of the Valpolicella?"

The cheerful man nodded. "Si, of course. Would you like to see the menu or I can bring you the specials?"

"Any special requests?" Sebastian asked.

"No, I trust your judgement." She sat in the chair Lucca held out for her and rolled her eyes. *Really! Could you sound a bit less like a romance novel?*

A younger version of the portly Lucca brought a bottle of wine to the table. Sebastian sat next to her, back to the wall. "Thanks, Marco." Sebastian poured two café glasses and slid one over to her. "Drink."

Sipping the light red wine, she mused over the prophecy. She had tumbled into a world of intrigue. Less than twenty-four hours since she had met him. The waiter, Marco, set the café table and left a basket of bread. He smiled at Cordelia and lit two delicate tapers.

Sebastian met her gaze as he rubbed a hand through his unruly mop of jet. She thought he struggled with something, but still couldn't pick up any distinct thoughts from his head.

They sat silent. Lucca returned with a cart full of dishes. Lifting lids off of the dishes, he released the tempting aroma of hot food.

Cordelia's stomach growled.

She saw the corner of his mouth trying to twitch up into the small expression of his humor. "A little hungry?"

"Yes." She met his scrutiny. Her hunger announced its urge to taste the food again.

He said, "We have things to talk about."

"Yes." She didn't bother to contain her sigh.

"Talk is fine, but eating feeds the soul," Lucca said, dishing out large portions of lasagna. "Mangia! Eat, eat!"

Taking a plate from Lucca gladly, to her pleasure, he ladled extra sauce over the lasagna from a different pan. "I love it that way."

She caught the ghost of a smile spread across Sebastian's face.

Lucca answered, "It's the only way he eats it."

Alongside the lasagna, Lucca served them delicious green beans and another fresh loaf of bread.

Sebastian sprinkled some Parmigiano-Reggiano from a bowl onto his lasagna and then sipped from his glass. "I'm not sure what to ask."

"I'm not certain what to tell you," Cordelia answered before plowing a large bite of lasagna into her mouth.

"I've never understood women who ate daintily," he said, watching her display.

She paused mid-chew. "Are you saying I'm not dainty?" She saw he tried to keep his face shrouded.

He choked off a little laugh. "No. I appreciate a good appetite."

Cordelia snorted into another large bite of lasagna. "Pathetic save."

Sebastian took a bite from his plate. Cordelia saw doubt on his face. She questioned her own judgement and thought it might be too late to change anything. "Okay, let's start with the Colosseum. You didn't faint out of nowhere."

"The psychic energy generated by violent games in the height of the Roman Empire still exists. Sometimes, when I'm in places of extreme emotion, positive or negative, a wave of energy dips out of time and hits me. Bam, I'm down."

Sebastian took another bite, processing her explanation. "So …from somewhere in the space-time continuum, emotional energy bubbles up and you feel it?"

She failed to detect any sarcasm. "I'm not certain about your use of the space-time continuum. It seems a little too sci-fi but I suppose that's as good as any. Yep, that's one thing that happens to me."

Sebastian cleared his throat and took another sip of wine. "In order for you to detect these residual moments, you'd have to tap a higher sensitivity. Psychic?"

"Yes." She didn't see any point in mitigating the truth.

"Can you read my mind? Tell me my future? Give me winning lotto numbers?" he asked.

Cordelia laughed. "No, I can't read your mind." *Because you're not like any person I know.* "I might be able to look into your future, but the future is constantly changing. The future I see would only happen if you did nothing to alter it. For example, having a bomboli for breakfast instead of eggs could rewrite what followed." He almost smiled at her reference to their morning. "You don't need the winning lotto numbers. According to public financial records, Global Surety Enterprises made over twenty million dollars last year and I suspect you made double that."

His eyebrow rose. “You checked up on me?” He mused for a moment. “I understand what you mean about the bomboli. Approximately, thirty-eight million to be exact.”

The conversation lapsed as they stared at each other, unasked questions and unspoken answers swirling around their heads.

“Where do we go from here?” Cordelia broke the silence.

He sat for a moment. “It wasn’t an accident we met you at the Colosseum.”

A flicker of apprehension rose in her. “What do you mean?”

His face showed uncertainty and he remained silent.

The display of emotion from him worried her more than his hesitation. “Tell me.”

CHAPTER NINETEEN

Sebastian didn't know how to say it. He knew using her without her knowing would be impossible.

She sat calmly waiting with no expression on her face.

"We needed your help." He started but before he could explain further Cordelia snorted. She wrinkled her nose as if catching an odious scent.

"No," she said. "Not an actual scent yet."

Sebastian stared at her. "Are you all right?"

Her voice had a faraway quality. "A trap."

He shifted into alert mode. "What? Where?"

Cordelia shook her head. "I don't know. Something's not right …I can smell it; it's threatening. This is crazy."

"Considering this morning it doesn't sound crazy. How much time? Will they attack the restaurant?" He pulled his phone from his pocket.

Cordelia looked out to the street. She indicated with her head. "This hasn't happened before … I can't be sure, but I think across the street. Men are waiting." She pointed.

Pushing a speed dial number, his hand tightened around Cordelia's. "Alonzo, you in the office?"

"Si."

"Get the GPS beacon up on this phone." Sebastian looked at her with grim determination.

"Done. What do you need?"

"Park and Crosse on duty?"

"Ah, no. Jackson and MacColgan are mobile. Park and Crosse are here. Ten minutes ETA. You need us?"

Sebastian thought a minute. "Christ, MacColgan? Okay, send Jackson and MacColgan to pick up Cordelia. She'll have my phone." He paused seeing movement outside. He squeezed Cordelia's hand. "Send Park and Crosse to rendezvous with me at this location. Tell them to be ready for a fight."

"Si. Cleanup crew?"

"Just to be on the safe side." Sebastian ended the conversation and handed the phone to Cordelia. "Put that in your bra. Don't lose it."

Her chuckle sounded nervous. "Wouldn't a pocket be more appropriate?"

Sebastian glanced at her out of the corner of his eye. "You don't have any pockets."

Cordelia tucked the phone into the cup of her bra. "I feel like I'm in a bad spy movie."

"We'll make sure you're wearing something with pockets next time." He called Lucca over. "My friend, we have a little problem." He nodded toward the door.

Lucca gave him a determined look. "My boy and I can help."

"We've got it covered," Sebastian said, placing a hand on his shoulder. "But I thank you for the offer."

"Saints protect you, il mio amico," the stout man said.

Sebastian took Cordelia's arm. "Let's go." They stepped out into the street. "Now, listen. Two agents are tracking my phone. Depending on their number, there will be a front and rear assault. I'm going to eliminate the threat from the fore. You make a break for it. Run as fast as you can toward the hotel and look for a blue Porsche Cayenne." He checked to be sure she understood. "At least you aren't wearing heels."

She took a deep breath. "What're you going to do after I start running?"

An edge of steel crept into his voice. "You don't want to know. Don't look back, don't slow down, just keep running. If you get to the hotel before Jackson and MacColgan pick you up, stay in the lobby until my men arrive. You'll know MacColgan, he's a redheaded Irish rogue with bedroom eyes."

She asked, "You know this from experience?"

"Mac reminds me every chance he gets. I've no doubt you can handle him."

Aware of closing footsteps behind them on the sidewalk, Sebastian loosened his grip on her hand. He shifted his gait, soft, silent, and alert.

He heard her cry out but didn't take his eyes off of the two approaching men, sensing rather than seeing her swing around with momentum. He heard the distinct crunch of bone followed by gurgles. *Good job*. Sizing up his own threat, he realized she hadn't started moving. Sounds of a tumble came from behind. She must've pulled the man's feet out from under him. At that moment, he picked up the sharp smell of danger with his keen senses. Cordelia had hit it right on the spot. Her lack of experience with scent made it impossible to describe. His nostrils flared. Heart pounding, he curled his hands at his side. She needed to get moving. He gathered his wits and shouted, "Run!"

Sebastian watched Cordelia's back as she shot past him fueled by adrenaline and fear. She didn't look back. He felt the man at his back regain his feet. The two men in front of him hesitated, and their dismissal of Cordelia confirmed their target. As the harsh scent became stronger, his keen hearing picked up a rambling shuffle from the alley on the left. His assailants waited for reinforcements, just one from what Sebastian could detect. He quelled the battle rage mushrooming deep within his diaphragm. He needed to see what he faced before taking any risks. Through the blood haze filming over his eyes, he saw the men in front of him had radios. He discerned the nearly imperceptible earbuds. One of the men spoke into the transmitter attached to his collar. Sebastian couldn't make out what the man said with the oncoming shuffling, but he identified the Slovak intonation.

He processed the information, as the thing he smelled emerged into view. Sebastian's eyes narrowed as he took in this new threat. He allowed the barrage of fury to overtake him. The burning furor, once alien to him, crashed over his body in a surge. In a blink, the creature blitzed through the two front guards. A blurred sense of shifting caused a cry from the three men intermingled with an inhuman snarl.

****

Cordelia didn't look back. The sounds of Sebastian's fight with the other men faded. Aware of a sharp, musky scent, she increased her speed to put more space between her and the fight. Glad of her running and fitness training, Cordelia could make out the lights of the hotel perhaps a block ahead of her. She started as a cobalt blue SUV appeared at her shoulder matching her pace. Cordelia allowed a glance at the vehicle and saw grinning at her a creamy face so freckled she stared. As handsome as freckled, the wide disarming grin was topped by flaming, crimson hair that curled and tangled.

"You must be Cordelia Fiore. I cannot imagine another lovely lady running along in the Italian night."

Cordelia, surprised by the thick, leprechaun brogue and cheerful tone, stopped dead in her tracks. She leaned her hands on her thighs catching her breath as the elegant Porsche pulled up to the curb beside her. Sebastian was right: MacColgan did have bedroom eyes.

"I'm Seamus MacColgan. I believe you're expecting me."

Seamus MacColgan filled the driver's seat. He matched Sebastian for height and outweighed him by a good twenty or thirty pounds. She couldn't imagine the seatbelt going around Seamus's shoulders. Another large and imposing man leaned forward in the passenger seat. "Don't mind Seamus, Ms. Fiore, he's incorrigible. My name's Anthony Jackson. Do you need help into the car?"

Cordelia thought Anthony Jackson's staunch Boston accent and midnight skin to be the perfect foil for his partner's irreverent Irish intonation. She shook her head both as an answer to Jackson's query and in response to two such outrageous characters. "Just give me a minute to breathe."

The two men nodded in concert and relaxed when she opened the back door and slid into the car. "Sebastian?"

Jackson explained, "Park and Crosse are backing him up. They'll help Sebastian take care of the situation. Alonzo instructed us to take you back to Sperlonga. Thomas and Rachna expect us."

Cordelia craned her neck to look back at the direction she had been running toward. "My hotel, my things are there."

Seamus winked at her in the rearview mirror. "Now, don't you go worrying. Alonzo's efficient. I imagine you'll be finding your clothes and such waiting for you at the Shaws'. It's your job to sit back and relax."

Jackson added, "You let us know if you need anything on the way. We'll be happy to stop. But Seamus is right, no need to worry."

The enormity of the situation landed on Cordelia with full force. "I …I think I killed a man, back there, I think … I think I crushed his larynx."

Jackson's cool Bostonian demeanor broke for a moment as his eyes filled with respect. "Yes, we believe you did."

"A right smart blow if you ask me," Seamus chimed in, wistful of missing a good fight.

"I think I might be sick," Cordelia whispered, opening a window to let the wind blow in.

"Now, my dear," Seamus consoled her, "you defended yourself. Killing's never an easy thing, but being on the living end of a fight is nothing to feel ashamed about."

Jackson nodded. "Not one of us could do much better, Ms. Fiore. You handled yourself well. Sebastian's advantage is that you could defend yourself and get away."

Cordelia held onto that nugget. Sebastian could focus on his own fight. She didn't need rescuing. *Hadn't she trained for years? Enzo would've spit on the dead man before walking away.* Shrugging off the pinch to her conscience, she leaned back into the leather of the seat. She said, "Well, at least my father'll be glad to know that I can give as good as I get."

Seamus grinned into the rearview mirror. "That, I'm sure, is not the least of your talents."

She rolled her eyes and thought about Sebastian's curse at MacColgan. She believed Seamus trustworthy. In this crazy rabbit hole, one thing Cordelia knew was that Sebastian surrounded himself with people he trusted without question. Her thoughts swirled around the man she left standing in dire uncertainty. The staunch men in front of her showed no concern. In fact, they engaged in a good-humored debate on the ideal speed-to-fuel ratio in low whispers. *Okay, he's fine.* Cordelia settled into the embrace of the velvety leather seat and closed her eyes.

CHAPTER TWENTY

Sperlonga

She woke when they arrived at Thomas and Rachna's villa. The sunrise announced its inevitable presence with a soft rosy glow on the eastern horizon. Thomas and Rachna stood in the driveway awaiting the trio. Anthony Jackson and Seamus MacColgan stepped out of the vehicle arguing about who should wake Cordelia. A pointless discussion— Cordelia roused as soon as the rhythm of the car's engine changed. She stretched the kinks out of her stiff neck and watched Thomas, head low, in deep discussion with the men she thought of as Frick and Frack. Rachna gripped a large ceramic coffee mug steaming in the early morning air and moved toward the vehicle. Cordelia stepped onto the gravel of the driveway that yesterday she'd fallen face down upon.

"Here, drink this." Rachna held out the earth-colored mug.

Cordelia took a sip of the strong cappuccino as Rachna led her up the driveway with an arm wrapped around her shoulder.

The three men remained in the driveway speaking in low tones as the women passed them to climb the stairs to the front door. Cordelia stationed herself in the large, curry-colored chair that Rachna rested upon yesterday when the blank-faced group clumped up the stairs. An emerald cashmere sweater hugged her shoulders while she clung to the coffee mug, her only link to reality. Without Sebastian's presence, she thought, she could pretend she imagined all of yesterday. Rachna carried a tray with fresh coffee and mugs into the sitting room placing it on the side table. She poured herself a piping mug and settled on the settee with her feet tucked under her. Seamus and Anthony poured coffee and planted their individual bulks into matching wing-backed chairs across from Cordelia. Thomas reached for the last mug, but his cell phone pierced the weary silence before he could pour.

"Shaw."

Cordelia could hear the rich timber of an Italian voice spilling out of the earpiece. "The situation's clear. We're cleaning things up now. Sebastian's heading your way. Crosse drove him. It was pretty rough."

Thomas nodded. "Understood. I'll send Jackson over to open his villa. Let's meet here tomorrow morning."

"Ciao."

Thomas slipped his phone into his pocket and continued with his coffee. "Tony, when you finish, head over to Sebastian's place and open it up. Be sure everything's stocked, he's going to be bone tired and needing some recoup."

Anthony downed the last drop of coffee and heaved up out of the chair. "The usual good?"

"Should be. It probably won't be necessary, but make sure his medical kit's stocked. If it isn't, give me a call. I'll send Seamus over with some things."

Anthony gave a slight bow toward Cordelia. "It's nice to meet you, Miss Fiore. I'll say again good job last night." He punched Seamus on the shoulder on his way past.

Seamus looked at Thomas over his mug. "Surveillance and perimeter?"

Thomas blew the top of his mug. "Please. I know it's been a long night. I'll have Crosse spell you depending on the shape he's in. Let Alonzo know we'll need some shift relief out here. Gellat should be in town. That means we have a full complement."

Seamus rose and set his mug back on the tray. He nodded to Rachna. "Thanks for the coffee." Then he winked. "I'll be keeping my nose out for breakfast."

Rachna grinned at Seamus's back as he made a quick retreat from any reprisal Thomas might make. "You know, Priyatam, if anything happened to you, I could see replacing you with Seamus."

Thomas snorted into his coffee mug. "Ouch."

Rachna smiled over her mug at her husband. Cordelia chuckled.

Thomas turned to Cordelia. "Don't tell me you agree."

Cordelia shrugged. "Sebastian said he had bedroom eyes and that accent, please." She rolled her eyes.

Thomas said, "Sebastian's right. Women are crazy."

The exhausted tension evaporated from the room. Sebastian was returning to Sperlonga.

Thomas sat next to his wife with one hand around his coffee mug and the other on her knee. "Sebastian'll need a nap and a hot shower when he gets back. Cordelia, Alonzo sent your things by courier. They should be here any minute."

Cordelia shifted a bit, adjusting the wrap a little tighter. She took a breath knowing that once she asked there'd be no turning back. "Okay, so what's going on?"

Thomas and Rachna shared an impassive look. Thomas spoke up. "I know this is all a bit … well, crazy. There's no other way to put it. I think it might be better to discuss this with Sebastian."

Cordelia braced herself. "Thomas, I've known you for a little over thirty hours. I'm staying in your house under guard. I killed a man. I've managed to move on faith up to this point because my gut instinct says you're the good guys if there's such a thing in this world. I'm on a razor's edge with a little sleep and a large dose of caffeine. I've trusted you." She gave a meaningful look at Rachna. "Time to trust me."

"She's right, Thomas. There's a lot that we can share with Cordelia. We can wait for Sebastian to cover the rest. She can't walk away from this. We both know that isn't possible. She deserves to know."

Thomas looked from his wife to Cordelia and sighed. "Cordelia, what do you know about Senator Matthews?"

Cordelia thought a moment, confused about the jump from being attacked to the effusive and charming Senator from Michigan. "Senator Matthews hired me to appraise and arrange the auction of several pieces of art. He's planning on using the capital from this sale to fund an urban renewal project involving low-income neighborhood schools. Personally, I think he's full of shit. Those schools will be left in the same condition they're in now."

Thomas nodded in agreement with Cordelia's take on the press-hungry Senator. "You might think we're the good guys, but we didn't come across you in the Colosseum by accident. Our company put together a detailed dossier on you and several others as entry points into Matthews' business records." He paused to let that information sink in.

Cordelia took a minute to recover her composure. She nodded without surprise. "Sebastian started to tell me this at the restaurant."

"When Sebastian and I were in the service, we retrieved components of a biochemical weapon some Islamic terrorists managed to get. Special training qualified us to make the insertion and recover the pathogens in question." Thomas sighed. Rachna patted his hand. He continued, "Our team infiltrated the location, but in the course of our mission, the pathogen, a bacteria genetically modified to be deadly, was released. Five members of our unit died, along with many of the insurgents." He closed his eyes for a moment.

Cordelia stated, "You're alive."

"Yes." Thomas nodded. "Along with Sebastian and me, three others survived: our commanding officer Jeremy Hawthorne, Lorena Gellat, and Jeffery Davidson. Our immune systems absorbed the bacteria and developed an antibody preventing us from having any symptoms. Jeffery died a year after our deployment from a type of leukemia that affects patients with immune deficiencies. Even though he didn't present symptoms right away, the bacteria affected his immune system and he developed cancer."

Cordelia didn't have to imagine the loss they felt. She knew survivor's guilt. Sebastian's curt and reserved manner made perfect sense. She kept most people at arm's length for a long time after her mother died. Nonna pointed out how lonely living apart from people would be. Life meant loss, but life also meant joy, energy, and light. She had a moment of clarity. "Jeremy Hawthorne's dead."

Thomas nodded. "Not from the pathogen, he died … " he paused to choose his words, "on an assignment during our stint with the NSA."

"This goes back to the Senator how?"

"We traced the virus that killed our unit to a medical research company called Biogenesis Corporation. Right after we discovered the connection a hit-and-run accident injured Sebastian and killed our primary witness," Thomas continued. "David Williams used to work for Biogenesis as their head of accounting. Three years ago, he became Matthews' personal business manager."

"You think that Matthews is investing in Biogenesis Corporation through David Williams and that someone linked to the company is cooking up biological weapons for the highest bidder?"

Thomas nodded, impressed. "Something like that."

Cordelia's calm demeanor belied her anger. She didn't know who ranked higher on her list—Williams and Matthews for using her or Sebastian, who should've approached her upfront in the beginning. A man like Sebastian would demand to know every tiny detail of her life. If he had a dossier containing information about her, he must know she'd never participate in something so awful. Surely with his insight and background, he could've determined that she would help him.

Before she could launch into a torrent, the front door flew open and Seamus stumbled in under the weight of Cordelia's luggage. "Whew, you couldn't have been a light packer?"

The sight of the abundant Irishman with her bags set Cordelia into a fit of giggles that started softly at first, but fueled by tension, exhaustion, and hunger turned into full-fledged guffaws.

The surprised look on Seamus's face made it clear while he enjoyed a joke, he didn't want to be the butt of one. He dropped the luggage in the middle of the room with feigned disgust. Seamus's incredulous, gaping face set Rachna off, and she began to giggle. Thomas too became infected by the laughter and let go into gales of deep chortles.

Seamus shrugged it off with good humor and remarked, "I haven't caught a whiff of any breakfast."

Rachna, pulling herself together, with a giggle or two still escaping, stood up. "No, you haven't and I'm starving."

"I'll help." Cordelia wiped a mirthful tear from her eye.

Thomas, reining in his laughter, clapped Seamus on the shoulder. "Come on, I'll help you get this luggage into the guest room."

Seamus looked at the pile of bags and rolled his eyes with a groan.

Thomas and Seamus placed Cordelia's luggage in their guest suite, then joined Rachna and Cordelia in the kitchen. Lorena Gellat arrived to run perimeter. Seamus slumped into a chair in the corner of the warm, aromatic kitchen and began to snore.

Rachna and Thomas shooed Cordelia onto a stool at the counter and made breakfast with the well-coordinated dance of couples who know each other's rhythm. She sipped her coffee while her thoughts eddied in circles. Sebastian rested at his villa safe. She felt equal amounts of relief and outrage. She had survived an attack and done well. She shouldn't have been involved in the first place and she killed a man.

Watching Thomas and Rachna tease and laugh gladdened her, but the trust she'd placed in them wavered. This is what hysterical must be. One step left, I'll scream and break things. One step right, I'll either laugh insanely or cry a river. Her psychic sense tingled in an unfamiliar way, but struggling with zero sleep and indignant anger left her thin and stretched. She pushed her concerns away. *What exactly are you going to do about it now? Not a damn thing.*

Thomas slid a plate steaming and heaped with a Mediterranean-spiced pile of eggs and potatoes in front of her. Her appetite snapped to attention. "This smells delicious!" Her stomach growled its agreement.

Thomas nudged Seamus with his foot. "House specialty. Wake up, you unruly leprechaun." Thomas held a plate under the ruddy Irishman's nose.

Between the kick and the smell, Seamus popped awake and wasted no time in shoveling food into his mouth. "Mmmmm …thith id good," he managed to mumble between forkfuls.

Rachna signaled Lorena in for a plate and a fresh cup of coffee. The brisk woman devoured her plate and took her cup of coffee back outside with her.

Seamus stood up stretching. "I'm going to head over to the flop house and grab a nap. Tony and Trevor need to be spelled. Lorena's good until tonight. We can work out shifts depending on how long we're holed up. Sebastian'll be up by dinner. Do you suppose we'll have enough information to make a plan?"

Thomas started washing dishes. "We shipped the remains to Ian an hour ago. I imagine Sebastian'll want to follow. We'll activate our London office. They only have one team out. I expect two or three days in England and then we'll see." He sighed looking out from the balcony over the Italian coastline. "I'll have Park and Crosse stay here on point with Rachna. We'll see what we sniff out."

Seamus nodded. "I'll let Lorena know she's on for the day. Want me to call Park?"

"Yep, and tell Alonzo we'll be heading into the city, probably tomorrow. He can get us what we need."

"Sure thing." Seamus headed out.

Cordelia managed to eat between yawns and Rachna laughed. "Come on, you, I'll show you the guest suite. You need some sleep."

CHAPTER TWENTY-ONE

Sebastian's head pounded. He admonished Crosse more than once for his driving in a thick and gruff voice. His body ached from head to toe; he could feel the jostling bumps in the road bone deep.

Crosse chuckled. "We're almost there. Jackson has your place open and stocked. A hot shower and stiff drink will work wonders." Trevor Crosse had been with Global Sureties since the beginning. Crosse, an Army Ranger who crossed paths with Hawthorne and the Black Wolves during a tour in the Middle East, met the ideal requirements. Their past as Marines couldn't be helped, but he couldn't deny their upstanding and effective operations. His decision to become a career officer or move into the civilian world loomed when Cole approached him with the job at Global Sureties. It worked out. A perfect combination of what he loved about the military with the flexibility and pay of the private sector, he didn't regret any of his choices. Some of those choices linked him to Cole permanently. Crosse thought about the consequences of his choice. He liked the clannish nature of the job. No, not a job, a family.

"Yeah, yeah, yeah," Sebastian mocked. "Easy for you to say, you managed to avoid any serious fighting."

Crosse snorted. "Because you eliminated the threat. Sure, I bagged one of them, but the other three you finished and as for the last ...well, we mopped up the pieces you left for us."

Sebastian grunted. "Cordelia Fiore took one of those guys out."

Crosse noted the slight note of pride in that mumbled statement. "Maybe we should recruit her. Not a lame duck and that psychic trick, no matter if it's a hit or miss thing, could come in handy. It did tonight."

"No," Sebastian said, firm and icy. "Cordelia Fiore's not going to be around long enough to be put in any more situations. Not if I can help it."

Crosse shrugged. He'd never seen Sebastian Cole concerned about a woman, until now. *Who am I to judge Sebastian?* His boss had it bad. Plain as the bruises on his face. "Right, boss."

Sebastian winced. "I told you not to call me that."

"Yessir." Crosse drove the rest of the way silent and amused. Despite his distant and cool manner with his team, they saw the deep connection Sebastian shared with Thomas. He treated them fairly and compensated them generously. Crosse felt underneath the glacial persona Sebastian cared. No one would approach him with this idea of course. He could shoot any one of them between the eyes. Crosse snickered at that thought.

"What's so funny?" Sebastian growled.

"Nothing, sir, absolutely nothing." Crosse smiled as he pulled onto the street where Sebastian's villa stood.

****

Sebastian stumbled into his villa with Jackson's help. He growled to both Jackson and Crosse to get some rest. The door closed behind him. He tugged his soiled clothing off, leaving a trail behind him on the floor. Hobbling into the living room, he made his way into the kitchen. Sebastian opened the French doors to let the ocean air into the room, mindless of his nudity. His phone chirped. "Cole."

"Nicola stocked your fridge and there's a twenty-year-old Glendronach on the counter," Thomas said.

Looking out on the wide, open sea, Sebastian opened the bottle and poured a three-finger glass. "Thanks."

"You okay?" his friend asked.

Sebastian drank deeply. "Yeah. Beat."

"Takes a lot out of us," Thomas said. "Cordelia's settled. I told her about Matthews and what we were after."

Climbing the stairs, he asked, "How'd she take it?"

"She said you started to tell her at the restaurant. She didn't throw anything, but she's pissed," Thomas said. "Rachna thinks you might walk softly the next time you see her."

"Your wife is right. Cordelia crushed a man's larynx and broke another man's wrist." He confessed, "She's impressive."

"I'll say. Whatever we decide or rather whatever she agrees to, you might have problems with MacGolgan. He's smitten."

"Hmph," Sebastian replied as he sauntered into the bathroom.

"You know you're intrigued," Thomas said with humor.

Sebastian grunted. "I'm going to take a shower and pass out."

Thomas advised, "Don't overdo the scotch."

"Hanging up now." Sebastian ended the call. He set his scotch on the counter to enjoy after his shower and stepped into the scorching deluge.

The water released his residual tension. He scrubbed with the amber and chocolate scented soap Rachna made for him. He recognized the missing element in Cordelia's scent. She smelled of amber, vanilla, gardenia, and a hint of chocolate. His nose wrinkled as the steam carried the scent along air currents and throughout the master suite. *Get that bloody woman out of your head!*

Rachna had redone his villa at the same time she renovated theirs. Rubbing a towel over his head, he pulled the heavy drapes across both banks of glass to shut out the light. His eyes grew accustomed to the dark, pupils widening to sharpen his focus. He grabbed his scotch and moved with a little stiffness to the king-sized bed imposed in the space between two sets of glass doors covered with luxurious coffee-colored velvet. Downing the scotch in two burning gulps, he slid between the Egyptian cotton and folded his hands behind his head. Cordelia amazed him. Sebastian tried to tamp down his growing admiration. She kept cool and effectively acted. She eliminated one of their attackers. She ran when he told her to run and hadn't pulled a tragic heroine act.

Shifting to his side and forcing his eyes closed, he thought through the events of the last couple of days. Cordelia might or might not have direct information about Matthews' finances. Haunted by her apparent prophecy, he wondered who hunted whom.

His thoughts drifted back to the hit and run. Memories of his accident remained vivid in his memory. He adjusted his head on the pillow, his elbow propping it up a bit. The fingers of his right hand drifted on their own to the smooth, narrow ridge starting below the base of his neck. At this angle, he couldn't trace the full vertical length of the six-inch scar, but he traced it thousands of times in the past four years, each subtle ridge and bump memorized.

Fuck it. He would put Cordelia on the next flight to Vancouver. Seamus could take her in handcuffs if necessary. The scotch and the shower worked their magic. His mind settled on an action, quieted his mind enough for him to succumb to sleep.

CHAPTER TWENTY-TWO

Cordelia took a short time to pull her clothes off and step into the scalding shower. She stood under the water easing the knots in her shoulders. She needed to call her office to check on the Matthews job. She needed to call Enzo. Stepping out of the shower with the steam swirling around her, she thought about Sebastian. A towel wrapped around her head, she slipped between the sparkling cotton sheets without dressing. The fluffy down comforter settled over her. Its weight offered cozy relief from the things that tumbled around in her head. She sank into the pillow with a sigh.

A few hours later Cordelia stretched long and catlike from her dreamless nap. She was confused at first about her surroundings because of the darkness, but then she remembered. The comforter settled with soothing heaviness crooning *Stay, sleep a little more … there's no reason to get out of bed.* Not true; she had a reason.

She felt outward in the villa and sensed nothing. Thomas and Rachna slept. Seamus left hours ago to get his own sleep. Cordelia picked up a hum outside of the villa, one of Sebastian's staff. She threw back the covers and slipped her feet to the cool tile floor.

Cordelia made her way to the bathroom and flipped on the cheerful light. Earlier, in her punch-drunk state, she hadn't noticed the lovely Moroccan tile. Nor had she paid much attention to the organic, aromatic soaps and lotions carrying the same image of Kali gracing Rachna's back. Cordelia had used the shower gel with a lovely blend of bergamot and ylang ylang without making the connection. Now with clarity, she opened bottles to sniff the variety of oils, lotions, and soaps.

After completing her exploration, she took a glance in the large oval mirror. Her hair, damp when she went to sleep, curled around her face. The lack of dark circles surprised her. She napped longer than she realized. A quick splash of cool water livened her up a bit. Cordelia stepped out into the room and looked to see where her bags had ended up. Flipping a switch on the wall, she illuminated a spacious closet hidden behind two sheer lace curtains. Her bags sat organized in a row on the floor.

Assessing her belongings, she felt admiration for the mysterious Alonzo. Everything placed as she had them in the drawers at the hotel. She smiled in appreciation of the efficiency. Cordelia made a silent note to thank him if she ever had the chance.

Cordelia threw on a chocolate knit skirt skimming her ankles with a wine-colored tank top. She slipped on her Unasweeps retrieved from her shoulder bag. After catching a bit of a chill in the evening breeze, she grabbed a cardigan with sleeves long enough to brush her fingers. She made her way toward the front door. The person on perimeter would know where to find Sebastian. Without overthinking, Cordelia stepped out into the night air heading in the direction where she sensed the guard.

She figured the guard would be better approached in a straightforward way. Cordelia caught her foot on some ground-level foliage and pitched forward. Rather than landing on her hands, she fell into another body, who stayed her tumble. Cordelia righted herself with the help and brushed her hands down her skirt.

"Thanks."

The guard, a woman, replied nonplussed. "No problem. Should you be out here?"

"Probably not. I forgot how dark it is without city lights. I couldn't find my phone. What time is it?"

"Just after ten. Not late, just dark."

"Everyone's sleeping. I thought you could tell me where to find Sebastian." Remembering her manners she extended her hand. "I'm Cordelia Fiore."

The guard chuckled as she took her hand. "Lorena Gellat. Sebastian, huh? I'm pretty sure he'll be over when he's ready."

"Could you show me to his villa?"

Cordelia worried the woman might not help, but then Lorena grinned. "I'll walk you over. I wouldn't want you to get lost in the dark."

This isn't a woman who follows the rules. "I'd appreciate it. I won't tell him."

"Sebastian doesn't scare me." Cordelia sensed rather than saw her grin.

From the angle of Sebastian's villa, Cordelia guessed it looked out onto the sea rather than lower Sperlonga. They stepped onto the driveway. Sebastian's stairs to the front door glowed from the porch light. Lorena said nothing. Cordelia wondered how the woman could see in the dark. She didn't carry a flashlight.

"Here you go," Lorena said.

"You've been with Sebastian a long time," Cordelia remarked, thinking the tall, Nordic beauty carried a dangerous edge in her movements.

"Marines together." Silence stretched, then she said, "I went off the grid, but Sebastian tracked me down. He still believes in being on the right side of things."

Cordelia looked startled.

"I've floated in and out of the world."

"So you're back in the world here? Wearing a white hat?" Cordelia thought about Sebastian motivating this woman to change.

"It's all relative. Sebastian and Thomas are good guys through and through. White hat? Meh, in the end it's about perspective. Good night." She turned back. "By the way, I was on your side. I figured you as the type that would help." Then the enigmatic woman disappeared into the darkness.

Cordelia couldn't help wonder about her. Sebastian said something similar the first day she met him. *Life is rarely black and white. I've made decisions based on intuition, irrelevant to right or wrong.* Her imp piped up again. *Yeah, but would you recognize the line anymore?*

****

Sebastian roused to the sound of his door knocker. *Christ, can't a guy get more than a few hours of sleep?* He rubbed his eyes and swung his legs over the side of the bed. A fresh pair of laundered jeans rested over the back of a leather club chair in the corner. *Ah Nicola.* She had been through the villa while he slept, tidying and leaving him clean clothes in her wake. The knocker pounded. He pulled the jeans on without bothering to button them. Running a hand through his hair, he padded through the villa to his entry way without flipping on any lights. A soft glow radiated from the kitchen. Nicola left the under counter lighting on low. He didn't bother looking through the peephole. Throwing the door open, he snapped, "What?"

His eyebrow rose at the sight of Cordelia. Bare-chested and barefoot, he stood with his jeans hanging above the taunt muscles dipping into his hips. Sebastian swept his arm toward the interior of his villa. "Come in." *Jeez, I gotta start paying attention to how I answer the door.*

Cordelia seemed to recover. As if he could read her mind, Sebastian buttoned up the rest of his fly with a sheepish look. He reached to a light switch on the wall and slid the switches up to raise the lights. Cordelia busied herself with a scan of his villa. He followed her gaze imagining how his place appeared to her.

Rich, earth tones carried the decor. Sebastian's balcony looked out over the sea, nothing breaking the serene line of the horizon. The rest of the furniture complimented the walls covered in smooth, buttery caramels and creams. An occasional shock of color, a bright blue cushion, and an embroidered blanket with deep persimmon swirls drew the eye. Sebastian liked clean lines and plush fabrics.

"Are you hungry?" Sebastian inquired, sweeping past her into the kitchen. "Because I'm starving and I'm certain Nicola's left me something delicious."

Cordelia followed him. "Nicola?"

Sebastian nodded, scanning a wine cabinet looking for something. "My housekeeper. Rachna found her. She keeps the place tidy, does my laundry, and keeps my kitchen stocked when I'm in Sperlonga. I can cook." He looked at Cordelia's raised eyebrow. "I *can*. I just don't always have the time. Nicola throws things together that I can heat up."

Cordelia snorted. "Must be convenient."

"Do you always cook and clean your own place?" he demanded.

"When I'm home. Of course," Cordelia conceded, "my friends own a restaurant right down the street. I don't have to cook."

Sebastian nodded as if this admission made his point. "Pick some wine if you'd like something to drink." He indicated the wine cabinet built into the wall.

An efficient space with clean lines and stainless steel appliances, the kitchen maintained spare economy. The earth tones continued through the kitchen with deeper, more dramatic touches of black and steel. An open bottle of twenty-year-old Glendronach sat on the counter.

"I wouldn't mind wine with food, but if the scotch is open I could stand a stiff drink."

Sebastian couldn't keep his eyebrow from lifting. He never met a woman who drank scotch. "Sure." He tried to hide the surprise in his voice and pulled out two crystal whiskey snifters.

Cordelia leaned against the counter as he poured the rich, amber liquor into the glasses. "You going to feed me?"

Handing her a glass, he grinned. "How about a rare filet mignon with some of Nicola's buttered spinach .... maybe a toss of homemade pasta?"

Cordelia's stomach growled.

"I'll take that as a yes." He chuckled.

Cordelia sipped the scotch. He could sense the comforting heat spreading from her mouth and throat out into her limbs. *The beauty of scotch.* He set to moving about the kitchen. He pulled a remote from a drawer near the wine cabinet and with a click of a button filled the room with the quiet sounds of John Coltrane and Duke Ellington playing "In a Sentimental Mood."

Cordelia pulled a chair out from the table looking like she wanted to say something.

"Spit it out." He took a sip of his own scotch.

"I have a question, well I have a lot of questions, but I don't want to ruin this." She gestured around the kitchen.

"This what?"

"You're not easy to be around, but like this ... it's ... comfortable."

"Good to know. Sometimes difficult." He made an imaginary check with his finger.

She blushed a little. "You're not exactly congenial."

Sebastian paused at the sink with a cutting board. He took a sip of his scotch and pursed his lips as the spicy heat slid down his throat. "I can't afford to be."

"What's that supposed to mean? I'm not some delicate flower. I killed a man yesterday. I may not be accustomed to fighting for my life, but I think I've proven that I can handle myself." Her voice rose with anger.

Sebastian drew in a deep breath and sighed. "You have no idea."

"Senator Matthews? I know enough to be certain I'd have helped you without all of this subterfuge." She took a breath. "Who put together my dossier?" He saw the sudden flash of intuition as things clicked into place. "That woman Lorena, she investigated me. You trust her." He didn't flinch at the bitterness in her voice. "Didn't she tell you I could be trusted?"

Sebastian avoided looking at her and took a butcher's package out of the refrigerator. "Not part of her job." He glanced at her and sighed with exasperation. "Leave it to Thomas."

Cordelia stood up and poured herself another scotch.

"You might want to take that slower," he remarked, his back turned toward her.

He felt the disdain in her question. "How slow would you recommend? Would you recommend another drink before I take this bottle and smash it over your head?"

Sebastian gave a deep, rueful laugh. "I need to be bashed in the head with a bottle?"

"I think a bat might be more … satisfying, but yes, you need hit in the head." An icy edge filled her voice. "I'm not going anywhere."

Sebastian whirled around waving a trimming knife at her. "You said you couldn't read my mind."

"It doesn't take a mind-reader! You're so focused on the idea of me getting on a plane anyone could see it." She stood to face him toe to toe. "I'm not going anywhere."

"You could've been killed." Sebastian turned to the stove to hide the look on his face.

"You couldn't have been?"

Sebastian threw a bunch of spinach into a colander with force. "That's not the point."

"What's the point here? You're trying to stop a bad guy from poisoning innocent people. I'm not sure what I can do, but you seemed to think I could help a few days ago."

"That was before," he said, adding butter to a sauté pan.

"Before what? Before someone followed you? Before a group of men, and goodness knows what else, attacked us and tried to kill you? Before I saw …" Her voice died without completing the last thought.

Sebastian poured himself more scotch and took a deep drink. "Yes, Cordelia, before all of that. I didn't think about the consequences of involving you. We thought we needed you to … Never mind."

"Why not now?" she interrupted hotly.

"I met you." He turned meeting her eyes.

He watched her anger deflate with a whoosh. A defeated sigh escaped her. Her face opened to him at that moment. He fell; no, he plummeted into her mind. He allowed her behind the cool, disinterested shell he kept on the surface. Intense heat didn't just radiate off of him, but it burned in the center of his being. At that moment, his defenses down, he stood before her with his soul naked of any guards or boundaries. She moved toward him like a moon pulled by gravity toward its planet. Aware of the moonlit kitchen, the soft voice of Sia Furler floating in the room, and the sound of the surf sweeping below them, he watched her drift across the room.

His eyes burned with an inner light in the cool glow of the moon; Sebastian stood rooted to the floor. He drew in the scent of amber and vanilla. Cordelia stood a hair's breadth from him. They stood frozen, eyes locked, the barest of space separating them. He imagined he could feel the light touch of her mind inside of him and managed to pull a weak wall around a remote corner of his brain. Her hand reached up to rest on his heart and he gave himself up to a different kind of impulse. Sebastian's mind went blank of everything outside of her. His arms wrapped around Cordelia, crushing her to him. She turned her face up to him; he fell upon her with his lips and teeth.

For a brief moment, nothing outside of the heat and her taste existed. Caution tickled the back of his awareness. He ignored it, giving in to the sensation of her tongue, to the delicate intensity of her teeth. His hand rested at the base of her neck, tangling in her hair.

She pushed some distance between them gasping a little. “Sebastian,” she said, her voice ragged. She cleared her throat said, “Sebastian!”

Sebastian returned to his senses and leaped back from her. His heat up, he pushed back at red tunnel vision. Forcing deep pools of air into his lungs, he whooshed them out again. He saw a hint of fear in her eyes and swore, “Goddamn it.” Two sides of his brain fought: one filled with desire to take her in his arms again and one filled with bitterness and cynicism. He didn’t trust himself to speak. He tamped the urgency down and focused.

She turned to face the open French doors. “Someone’s watching.”

His control almost regained, he grabbed his phone and dialed a number.

He heard Crosse’s voice. “Boss?”

“South perimeter breach.” Sebastian disconnected and turned off the flame on the stove. Cool and remote, he shut out the scorching ache and looked at Cordelia all business. “We need to get out of here.”

CHAPTER TWENTY-THREE

Slovenia
Biogenesis Corporation Headquarters

Vivienne Carlson gripped the arms of her chair, close to losing her knife-edged control. "A total loss."

"Yes, ma'am." Dominic Baptiste cringed.

She took a slow breath. It would be foolish to allow her emotions to take her. "What about Cole?"

"Gone to ground. They'll head out of the country to regroup and pull together more resources. England. He still has the woman with him. I'd dump her, she's a liability," Baptiste said.

Vivienne felt her teeth grinding together and forced a deep breath into her lungs. She shook her hands and head, desperate to let go of this sickening feeling. Cole belonged to her. She made him perfect. This woman couldn't understand who he was or how important he'd become. Vivienne's hand came down hard on the surveillance photos. She took a few deep breaths. "All of the operatives lost."

"Yes, as well as the …" Baptiste trailed off.

She cut him off with a wave. "Yes, I know. You say Cole should get rid of this woman."

The man took his time. "It's what I'd do. She isn't one of his staff. She has no training. She's a weakness, a target."

Vivienne pursed her lips thinking. "You're right. She is a target. One we'll exploit. We'll wait for a moment to take her. He's a cliché. Sebastian Cole will knock on my front door."

"Orders?" Baptiste asked.

"You know where he's going. Send out teams and find an opportunity to take her. If a partnership is out of the question, I will own him. He is the missing factor in my research. Get her and I'll have him." She relaxed back into her chair.

"Yes, ma'am." Baptiste turned to leave.

"Baptiste."

"Ma'am?"

She held out the photos in her manicured hands. "Take these with you." As soon as he had shut the door, Vivienne Carlson forced the tension in her body to release. Leaning forward, her fingers stroked a crystal gem-cut paperweight on her desk. Sebastian Cole would not prevent her success. She'd found the secret to effectively strengthening the human immune system. He was her proof and she would recover him. She wasn't going to fail. Her fingers tightened around the glass. As if watching someone else, Vivienne hurled the weight across the room. Slivers exploded as it shattered against the door.

****

Baptiste dropped the photos on Andre's desk. "Shred these."

Andre spread the photos out looking at the couple frozen in black and white. He recognized the man, Mr. Miller from Control Robotics. Andre couldn't forget a man like that. Neither could Dr. Carlson. He listened to the tinkle of shattering glass from the other side of the door. He noted the woman in the photo. Not typically beautiful, but something about her hypnotized. Even in black and white, she seemed warm and full of life. From the look on Robert Miller's face, he thought so too.

Andre's eyes fell on the photo of their kiss. It brought to mind the Hollywood kisses that he loved to see in his old '40s films. He couldn't get enough of Ingrid Bergman falling into Cary Grant's arms, whether in a comedy like *Indiscreet* or something dramatic like *Notorious*. The urgency drifted off of the screen. The same feeling encompassed the photo and touched him. Another piece of crystal smashed against the door. He thought back to the street Dr. Carlson took him from so many years ago.

He poured a fresh cup of tea and paused at the door to listen. The office grew quiet. Rather than shred the photos, he slipped them into a file folder and slid the file into his desk drawer. It seemed a shame to destroy such a moment. Andre entered her office. She hadn't summoned him, but it had been still for a while. "Dr. Carlson?"

She sat ramrod straight facing the bank of windows looking out onto Prešeren Square. She looked deflated. He never thought of her as a tiny woman, but at this moment she looked small.

"You'll clean this up?" Her voice was low and calm.

Without a trace of his thoughts reaching his voice, he answered, "Of course, Dr. Carlson."

She rose, stretching to her full height. "Very good. I'll be in my lab." She turned without a glance at him and walked through the detritus of her anger.

Andre stood in her office watching the sun start its descent past noon. Warm from the sun's rays, the room felt cold to him. He used to cringe from her wrath, but seeing her like this, jealous and desperate, changed something in him. A hollow space bloomed inside of him where loyalty and devotion used to nest. She taught him he owed her everything. Her towering power faded. He looked at his hands, wondering if he would see it slipping through his fingers.

Only fourteen years old when she pulled him off of the street, he rarely thought about the odd group of street rabble that made up his surrogate family. He took her business card and never looked back. He thought about the long hours studying not just English and Slovenian; she insisted he become literate as well in French and Italian. He poured through classic literature and history. He went to business school but made no friends. She nurtured his street-born suspicion of strangers. Often he spoke only to her in an entire week.

She demanded that he walk, speak, and, above all, obey with grace. He winced a little remembering how her temper flared when his street swagger popped out occasionally to challenge her. On generous days, he might not eat for a few days. His mind slid around other memories of her. He flexed his shoulders, old pains creeping out of the cobwebs.

Looking at the pieces of shattered glass and porcelain strewn across the office floor, he remembered a bit of William Blake. "Thy friendship oft has made my heart to ache; do be my enemy — for friendship's sake." She hated William Blake. She forbade him from ever reading it as part of his studies.

"He was a romantic mystic with no concept of the concrete. I won't have you filling your head with idealistic twaddle." She smacked him in the head with Blake's *Songs of Innocence*, and then tossed it into the fire with contempt.

A little piece of his heart charred. From then until now, he read Blake and the other romantics in secret. "Thy friendship oft has made my heart to ache." The little piece of ash felt a kinship with the shards of glass crunching under his feet. He wondered if his mentor might feel about Mr. Miller what he felt about the beauty of Blake's poetry. For the first time, he thought of her as mortal. Andre lifted his chin and looked again out at the waters of the Ljubljanica moving by the pedestrians walking along the bridge. All of his loyalty and the destruction his loyalty nurtured pulled down on his shoulders. In eleven years, he'd never experienced a kind word from her without the twist of cruelty. Just once he would've loved to see a smile for him reach her eyes.

He pressed the intercom on her phone.

"This is maintenance, Dr. Carlson."

Andre smiled. Every person in the building knew her extension. "Mr. Rubin, it's Andre. There's been a little … incident in Dr. Carlson's office. Would you kindly send a cleaning crew up here?"

"I'll get someone right up there, sir." Mr. Rubin's voice warmed with respect.

"This will require more than one person, Mr. Rubin. Oh, and tell them to be careful. There's glass to pick up, a lot of broken glass." His courtesy proved an investment in people.

The maintenance manager didn't dare ask his question. "All righty, Mr. Juricic. I'll get some guys up there right now."

"Thank you, Mr. Rubin. They'll have to let themselves into the office on their own. I've an appointment out of the building this evening. Will you see to it things are secure up here when they're done?"

Andre imagined he could hear Mr. Rubin's head nodding. "I'll take care of that personally."

"Thank you again, Mr. Rubin." He disconnected the call and dialed another extension. "Miss Goodwin."

"Yes, sir, Mr. Juricic."

"Miss Goodwin, I've been called out for an appointment this afternoon. Would you please field any calls? Dr. Carlson's in her lab and not to be disturbed."

Miss Goodwin answered, "Oh yes, I'd be happy to handle the phones for you."

Andre gathered his things, safely storing them in his leather satchel. He slipped his arms into a light cashmere overcoat; the early summer evenings remained cool. A brief glance in the wall mirror near the elevator showed an impeccably dressed, almost lovely young man with a serene smile on his face. The elevator car chimed as it opened and he stepped in without a backward glance. The soft notes of Handel's water music drifted down around his shoulders. Stepping out in front of the security desk, Andre checked to be sure his calfskin gloves were nestled safely in his pocket.

A security desk officer snapped to attention upon seeing Andre approach. "Ali lahko kličem za vaš avto, Mr. Juricic?" *Can I call for your car?*

Andre waved a delicate hand at the guard. "Ne, hvala. Bom hojo danes. To je zelo lepo ven, kajne?" *No thank you. I'll be walking today. It's quite lovely out, isn't it?*

The guard tipped his hand to his hat. "Uživajte sprehod." *Enjoy your walk.*

Andre stepped out into the square thinking about which direction to go. Turning to the right, he headed south away from the chic cafés and shops that drew the crowds of young, hip Slovenians. He had some old friends to look up.

CHAPTER TWENTY-FOUR

England
Swaffham Airfield

Cordelia stood wrapped in a bulky cashmere sweater against the chill of the morning. The sun hadn't risen yet, but Sebastian marshaled the troops to an airfield twenty miles up the coast. The elusive Alonzo rounded up a private jet; a gleaming Gulfstream G200 sat under the hollow fluorescent lights in the hanger waiting for its passengers, a great shining bird. Trevor Crosse and Devyn Park stayed with Rachna in Sperlonga. Thomas, Lorena Gellat, Seamus, and Anthony Jackson would travel with Sebastian and Cordelia on the jet to Swaffham, England.

Alonzo had sent some crates and equipment to Norwich the night before, so they had made do with a charter company. They filed a bogus flight plan. Sebastian didn't want to leave too easy a trail for whoever followed. He couldn't send Cordelia home. If a team could get close to Sebastian's villa, then they could identify her. At least he could offer her protection if she stayed with him.

The kiss rooted in his brain. He had to concentrate on the details of their trip. Sebastian paid sharp attention to Jackson to avoid thinking about the intoxicating scent of gardenia drifting across the hangar.

"I've arranged for cars at Swaffham and Ian knows we're on our way. He and Lindsay will have rooms ready for us. Oh, and Sir Gerald will be meeting us with the cars," Jackson informed him.

"Good. Let's get the plane loaded. Have Lorena do a sweep on the plane and get Seamus to move the equipment." Sebastian turned toward the office where Alonzo finished up some details and stopped. "Did you say my father would meet us with the vehicles?" Sebastian asked.

Jackson said, "Yessir."

Sebastian shook his head and muttered.

Within minutes, they taxied to the runway. In the plane, Thomas, Sebastian, and Anthony sat in a pod of four seats facing each other at the front of the cabin. Seamus sat crumpled in a rear seat with a sweater over his eyes snoring as the plane reached takeoff speed.

Lorena positioned herself in a middle cabin seat across from Cordelia. Sebastian's sharp ears heard her quip, "Seamus could sleep in a hurricane."

The broad Irishman snored and growled like a dreaming dog. Sebastian listened to Cordelia's response. "I suppose with your job you need to get sleep wherever and whenever you can."

"You know, our jobs aren't this exciting," Lorena said. Sebastian silently agreed.

"Really, we spend a lot of time babysitting wealthy people who have too much time and money on their hands. Or we deliver artwork, consult on security systems, things like that. Most of our job is pretty dull. Not that we don't have investigation jobs for insurance companies and the like, but the majority of the time we're just visual muscle."

Cordelia said, "Must be disappointing."

"Oh no, don't get me wrong. I can deal with boring. Most of our teams have seen their fair share of action, myself included. Sure there're a lot of easy jobs, but I don't mind. It pays better and I'm not dodging grenades."

Cordelia laughed. Sebastian enjoyed her ease. She asked, "Where are we going?"

Lorena shook her head. "He's done it to you too?"

"Done what?" Cordelia asked.

Lorena laughed and looked over her shoulder at him. Sebastian pretended not to eavesdrop and leaned over some maps and papers. "No, it isn't like that. He's my friend and my boss, a good one. Sebastian inspires trust. You didn't ask him why we're jumping on a plane in the middle of the night. I didn't ask him. Not one of us has any doubt we need to leave Italy. Complete confidence." She shook her head amused.

"I knew we're going to England. I just don't know where or why," Cordelia said, her tone reticent.

"We're landing at an airfield outside of Norwich. It's a town northeast of London. Sebastian's family home is near there, and Ian, his brother, runs a medical research facility there. There are some things Ian's working on. It'll give us a chance to get organized without being spread so thin on security." She reached into a shoulder bag at her feet and pulled out a water bottle. "We have a full team in Norwich on detail at Ian's facility. Home office is in London. There won't be any holes."

"Is Ian working on the biotoxin Thomas mentioned?"

Lorena's eyes hooded a bit as she opened her mouth to answer. She looked at Sebastian. He gave her a minute shake and moved from his seat to join them. "Lorena, Jackson's asking where you put his bag." His eyebrow went up. "I think he's worried about his toothbrush."

Lorena took the cue with a smile. "He's such a primper." She stood up and slid by Sebastian and then turned back to Cordelia. "I'll bring you back some tea, help you sleep a little."

Before she sauntered to the front of the cabin, Lorena shot Sebastian a look.

Sebastian's eyebrows knitted together. "The cheek. I swear you're inspiring an irritating level of rebellion in my team." He sat down across from her, his knees skimming her own.

"A little rebellion's good. It keeps things fresh. Maybe you're a little too sure of yourself." Her steely look amused him.

"Hmph, you'd better hope not," he said, weighing his options. "Thomas told you about Matthews and the illegal funding."

"Yes."

Sebastian leaned into his hand and ruffled his hair. "I don't think this is Matthews. This feels personal. Someone's watching me and now they've seen—"

"They're going to try to use me," she said.

"You aren't safe," he agreed.

"What now?" Cordelia asked.

Sebastian rubbed the scruff on his chin. "They left some … clues when they attacked us in Rome. I sent those to my brother to see if he could find something useful. That's where we're headed. My family has an estate—"

Cordelia cut him off. "Lorena told me."

Sebastian frowned again. "Rebellion. We have a better chance of keeping an eye on you and we might catch a break with Ian's help."

"You're not happy about it," she said.

"Not especially, no."

Cordelia pressed her lips together, irritation on her face. "Then why? Just send me home. I can take care of myself and maybe if I weren't with you I wouldn't be in any danger."

Sebastian sighed. "I can't send you home if there's the chance you might be hurt."

Her tone softened a little. "So what's your problem?"

"You don't know my family. It's … complicated."

****

The sun was rising as the jet landed at the Swaffham airfield. After their conversation, Sebastian had settled into silence for the rest of the flight. Seamus, who hadn't moved an inch since the plane took off, roused himself no more rumpled than before.

Sebastian and Thomas exited as soon as the plane stopped moving, followed by Jackson. Lorena gestured for Cordelia to stay put for a minute and peered out the cabin door with a mischievous grin blooming on her face. "Sir Gerald!" she called out.

"Halloo, my bonny Lorena!" A booming, patrician voice echoed from outside in the hangar. "Sir Anthony neglected to mention the grace of your presence in this chipper group. You can ride with me."

Lorena laughed and waved for Cordelia to exit the plane behind her. "I have a surprise for you."

Cordelia blinked a bit in response to the bright hangar lights and focused on a tall, lordly figure standing near a 1964 Bentley Silver Cloud in perfect condition. Standing a little over six feet tall with platinum silver threading his thick wavy hair, he had a devilish twinkle in his sea gray eyes. The Bentley fit his stylish country gentleman panache. A deeper emerald argyle sweater vest that topped gray riding pants and a well-worn pair of paddock boots complemented his soft forest green tweed jacket showing off his still strong frame.

"Ho ho ho, what've we here? Not only did Anthony withhold announcement of your lovely company, but he neglected to mention the addition of a Mediterranean goddess to our happy troupe!"

Sebastian moved toward them with long strides. "Dad, can we get going? And the Bentley, really?"

Cordelia stifled a giggle. Lorena ignored Sebastian and introduced her. "Gerald, this is Cordelia Fiore of Vancouver. Cordelia this is Sir Gerald Cole of North Walsham, England. Sebastian's father."

Gerald Cole ignored Sebastian as well, making a deep bow over Cordelia's hand. "Mademoiselle Fiore, que bellisima. I'm enchanted to meet you." He turned to Sebastian. "You left a great deal of information out of your missive, young man. Lorena and the lovely Miss Fiore will ride with me. The rest can follow along, no need to bump around in those SUVs when you can glide."

Sebastian said, his tone frigid, "Dad, I prefer to keep Cordelia close—"

Gerald cut him off. "Fine, ride in the Bentley." He turned to signal to the others. "Troops! We are off. Last one to the manor will eat cold eggs!" Cordelia smiled at Gerald's wink. "We'll have a little nip of champagne, shall we?"

Cordelia let Sir Gerald assist her into the elegant automobile. Sebastian slapped his forehead as Lorena slid past him to take her place in the car. Cordelia gave Sebastian a little, satisfied smile. *Ha, now who's in control?*

Gerald looked at Sebastian. "Let's go, son; we need to shake a tail feather."

Sebastian made a strangled noise and strode off. He hopped in the lead truck and slammed the door.

Sir Gerald tapped on the glass partition separating the passenger cabin from the driver, and the car sailed forward.

He rounded on Cordelia. "A little bubbly? Cordelia Fiore. Italiana I presume?" Shamelessly charming, he couldn't hide bright intelligence in his shining eyes.

"Yes, sir, half. My mother was Irish."

"Ah, the fey folk! No wonder you're such a delectable beauty." He turned to Lorena apologetically. "Of course, Lorena, I'm speaking in an observational way."

Lorena laughed. "Observe away, Sir Gerald. Sebastian's going to be sour."

"Oh, my wayward boy, I can handle the young rascal." He winked at Cordelia, causing her to laugh again. "Back to you, Miss Fiore; you must do something with the arts. I can see it in your aura. Someone with such an aura must be artistic."

Cordelia didn't know what to say. "Ah, sort of. I authenticate art. I'm an art historian."

"A brilliant eye for details. Sebastian isn't putting anything over on you is he? That's why he's so disagreeable. He hasn't a clue how to work around you."

"I'm not sure what you mean," Cordelia replied, confused.

Lorena chimed in, "Oh yeah, he's in knots."

Gerald waved his champagne flute around. "Yes, yes, I see. Cordelia, could you love my son?"

Cordelia choked a bit on a sip of champagne. "Excuse me?"

Lorena pounded her back.

"You can't be ignorant of the fact Sebastian is in love with you? I assumed from your pinkish glow you're attracted to him. He's a strapping and handsome beast, takes after his father." He gave her an intelligent grin.

Lorena added, "They met in Rome a few days ago."

Cordelia glared at Lorena, who ignored her.

Gerald clapped his hand to his thigh. "Love at first sight! Across a crowded piazza, he noticed your grace. He felt compelled to speak to you." Cordelia thought his eyes misted.

"I don't know about the grace. I fell a couple of times." Sebastian's father had her off balance. Hawkish and impish by turns, she thought perhaps Sebastian wasn't wrong to be frustrated.

"A bit Bronte-esque? You stumbled, and he caught you, your eyes met, and connection forged?" Gerald mused.

"Mr. Cole—" Cordelia began, but he cut her off.

"Gerald please, my dear, Gerald. Lorena here won't drop the sir, but I would like it if you called me Gerald."

"Gerald—"

He put his hand up to stop her. "I don't mind the sir, but it sounds pretentious sometimes. As for Sebastian, yes he's in love with you. He doesn't know it yet, stubborn boy. You'll have to be patient. Give him some room. He has issues, mind you, but don't we all?" He looked at her.

Cordelia had no idea where to go in the conversation. "Um … yes?"

"Yes." He grinned. "There it is. My goodness, you're lovely and strong-willed. I can see the steel in your backbone! Give him a lot of trouble. Sebastian needs some trouble." He shook his head, a fond look on his face.

Cordelia glared at Lorena. The woman in question grinned. Cordelia expected to see the feathers of a canary hanging out of her mouth.

Gerald cried out, startling Cordelia. "Here we are! Home sweet home; ignore the large gate."

Cordelia gazed out at the entrance to the Cole estate. They traveled down a lengthy, tree-lined drive leading to a substantial gate. The gate opened automatically. The manor house stood at the far end of another stretch of the drive. A high rock wall spread in opposite directions and disappeared into the trees on either side of the gate. The house stood enormous and proud. She counted three separate wings. The center of the manor climbed into the blue English sky with a high peaked roof of green tile. Windows upon windows marked the sprawling edifice as the two outer wings reached out on either side of the main entrance. Constructed out of granite and stone, the manor stood the test of time. While primarily Elizabethan, it had Jacobean round-arch arcades and Cordelia could see at least two open work parapets.

"Lindsay has brunch queued for the dining room. Ian's been locked up in the laboratory." Gerald opened the door and stepped out onto the limestone drive.

CHAPTER TWENTY-FIVE

Cole Estate
North Walsham, Norwich, England

Sebastian couldn't contain the growling menace in his throat. "He drives me mad! Round the bloody bend!" The English countryside pulled out his British accent.

Thomas clucked. "Gerald's a force of nature and you know it. Hmm … reminds me of someone else," he continued as Sebastian glared at him. "Sure he's charming the ladies, but you know his senses and instincts are as keen as yours or mine. He's capable. You're just worried about what he might say to Cordelia."

"Right, that's exactly why I'm worried. Between you and that old codger, I'll be lucky to have any privacy."

Thomas gazed down the road. "If you're lucky, between me and the grand gentleman, you might come out of this with Cordelia. We know what's good for you no matter what you think."

Sebastian dropped his head in his hands and groaned. "Disaster. This has disaster written all over it."

Thomas whistled a little tune as he pulled the Rover into the Cole estate driveway behind the Bently. "You never know how to look at the bright side of things."

****

Cordelia, a little shell-shocked, stepped out behind Sir Gerald. His singsong joviality and his pointed questions left her off balance. Looking at the Cole estate up close didn't help her sense of vertigo. Gerald strode toward the ornate double oak doors framed by gray granite. Rising behind two heavy iron gates, massive oak doors stood ready to hold off an attack. A battering ram would have a tough time with those doors, let alone the gates.

"Cordelia, come along," Sir Gerald called out with an outstretched hand.

Lorena unfolded herself from the Bentley and gave Cordelia a gentle push to help her momentum. "He doesn't bite."

Cordelia moved closer to Sir Gerald as Thomas and Sebastian pulled up behind the Bentley with the other vehicles in their group. She could see the heavy iron gates of the driveway closing in the distance. Before Sir Gerald and Cordelia reached the granite steps leading up to the great doors, both doors opened to reveal a tall, stately man dressed in a Harris tweed blazer worn over crisp khaki slacks. He reminded her of a younger version of the British actor Ben Kingsley without Gandhi's robes.

"Gerald, you've brought us delightful company." He made up the space between them to take Lorena's hands. "Why didn't Sebastian say you were coming? Staying out of trouble?"

Lorena gave him a quick hug. "Sebastian keeps me busy."

Cordelia noticed an undercurrent but had no time to think about it.

"And who's this amazing woman?" He turned his discriminating gaze on Cordelia.

Sir Gerald moved in to take her elbow. "Lindsay, this is noted art historian Cordelia Fiore. Cordelia, this is Arthur Lindsay, author and Ian's better half."

Arthur Lindsay kept one hand on Lorena's and reached the other out to Cordelia. "Miss Fiore, welcome to our humble enclave."

"Mr. Lindsay." Cordelia took his firm handshake. "I'm happy to meet you."

With Sir Gerald framing her left and Lindsay framing her right, she had no choice but to follow them up the stairs. She shot a backward glance at Sebastian organizing his team and thought she caught a rueful glint in his steely gaze.

If the exterior of the Coles' estate stunned Cordelia, nothing compared to the interior. The two great doors opened up into a massive, domed entryway. The echoing round space rose above a glossy black and white tiled floor. She imagined stepping onto a colossal chessboard. Luminous white walls floated up to the fifteen-foot dome overhead. The ceiling, painted with Italian frescoes, hovered overhead. An officious butler of indiscernible age met them in the foyer.

Sir Gerald gave the manservant an easy dip of his head. "Reynolds, this is Cordelia Fiore, and you know our dear Lorena. Would you set them up in the south wing with views of the garden?"

"Sir," Reynolds responded with courteous indifference. "Yes, sir, Signore Giametti sent the bags ahead and they've been unpacked."

Lorena waved a hand. "Reynolds, did you color coordinate my closet? You know I like to look spiffy."

The officious butler made a displeased face then remembered indifference. "James unpacked your bags, Ms. Gellat. I'm sure he did an excellent job." Without further discussion, Reynolds made a military-sharp spin on his heel and disappeared down the main entry hallway.

"I love giving him fits." Lorena smirked and nodded to follow the butler. Cordelia gaped at the artwork and antiques. The butler didn't lead them upstairs; rather he veered off to the left and led them into the south wing of the house.

"The young Mr. Cole and Mr. Lindsay had this wing remodeled, making several large rooms downstairs to allow for better access to the gardens." Though Reynolds spoke in a bored, affected way, he exhibited pride of the house. "This part of the house was unused until the remodel. The family resides in the north wing. The formal sitting room sits to the right of the foyer. In the north wing, there is a library that serves as Sir Cole's office. Sir Gerald keeps his personal quarters in the northeast wing while the younger Mr. Cole and Mr. Lindsay live in the northwest. The older Mr. Cole stays in the guest quarters on the second floor of the south wing."

Reynolds' stately pleasure encouraged Cordelia to speak. "This wing looks authentic. It would be difficult to detect the remodel."

The butler puffed a bit more. "Thank you, ma'am. My brother is a carpenter. He designed and completed most of the work himself." He stopped at a closed door to the right. "These are your rooms, Miss Gellat."

Lorena gave him a quick elbow to the ribs. "Thanks, my good man." She opened the door and stepped across the threshold before he could glower.

"Ahem." Reynolds composed himself. He moved further down the hall. "And these, Miss Fiore, will be your rooms." He opened another door further down the right from Lorena's.

She stepped through the doorway.

"Please do not hesitate to ring if you need anything, Miss Fiore." Reynolds shot Lorena a quick look of disapproval. Cordelia had won some points with her compliments on the wing's remodeling.

"Thank you, Reynolds." She tried to absorb her surroundings.

Reynolds turned on his heel and vanished down the hallway.

Lorena leaned against the doorjamb. "I wonder if he learned that in butler school."

"They have butler school?" Cordelia asked, intrigued.

"Of course, though Reynolds' family has worked for the Coles for decades, so maybe he comes by it naturally."

"You put him off."

Lorena smiled. "Ah, Reynolds and I go back a long while. He wouldn't know what to do if I didn't goad him." She stretched. "If I know Arthur, and I do, he has a marvelous spread planned. I'm going to grab a shower before I go sniffing for something to eat." She looked at Cordelia. "You going to be okay on your own for a bit?"

Enjoying another ally in the Sebastian camp, she waved Lorena off. "I'll be fine. I think I'll walk the gardens a bit. I need to breathe." She looked into her rooms. "Reynolds said we have access to them, right?"

"Yep, just go to the sitting room. There are French doors leading to a private patio then on to the gardens. One of us will come find you when the food's ready." She began to close her door, but Cordelia stopped her.

"Thanks, Lorena." She could've said more, but the tall flaxen-haired woman nodded.

"Any time." She shut the door.

Cordelia shut her own door and took a look around the suite. A large sitting room with an elegant granite fireplace furnished in cool greens and blues opened through double doors to the gardens. The furnishings had a Victorian flavor. The carpet, luxurious and white, made her cringe thinking about keeping it clean. She had a mad urge to wiggle her toes in it. The French doors offered a view to a quaint cobble patio decked out with cushioned chairs and a small table. Cordelia pictured herself sipping coffee, or perhaps tea, a book opened on her lap.

The door to the left opened to the bedroom; she peeked in and saw her clothes hanging in the roomy closet. *Seriously, how do these people move so fast?* The king-sized bed invited a person to snuggle deep in the down comforter and piles of pillows. The greens and blues flowed into the bedroom in deeper tones. She could see double doors opened to what looked to be an enormous bathroom. Tempted by the idea of a claw foot tub to sink into up to her chin, she resisted and headed out toward the gardens.

Stepping onto the patio, she heard birds chirping and felt the soft tickle of a breeze on her face. She took a deep breath and sighed it out, letting some tension melt out of her shoulders. Just beyond the patio, she could see the expanse of the gardens spread out, a colorful patchwork of English blooms. Walking into the kaleidoscope of fragrance, she stepped with care on the cobbled path. Two whitewashed barns rose out of the garden opposite the manor. Cordelia delighted at the idea of horses and possibly goats. Animals offered their own soothing balm. She moved with purpose toward the first building. A riding arena bridged the space between the two stables and she could see horses poking their heads out of the stalls on the other side of the circumference of the earth. At the nearest barn, she met the sliding barn door with a feeling of pleasure. The fresh smell of hay drifted out on the breeze. She opened the smaller inner door to the stable and stepped through, confused by the space she found.

A glossy and modern medical laboratory took the place of the barn. In the center of the room, a dark-haired figure bent over an examination table. Thinking it Sebastian, she stepped forward. Her brain disagreed with her eyes processing the slighter build and hair that brushed the collar of a white medical coat.

The figure stood at the shaft of light and the sound of the door. The man, so similar in looks to Sebastian, had to be Ian Cole. He strode forward with a different kind of grace than his brother. He offered her a warm, welcoming smile. “Hallo, who’ve we here?”

CHAPTER TWENTY-SIX

"Cordelia. Cordelia Fiore," she stammered, off balance from such an open expression on an almost mirror image of Sebastian.

"Sebastian's arrived then, good." He closed the distance between them with long, easy strides. "I'm glad to meet you. I'm Ian Cole." He bowed over her hand. "This is a pleasant surprise. I didn't know Sebastian … I mean it's unusual for him to bring …"

Cordelia tried to keep the snark out of her voice. "I'm involved with the case."

Ian looked disappointed. "I'm sorry. Looking at you, well, it's easy to think Sebastian might be … ahem, sorry."

His stuttering and stammering charmed her.

She smiled and squeezed his hand. "This is your lab? I thought it was the stables."

"Ah no, I mean yes, it's my medical lab and no, not the stables." He gazed at the large, clinical space. "I did build it to resemble the barn. I like the barn; it's cozy with the smell of fresh hay and the sounds of the horses. We have goats and sheep too. Much more comforting than the city." Without letting go of her hand, he led her into the room. "My office is upstairs in the loft. This is my personal lab. I have a much bigger facility in town. That's where most of my staff works. This," he gestured with pleasure in his voice, "is just mine."

Cordelia stood in the midst of his laboratory still holding his hand. "Your lair?"

He chuckled. "Not really a dank, dripping vault, is it?"

"No." Cordelia looked around at the cheerful white space. The left side of the building had several refrigeration units—two with large stainless steel doors and two smaller units with glass doors. She could see chemicals and bottles of medicine with syringe caps. The rest of the room contained a variety of sinks and cabinets with countertop space. The ceiling is what gave the room a light, airy feeling. Between the traditional roof rafters, two banks of transom skylights offered a clear view of the clouds and the robin's egg sky.

Ian saw her gaze upward. "Isn't it lovely? Not that we get many days like this, but when we do—"

"You like to see it," Cordelia finished. She glanced at Ian then noticed the examination table over his shoulder.

He noticed her stare. "Oh yes, this is the sample Alonzo sent. Isn't it fascinating?" He let go of her hand and focused on his work. "You can see here his physical structure is human." He peered at what appeared to be a hand and pulled a light down closer from its mount on a rafter.

Cordelia moved closer to the table, horrified.

Ian continued without noticing her face. "I ran some tests, and it's definitely human. Or at least part human. I sent a DNA sample to town. We have a sequencer there. My staff'll be able to break down the individual strands of DNA." He gestured her closer with a wave of his hand. "The hirsute nature has to be from a different genetic species unless the man had some unfortunate ancestry." He chuckled. "Someone has been mucking about with recombinant DNA sequences." He spoke as if someone had tampered with a hot cocoa recipe.

"This attacked Sebastian the other night?" She steadied her voice.

"Yes, whoever sent this poor creature out against Sebastian didn't know who they were up against."

Cordelia found herself infected by Ian's curiosity. "Sebastian …killed it?"

"Oh easily, his transformation is more sophisticated than this unfortunate individual. Sebastian's body has fully integrated the genetic alterations. I took a rudimentary look at the cell structure, and while similar, Sebastian's is more evolved. Something in his biology adapted and assimilated the DNA codes." Ian looked up to see if Cordelia understood.

She nodded for him to keep going, not trusting her voice and not certain of what she heard. Sebastian's transformation?

"Sebastian's capable of a full transformation both to his altered state and back to his human state at will. This poor bloke doesn't have the same cellular flexibility. He transformed into this creature with no hope of changing back. The key to the DNA sequencing will be to find out what Sebastian has in his biology this fellow didn't." Ian's voice bubbled with excitement. Cordelia felt a little dizzy and sick. "The interesting thing is even if Sebastian hadn't killed it, the creature would have died. The body shows rapid deterioration. The immune system had attacked all of the cells and major organs in the body. Alonzo sent it … him," he continued. "On arrival, its core temperature was well over 117 degrees, and it had been dead for several hours. You and I, even with a fever, have a safe core temperature of—"

"104 degrees," Cordelia finished.

Ian thrilled at her understanding. He blazed on, missing the blank stare in her face. "Correct, and that's alive. Body temperature decreases upon death. His immune system would've done him in. Burned him up, so to speak."

"The creature ran a temperature because its immune system thought it was sick?" She remembered the heat radiating from Sebastian. She thought she'd imagined it. "Sebastian runs hot."

Ian paused a minute to think her statement through. "Yes, like our bodies would fight off a virus …" his voice trailed off, and Cordelia could see his wheels turning.

"Cordelia, you're brilliant!" He turned and grabbed both of her hands. "I was overthinking, but you're right. When we found Sebastian, I couldn't retrieve all of the research procedures from the hard drives. You've given me an idea! Right there in front of me the whole time! I'm such an idiot!"

Pushing down her shock, she couldn't resist teasing him. "Or such a genius?"

He laughed out loud. "Bloody right, thinking too much to see it. Viral vectors! It explains a lot!"

Cordelia frowned. "Now you do need to explain, genius."

"Right, okay, basic stuff first. Viruses find a path into the body, usually the nose, eyes, mouth, but the blood also. Transferred usually by touch or direct contact."

She rubbed her hands together. "Sing the ABC song when washing your hands?"

Ian chuckled and pointed a finger at her. "Exactly. So if you don't come into direct contact with a virus, you don't contract it. This thing's," he pointed at the creature on the table, "immune system worked overtime because it had a virus introduced directly into the system." He gestured her over to the table. She moved closer. The thing gave her gooseflesh.

"There's a scar at the base of the neck. You can't see it because of the fur, but it's there. Sebastian has the same scar. I knew there'd been an intrusion to the spinal fluid; I just didn't know why." He looked at Cordelia.

"Direct contact with the virus," she said, her stomach growing more queasy.

"Not just beautiful, but brilliant." He beamed. "Using a virus as a delivery method, we call it a vector and injecting the sequences into the spinal fluid could, theoretically, deliver genetic instructions in such a way to ensure mutation."

Cordelia reached a hand out behind her and pressed it into the cool stainless steel countertop to keep standing. "Someone forced this … man … to change?"

Ian's voice rose in giddy excitement. "They tried, but the body fought the virus, weakening the DNA sequence. It's bloody marvelous!" He turned to Cordelia. "Sorry, I've been looking at this for over four years. This specimen and your lovely keen eye have helped me get a fresh look at this. Ha! Helped me figure out a way of determining Sebastian's condition. I might be able to immunize him and the others. We might be able to reverse their condition. Even if I can't reverse the mutation, I could, at the very least immunize the people in close contact to prevent any more infection."

"Others?" she asked. Her brain shied away from the idea looming at the edge of their conversation.

A shaft of light shot into the room as the door opened. "Ian, have you—" Sebastian looked from Cordelia to his brother then to the body on the table. The two brothers spoke almost at once.

"What the blooming hell…" Sebastian's voice sounded harsh with shock.

"Come hear what we've figured…" Ian's voice died out at the stony look on his brother's face.

Cordelia met Sebastian stare for stare, unwilling to let him see her flinch. She went cold.

****

They all stood for a moment, silence hanging heavy in the room. Sebastian moved farther into the room.

"What have you figured out?" His voice fell in icy notes.

Ian, confused by his brother's rage, gestured to the figure on the table. "Cordelia gave me a hint I've been thinking about this backwards." Sebastian looked stony. "Ahem, yes, well she and I were discussing viruses and immunity. She mentioned fevers, and I don't know why I didn't think about this sooner, but with a few more tests, I believe I can prove the DNA sequencing triggering your … er," he slowed down a bit as he looked up to see Sebastian's face granite, "the … the change was delivered using a viral vector."

Sebastian remained quiet for a moment, then said, "The spinal fluid was the entrance point delivering the virus with the DNA sequences. Immediate access to the brain stem." He moved closer to Ian and the body. "Ian, they had me for almost two weeks. The injections could've been timed. A chain reaction."

The younger brother finished his sentence. "Allowing one set of mutations to infect before another set was delivered. If the DNA sequence can be broken down, the mutations—"

"We might be able to trace the path of the sequence. Can we reverse engineer it?" The two brothers thought as a unit. Cordelia stood entranced by the connection she saw between them. She watched Sebastian, guard down, close to his brother.

Ian put his hand on Sebastian's shoulder. "I don't know. You're different somehow. You survived, no, you've evolved." He nodded his head toward the table. "That poor bastard never had a chance."

Reminded of the thing on the table and what Ian said about others, Cordelia held back the dagger of fear at the edge of her mind and moved toward the open door.

Sebastian straightened. He pointed a finger at Ian. "You," his voice became resigned. "Just keep working on it."

Cordelia stepped out the door as his hand closed on her arm. She gasped at the speed with which he crossed the room. She jerked her arm out of his grasp and stepped into the weak morning sunshine. "And me?"

Sebastian rubbed a hand across his eyes. The loud rumble of her stomach reanimated him, and his eyebrow rose. "You need to eat something."

"You're an ass." She startled him and stalked off toward her rooms.

From inside the still open doorway, Ian started laughing and called out, "Blow me down, she's a keen eye for you."

"Bugger off, Ian," Sebastian called over his shoulder as he trotted after her.

Cordelia didn't know which thought to follow. They spun through her mind, dervishes twirling without direction. *Others.* Ian said others. Ideas began to click into place. A complex pattern settling one by one as they slowed. *Thomas. Seamus. Not Alonzo, not Rachna, but she must know. Not Ian or Arthur Lindsay. Sir Gerald? No. Thinking about it, everyone similar to Sebastian hummed. Lorena.* She'd become so accustomed to Sebastian and Thomas's white noise she didn't even notice Lorena put out a low hum too.

Cordelia stopped when she reached the patio and bent over, hands on her knees. She forced her breath to even out for fear she might throw up. *Think this through, Cord. You're fine. They've shown concern for your safety. There's a bigger picture.* She scoffed at herself. *Did you see that thing? Sebastian turns into something like that*! She took another steadying breath. *I've stepped into a terrible movie.* The little voice in the back of her mind snorted. *Stepped? Hell, you've fallen. Not just into a situation, you're halfway in love with him already.*

"If that doesn't fuck all," she said out loud.

"That sums it up." Sebastian's bitter tone startled her out of her reverie.

One thought bloomed into form outside all of the others. She planted her feet and swung around, landing a sharp right uppercut on Sebastian's chin.

He fell back a step or two startled, but clearly not hurt.

She didn't flinch, even though her hand throbbed. "Fuck!"

"You said that already," he said, rubbing his face.

She looked at him expressionless. "Explain."

He sighed. "I didn't want you involved."

"Too late." She folded her arms.

CHAPTER TWENTY-SEVEN

Sebastian sat across from Cordelia on the patio outside her room. "Thomas and Lorena quit the agency to help Ian figure out what they did to me. They had no idea what they were getting into. After bringing me here, I changed for the first time." Cordelia held her breath. Sebastian's voice grew weary. "I ripped the place up. Ian tried to keep me sedated, but something tore through me. I bit Thomas and Lorena. I don't remember it, but I did." He brushed his hair back. "I'm infectious. I transmit this to people when I shift. Bloody hell, Cordelia, they've always had my back, and this is how I've repaid them." He gazed out at the garden.

"You changed in Rome. You told me to run." She remembered.

"After four years I've learned to control it. Thomas and Lorena can as well. They actually feel it's an advantage. Can you believe it? We've mutated beyond human existence to become … what? And they think it's a great thing."

"Seamus too. He loves being different." She spoke the words as the realization crystallized in her brain. "The man has no shame."

Sebastian grimaced. "No, he doesn't. He convinced Lorena to bite him. I don't know how, but it's a bloody mess."

"Alonzo and the others who work with you, they all know."

"Yes, after we vet a person for the job. They spend a year or so working with us; if it seems like a permanent placement, we tell them. Most of them suspect by that time."

"You don't hire stupid people." The irony amused her.

He shook his head. "Can't abide stupid people. Someone on my team could be hurt or killed." He leaned into his hand.

"You become what? A werewolf? A snarling, drooling monster?"

"This isn't a joke, Cordelia. We aren't in some fairy tale. This is my life or what's left of it. They took everything I am …." the snarl in his voice came from deep in his throat.

She ignored his tirade. "Not a dog then. You know I imagined you as more of a predatory cat, a panther maybe. No wonder it always feels you're ready to tear someone's throat out." She stood up to go inside. She kept her tone light, but her head spun. Despite his situation, she refused to reinforce his self-pity. He took responsibility for the safety of his team. She knew he felt affection for his brother and, yes, even his father. Men like Thomas Shaw and Seamus MacColgan didn't offer their loyalties to monsters. Rachna loved Thomas and Sebastian too. Rachna trusted him. So did Lorena. I will too.

He jumped up to follow. "This is dangerous! You've no idea what you're involved in and I don't want to be responsible if anything happens to you!" He stepped into her room on her heels.

Cordelia whirled around placing both hands on his chest and shoved him as hard as she could. "You are so stupid!" She poked him hard in the chest. "If something happens it's because there are people out there willing to do this without caring about the consequences. You have no control over them. None of this is your fault."

"Cordelia, I'm a freak."

She laughed. “Who’re you to be talking about being a freak? I hear people’s thoughts, Sebastian. I can tell the future. I see the past. Listen, buster, you’re looking at the last person in the world who’s going to offer sympathy for being a freak. Whatever you are, you’re one of the good guys.”

He grabbed her arms. “You’re not listening.”

She could feel his heat through the sleeves of her shirt, and, she thought, his body’s heightened immune system. She felt the rhythm of his heart. “Yes, I am. The question is, are you?”

Cordelia pulled him with her gaze toward the bedroom, moving backward, careful not to break eye contact. Sliding her hands from his chest to his face, she drew him down to kiss. Heat scorched through her body. Moving with a purpose of their own, her hands tugged his shirt up over his head, tracing the skin of his chest and shoulders. Lips parted, mouths tasting and devouring, she broke contact to lift her own shirt. Up and away, his hands raised the soft fabric up and off. Her mouth found his again.

Far from the crushing insistence of his kiss at the villa, this teasing and delicate kiss sent shivers down her spine. She felt his hands move down her arms and across the small of her back. Wrapping her arms around his neck, she pulled him across the space between the door and the bed. Tangled in the hot press of their bodies, Cordelia felt the bed too late. She fell back, Sebastian falling with her. He slid his hand along her thigh lifting her knee up and around his waist. Sebastian buried his face in her neck. His nipping bites ignited a fire in her belly. She felt the hardness of his body’s answering desire and ground her hips up into him.

Her mouth found his neck, tasting with a mind of its own. He pressed her hands into the bed. His kiss bruised her lips with the force. She gasped, losing her breath. The shrill and cutting ring of the phone on the bedside table interrupted her descent into the luscious sensations of his fingers sliding up the back of her thigh. Breathing hard, he pulled away to focus on her face, and she saw him slam his control into place. She groaned, draping her arm over her face. "Shit."

He tsked her language and handed her the receiver.

"Hello?" She thought about throwing it at Sebastian's head.

"Brunch is ready," Lorena's cheerful voice rang out.

Cordelia sucked in her frustrated sigh. "Give me a minute. I'll meet you in the hall." She dropped the phone on the bed.

Sebastian, his shirt back on, replaced the receiver on the cradle and smoothed his hair back. Cordelia leaned up on her elbows giving him a dirty look. "Shut up."

"I didn't say anything." He smoothed his shirt.

"I can hear you thinking it." She flopped back down with a growl throwing her arm over her face again.

"You can't read my mind," he reminded.

"That's what you think."

Sebastian let out a breath as if to speak, but Cordelia cut him off. "Not one word." Her voice came muffled from under her arm.

He backed out of the room and walked out the open French doors into the garden.

Someone knocked on the door. "Cordelia?" Lorena opened it and peeked into the room. "You okay?" Once inside the sitting room, Lorena had a clear view of Cordelia lying on the bed half dressed with her skirt up over one knee. She moved in and looked around.

"Shit, shit, shit!" Cordelia muttered from under her arm.

Lorena drew a hand through her hair and whistled. "You can say that again."

"Help me out here," she demanded, pulling a fresh t-shirt on over her head. Cordelia frowned at her reflection in the bathroom mirror and pulled her tussled hair into a pony tail.

Lorena sat down in the chair in the corner chuckling and shaking her head.

"Hand me that charcoal sweater."

Lorena reached over to where Cordelia had thrown it and tossed it into the bathroom. "Food'll be cold unless you hurry."

"I won't be able to eat anything," Cordelia mumbled.

"Wanna bet? You haven't had a solid meal since Sperlonga. Neither have I, point of fact. My stomach's grumbling. I know you're starving. Lindsay puts on a great spread and we're both going to eat." She blew on her fingers and rubbed them against her shirt. "There's no way either one of us is going to miss out on a meal because Sebastian Cole's an asshole."

"Maybe I'm the idiot." She stepped into the room, tugging her sweater over her shoulders. "This is as good as it's getting. Lorena," she slumped onto the bed, "what am I doing here?"

"Look, we both know Sebastian could've put you on a plane to Vancouver without blinking an eye and you'd have been a distant memory." She stood up and stretched. "As long as I've known Sebastian, before all of this mutation crap," she gave Cordelia a look. No more pretending. "He never could settle on a woman. Oh, there were women, but nothing lasting. He had some reason or another it went south." She leaned on the doorframe and looked at Cordelia. "You're in more danger with us than you would be if we had just sent you home. He knows that deep down, but he's convinced himself we can keep you safe." She walked over and grabbed Cordelia's hands, pulling her to her feet. "No one's complaining for a couple of reasons. Frankly, you're the first woman he's been with that we like. And, girlfriend, everyone's talking about how you nailed that guy in Rome. No histrionics, no stupid questions, no 'I broke a nail' shit, AND you didn't puke."

Cordelia let her pull her out of the bedroom toward the doorway to the hall with a little laugh. "I felt like puking."

"But you didn't and in our business that's a plus. Even some of the tough guys puke the first time they have to kill someone. I saw it all of the time in Afghanistan." She opened the door and pushed Cordelia through. "Now, we're going to go enjoy Lindsay's meal, to hell with Sebastian and the horse he road in on. He doesn't know it; he's screwed. He's in love with you." She linked her arm with Cordelia's and headed down the hallway toward the smell of food. "Now, I can guarantee that he's going to fuck it up, but hang in there. He'll come around. And if he doesn't … you'll live."

Cordelia lifted her shoulders square with Lorena's and matched her stride for stride. "You're right, I'm hungry."

Lorena laughed.

CHAPTER TWENTY-EIGHT

"We know she's in Slovenia. Let's hit her quick." Seamus filled a large wing-backed chair in a corner of the library.

Thomas stood, leaning over the architectural schematics of the Biogenesis compound. "Make it look like a burglary, corporate espionage. Wouldn't be a problem."

Ian flipped through the stack of blueprints. "No guarantee where she's keeping her data and experiments." He pulled out a blueprint of the building. "This is the primary facility. It's not reasonable to search a building this size. She has a lab here and in the corporate building on Prešeren Square. We've no idea where she's hiding her work. It's a safe bet it isn't in either of the corporate sites."

Lorena leaned against a bookcase. "Let's flush her out."

Sebastian kept looking at the schematics. "With what? Carlson's smart and ruthless. There's no telling where she's holed up."

Moving forward, Lorena gave Cordelia a wink. Buckle up. "Bait her. We're being tailed. Sooner or later, they're going to find out we're in England. Let's slip up, put what she wants within reach. See what happens."

"She's desperate. She made a mistake with the ambush," Ian agreed, his eyes glittering with mischief. He caught Lorena's wink too. "Could be so tempting she'd slip again. You're irresistible."

"These guys aren't great. We've managed to spot them. No reason why we couldn't follow them back to her." Seamus leaned forward. Cordelia saw the idea appealed to him.

"We didn't spot them; Cordelia did," Thomas pointed out.

"Now we know," Lorena said.

Ian finished her thought. "We can ensure we could track them."

Sebastian put his hand up. The room paused. "We don't know what she wants."

Thomas snorted at the same time Lorena barked out a cough to cover her laugh.

Ian resisted the urge to roll his eyes. "Sebastian—"

Cordelia beat him to it without humor. "She wants you."

Sebastian looked up at her. He paused a moment, something settling behind his eyes. "You shouldn't be here."

Seamus moved to stand next to Cordelia's chair. "We took a vote."

"Yep," Lorena added. "We like her."

Sebastian shot Thomas a cold glare. "Vote?"

The shaggy Englishman nodded, laughter threatening to explode. "We've decided to keep her."

Sir Gerald breezed into the room followed by Reynolds and James loaded with trays of tea and snacks. He surveyed the room ending with his oldest son's face. "Ah, you've told him."

Cordelia put her face in her hand, shaking her head.

Lorena, buoyant with humor, broke the silence. "Sebastian, we've voted you off the island. We're keeping Cordelia."

"Enough." Sebastian's low, cool voice sobered the mood. "A trap it is, but Cordelia's going home." He scanned the members of his team ending any discussion. "Lorena, you'll take a team and put Cordelia on the plane. If Carlson wants me, let's make sure she gets a shot."

Thomas started thinking. "Everyone will need a subdural tracker. Sebastian, you'll be marked. Let's assume they know we're here. A trip to London office would provide an opportunity to snatch you."

Seamus approached the desk. "We have enough manpower to position teams at both facilities. If you end up at either location, we'll have an immediate response. It would only take the rest of us a short time to join up at either location."

Thomas pointed to a place on the map. "I'll position myself on standby in the middle of the two sites. Better the chances of me getting to you if there's a different location. I'll have Flora and Collins with the teams waiting at the labs."

Cordelia stood up. "Looks like you have this under control. I'll go pack." She gave a last look at Sebastian, who concentrated on the map, then she left the room.

"Smooth, Sebastian. You've got moves that bring tears to a woman's eyes." Lorena followed Cordelia out.

Pulled from the focus of the operation, Thomas gave Sebastian a sympathetic look.

"What?" he demanded.

Sir Gerald patted Sebastian on the shoulder. "I've got a way with the ladies. Thought you might have the gene but seems to have skipped you, old chap."

Sebastian's shoulders sagged in resignation. "Look, are we doing this?"

"Hell, yes," Seamus barked.

Eyes turned back to the plan.

****

Three SUVs lined up on the gravel drive. Cordelia's hand was tucked into the crook of Sir Gerald's arm. He patted her. "You won't be a stranger. This hubbub will settle down and you'll come visit me soon. Or perchance, I'll pop into Vancouver. I hear your father has a sterling bookstore."

Cordelia didn't feel sincere when she said, "I'd love that."

Lorena drove Reynolds crazy trying to direct the butler in the art of loading luggage.

Cordelia turned to take a last look at the manor.

Sir Gerald followed her gaze. "He's not very good with people in general, but Sebastian's the best when it comes to this sort of thing."

Lorena opened the passenger door. "Let's haul ass."

Sir Gerald kissed Cordelia's cheek. "Ciao, bella."

She stepped into the vehicle. "Ciao."

"You'll call when it's done? Never mind the time difference," Lorena said, waving as she walked to the right side of the SUV.

Once in the car, Lorena adjusted the mirrors and moved the seatbelt around the pistol holstered at her ribcage. Cordelia's eyes fell on the gun. "It's a Bersa Thunder 40. I'm trying it out. I typically carry a Glock, but I like to see what's out there. Some women shop for shoes; not me."

Cordelia, not being a shoe person or a gun person, nodded as though she understood.

Lorena laughed. "It's lightweight. It packs a punch and it's compact enough to conceal under some evening gowns." She pulled it from the holster. "You ever fire a gun?"

"Nope. Didn't think of it as a life skill. I can drive a stick shift, swim, throw a punch, and I can ride a bike. No one said, 'Cordelia learn to shoot a gun … critical life skill.'"

"Someone should've. You don't have to love guns, but someone should've taught you how to handle one." She laid the gun flat in her left hand. "It weighs about thirty ounces but isn't a small gun." She opened the ejection port. "No round in the chamber." She pressed a button and the magazine slid out. "No magazine." She handed the gun to Cordelia.

"It's heavy," Cordelia said, thinking how easily Lorena handled the gun.

"Not as heavy as some, but it's stable. Hold it in two hands, one over the other like a golf club." She took the gun and wrapped Cordelia's hands around it. "It's a semi-automatic, so outside of a misfire or jam, just make sure you have rounds in the magazine. I carry three extra magazines." She lifted her shirt to show Cordelia the cartridge sleeves on her belt.

"Um, okay." Cordelia tried to balance the weight of the gun.

Lorena touched two spots on the barrel. "There's a front sight and a rear sight. Look down the barrel."

"It's heavy," Cordelia repeated when she held the gun out in front of her.

"I told you, you get used to it. Look down the barrel. Do you see the front sight?"

Cordelia nodded.

"Hold the gun in your right hand with the left hand folded over it. Not too tight, you're not swinging a bat. It's important to focus on the front blade. Keep it crisp and align it in the center of the rear sight blades. Try to keep equal bars of light on either side of the front blade."

Cordelia aimed the gun toward the windshield.

"I prefer keeping both eyes open, better distance perception that way." A small smile lifted the corner of Lorena's mouth. "I would recommend pulling your tongue back into your mouth. You might bite it."

Cordelia laughed and retracted her tongue. "Now what?"

"Okay, this is the hard part. Don't focus on your target; focus on aligning the front blade. The target should be slightly blurry. There are two planes of targeting, vertical and horizontal. The horizontal plane's taken care of when you frame the front blade between equal bars of light. The vertical plane is like the horizon. You can aim center of mass; that's in the middle of what you're trying to shoot. Some people aim six o'clock, my grandpa called it pumpkin-on-a-post because you're sighting the entire target right above the front blade. Either way, gently squeeze the trigger. If you jerk it, your shot will drop low. You'll have to go to a shooting range and practice to figure out what kind of shot you are. For now, if you have to, aim a little high. You'll jerk the trigger."

"I won't need this." Cordelia tried handing her back the pistol.

"This is the clip and the clip release button. Clip slides in." There was a distinctive snap. "Hit the button and gravity does the rest." The clip slid out. "This is the safety. Keep it on until you're sure you'll need the gun. You might not need it today, but I'm a firm believer in Mr. Murphy. Just take it and don't keep it in your purse."

Cordelia slid the gun into the deep interior pocket of her jacket. "Happy?"

"Is anybody?" Lorena started the car and started down the long gravel road.

"What's the plan?" Cordelia felt awkward with the weight of the gun in her pocket.

"We're heading to the airfield where we landed." She shook her head. "Time's getting away from me. Alonzo has the jet ready with a flight plan to London."

"I live in Vancouver."

"Yeah, the plane will divert in the air. No need to take out a sign when people are watching. We're counting on their focus on the house and London. We're only two cars with a flight plan to the city. We could be carrying anything, with a flight plan to Vancouver we're carrying you."

"Bait and switch."

"You got it. You know you're good at this." Lorena kept an eye on traffic, farm trucks, freight trucks, and the occasional car. She stopped at the crossroads giving a glance at the farm lorry approaching from the right. She took her foot off the brake and accelerated.

Cordelia's brain took a full thirty seconds to connect the screeching, crunching sound of metal to the whiplash of her head into the passenger window. Stunned, she tried to focus. The pressure in her head registered with her eyes, and she realized she dangled sideways. The SUV had rolled and spun so it rested on the passenger side. Lorena pressed close to her as the space in the SUV compacted inward. She reached out to touch Lorena's cheek. Blood on the corner of her mouth alarmed Cordelia.

"Lorena." The ragged sound that came out of her mouth surprised her. "Lorena." She flooded with relief when Lorena's eyelids fluttered.

"Yep." A cough sprayed more blood. "Still here." The sound of four quick snaps confused Cordelia, but the sound revived Lorena. "Is my bag," she coughed, "is my bag here?"

Cordelia looked around at the broken glass and detritus of equipment tossed around Lorena. "I think so. Everything's all over."

"Is there something that looks like an otoscope?" she asked.

Cordelia's heartbeat raced. "A what? Lorena, you're hurt."

Lorena shook her head. "I'm dead." Another bubble of blood escaped with her shallow breath. "An otoscope, the thing the doctor uses to check your ears."

Cordelia scanned the flotsam and her blurry focus fell on the thing she thought Lorena wanted. "Yes, near your right hand."

Lorena winced as she shifted her hand around to find the object. She swore when she heard the sound of voices approaching the wreck. "Give me your palm."

Cordelia reached out her hand. "Lorena, help's coming; you're going to be fine." She gasped at the sharp pain high in the meaty part of her hand. "What—"

Lorena dropped the tool and held her hand up. "Cor … they took the wrong bait." She coughed.

Cordelia struggled to suppress her own pain. She tried to calm Lorena. "I hear people. They're going to get us out of here."

Lorena gave a humorless laugh, full of her own blood. "Coming for you; remember, aim high." A gurgling choke made her pause. "He'll come for you, he'll—" Her sucking gasp chilled Cordelia's heart. "He'll fuck it up … but he'll come."

A baton smashed through what was left of the windshield showering the two women with glittering squares of glass. Cordelia winced. "We need help."

A hand reached into the vehicle aiming a large pistol fitted with a suppressor at Lorena's head. Lorena turned her gaze to stare at her murderer. "Nice Glock."

Cordelia squeezed her eyes shut against threatening tears as burly hands reached in and sliced her seatbelt. She didn't notice the additional scratches and cuts on her body as they dragged her out through the scraping teeth of the window. Keeping her eyes closed, she felt a sharp sting in her hip and then things went black.

CHAPTER TWENTY-NINE

Cordelia struggled to open her eyes. Whatever her abductors drugged her with was still clinging to her brain. As her mind cleared a little, she began to panic. She couldn't move. Could she feel her arms and legs? Yes, the feeling was coming back to her. It took all of her concentration to wiggle a finger, but the effort dragged her lids down.

Wake.

Cordelia jerked at the thought drilled into her head. It didn't feel like hers; the drugs clouded things. She focused on trying to open her eyes again.

Quiet. Trouble comes.

This is ridiculous. I'm hallucinating. Open your eyes, Cord. As she poured her energy into trying to pry her lids up, she heard voices approaching. The door opened. It didn't take much effort to remain still.

"She's a little worse for wear, Viktor," a cool, impersonal voice remarked.

"Extraction turned out more complicated than we planned, but she'll heal. Most of her injuries are superficial. No broken bones, no internal injuries, just peripheral lacerations. I can treat those if you like and have her cleaned up."

"Unnecessary unless there are embedded glass fragments. She might heal during the insertion. Of course, she might not." The remote nonchalance in the woman's voice unnerved Cordelia. This time she did have to tamp down an impulse to struggle. "Wake her up. We need to have a chat."

The second presence, Viktor, moved into the hollow-sounding room. He seemed to leave her immediate vicinity and then moved back to sounds of drawers and clinking of glass. Vials, she thought from the small, tinny sound. Panic began to bubble up from her belly.

"This'll counter the sedatives."

A cold sting started in her arm and then she felt it flow through her veins. Her awareness followed the icy path of the drug as it left a trail of sensation. Freezing alertness spread through her limbs inch by agonizing inch until her eyes flew open. The cuts and scrapes from the glass began to bite. Her head was immobilized by a strap around her forehead. Straps held her hands, her ankles, and her waist.

Forcing her eyes to the furthest corners of her sockets, she saw nothing remarkable about the room to the left. Scanning to the right, she saw an amazing creature behind the bars of an immense cage. The size of a mountain gorilla, the creature's silky fur shone with a burnished cinnamon. A couple of blankets lay folded in the corner. Food dishes were placed at perfect angles near a faucet and sink.

A petite woman with champagne hair cut in an angular bob moved closer to Cordelia. "Ah, you've noticed Elsa. She's my first success in recombinant DNA." The woman's spiteful gaze pierced Cordelia. The woman spoke with a cool distance, but Cordelia knew she hated her with draconian force. It radiated out of her eyes and flowed into Cordelia's brain, still woozy from the sedative.

The flaxen pixie said, "Nothing to say, no demands or cries of release."

Cordelia tried to work up enough saliva to swallow the sand from her throat. Her voice croaked out, "It's a waste of time."

The woman chimed out an insincere laugh, piquing Cordelia's tender fury along with her mounting fear. This woman wanted her dead. Cordelia's mind clouded for a moment with smoldering pain. Straps cut into her wrists. Her cuts and bruises rose in heat with her unease. The searing wound in her hand throbbed. Lorena stabbed her with something. She said Sebastian would come. A brief flash of hope flared in the mire of her pain and fear. She stomped down the flicker forcing her face to freeze.

"Oh, smarter than we look, aren't we? Still, he's so much better than you. I'll have him in the end though."

Cordelia saw this woman with penetrating clarity. In her mind, she owned Sebastian. She viewed him as her creation and desperately needed to possess him. There is hunger and turmoil. The painful taste of desire unsatisfied. She had watched them. The men following Sebastian took orders from her. Whatever this woman saw between Sebastian and Cordelia threatened her plans.

Careful, careful.

The thought bored into her head. She couldn't look at Elsa without breaking contact with this woman. She shook off the tangent and tried to focus her thoughts. She drew a rattling breath. "Whatever I mean to him, he'll come. He wouldn't come for you."

The spittle hit Cordelia in the face. The frosty visage slipped but snapped back.

Pain. Pain, Elsa warned.

Cordelia didn't need the additional thought in her head. She fanned the madness in this woman. If Cordelia could keep her off balance, she might make a mistake. Any advantage gained would be slim.

"Of course he'll come for you. He's the consummate hero." Ice chipped in her voice. "But I'll have him."

"Never willingly." The gravel in Cordelia's throat loosened.

The woman snapped her fingers. "Enough. Save your breath. I've observed the insertion is painful." She walked out of Cordelia's vision.

The sounds of preparation out of her sight threatened to balloon her panic.

Elsa, do you know what's going to happen?

Elsa knows. Pain. Big pain.

Okay, not helpful. Cordelia's anxiety cranked up another notch. Her entire body jerked when she felt a freezing swipe at the base of her neck.

"This is a topical anesthetic." The man's voice hinted at a touch of pity. "This'll numb the area before the incision. I'll be putting in an IV drip that's a blend of nutrients, amino acids, and a bit of morphine." He came to swipe her left arm. Using scissors, he cut away the ragged cloth of her sleeve. "The morphine only dampens the discomfort."

Cordelia kept silent.

"Really, Viktor, your concern is touching, though it's not important. Get on with it." The woman's cool tone overflowed with disdain.

"Yes, Dr. Carlson. Habit." The man skulked out of Cordelia's sight.

Others come.

Cordelia looked back into the creature's eyes. Not the creature, Elsa. *Who's coming, Elsa?*

Others come. Others like Elsa.

When are they coming? Cordelia held onto the hope Sebastian might arrive before Carlson could do anything.

Others come. Pain, Cordelia. Pain. Sorrow surrounded the thought.

Cordelia's mind grew fuzzy as the morphine hit her system. The impressions from Elsa amped her fear up to panic. Cordelia strained against the straps. All thoughts of Sebastian and rescue fled her mind, replaced with foreboding. She thrashed to no avail. Her mind sank a bit deeper into the fog as she felt a tug at the base of her neck. A brief kiss of ice preceded the liquid flame down

Cordelia's spine. The molten tendrils spread into the skin along her back and extended outward, a spiraling galaxy of agony. The magma continued up the cervical vertebrae on a creeping path toward her skull. She felt the torrid fingers of heat slipping around her temples and gouging behind her eyes. She didn't bother trying to keep silent. Cordelia's head strained backward against the strap, her mouth opening in howling despair.

The last clear thought in her head came from Elsa.

Hold on. Others come.

****

Sebastian paced near the Rover. His mind flipped in loops while he and Thomas waited to find out if Alonzo could get a GPS location on the tracker they hoped Lorena used on Cordelia.

"Could you just stop? I'm coming unhinged watching you." Thomas sat with a laptop on his knees.

"Three hours, Thomas. They're not at either facility. It'll take us at least one more to find her and mobilize." Tension crackled around him.

Thomas sighed. "We'll find Cordelia and we'll get Carlson."

"Not in time." He slammed his hand on the truck.

"You can't think about that. We have to keep cool about this and do it right. Hawthorne would tell you to take it down a notch, Cole."

Sebastian ran his hand through his hair. "Yeah, yeah. Taking it down." His phone chirped. "Cole."

"Mr. Cole," said a graceful, accented voice on the other end. "I'd like to offer you some assistance. You're looking for Vivienne Carlson."

Thomas stepped out of the Rover. "Who is it?"

Sebastian put a hand up. "Why should I trust you?"

"We've met before, Mr. Cole. I'm Andre Juricic. Several years ago, I worked for Mr. Weber at the Manhattan office of Biogenesis. Do you recall?"

Sebastian brought to mind the image of the young, refined assistant who brought him coffee. "I remember."

"I've been employed by Dr. Carlson for many years. Do you understand?"

Thomas called Park on his phone. "Hey, get a trace on Sebastian's phone. I want to know where that call's coming from."

"I understand. Why help now?"

Andre paused. "Let's say, for brevity's sake, I've had a paradigm shift. I no longer agree with Carlson's truth. I'd like to help you stop her."

"How do I know this isn't a trap?" Sebastian looked at Thomas. Thomas gave him a thumbs-up. They had Juricic's position.

"Some interesting photos crossed my desk earlier this week. Can you imagine what I saw in those photos?"

"This is ridiculous. What do you want?" Sebastian's frustration bubbled closer to the surface.

"I want to end her. To prevent her from doing to anyone else what she's done to you."

Sebastian thought his teeth would crack from the pressure. "We agree on that point, but you're too late. She has Cordelia."

The unexpected hiss of anger from Andre surprised Cole. "She moved faster than I anticipated. I know where Vivienne's holding her. How soon can you move?"

"Now."

"You've traced the call, yes?"

Sebastian snorted. "Yes."

"We're outside of the security perimeter. Sadly, you're at least an hour away."

Sebastian strode toward the Rover signaling to Thomas to stow the equipment to get moving. “We’re moving.”

“In those photos, I saw love, Mr. Cole.” Andre hung up.

CHAPTER THIRTY

"You have security codes that'll get us in without triggering anything?" Sebastian looked at the building schematic spread out on the hood of the Rover.

Andre stood near Sebastian. His uncle, Niko Mdivani, stood opposite them with Thomas. Turned out, Niko had worked with the Global Sureties team. Having a Slovenian thief lord as an ally proved valuable from time to time. *One big happy family.*

"Yes, we can get deep into the compound without raising any alarm. It'll be different close to the lab. There are motion triggers at odd intervals and laser trigger alarms too numerous to avoid. At that point, we'll have to move fast," Andre said.

Sebastian scrutinized the layout. He tapped his finger on the page. "The lab is three floors down, but her office is three floors up. Where will Carlson be?"

Andre took a brief glance up at Sebastian. "Cordelia will be in the lab. Carlson will be in her office between each administration of the DNA sequence. They call it insertion. Dr. Carlson's only present at the initial stage of insertion."

Sebastian didn't blink. "We'll need two teams and a team in Ljubljana for the Biogenesis offices. It won't do to take care of things in this lab without bringing the whole thing down."

Thomas leaned forward. "Thanks to Niko," Niko tipped his head, "our team has backup at the headquarters building. They can go in, download files, pull databases, and basically strip firewalls for full access." He put his finger on the second lab site. "Taylor and Mars will take the second site with Francek and Grubelnik. Same drill there, though the lab is full of animals and staff."

Niko spoke up. "I've called Dalmatin. That's his territory. Carlson's been plucking our folk off of the street. Andre isn't the only one, almost every family can claim a loss. Everyone in the underground has an interest in shutting her down. Dalmatin's agreed to have personnel available if your second team needs help."

Sebastian looked up. "I've got Alonzo ready to make the call to Interpol and the Slovenian government fifteen minutes after the breach. That'll give our teams time to get what we need." He looked up at Thomas. "Seamus." Sebastian looked around to see the rogue's feet hanging out of his Rover. "Someone kick that asshole."

Jackson slammed the door shut on the size thirteen boots. Seamus swore and tumbled out of the Rover. "Yeah, boss?"

Sebastian's impassive glare made the giant leprechaun shrug.

"You and Jackson'll take the lab. Four of Niko's men will have Ian right behind you."

Seamus and Jackson shared a look. Seamus asked, "You sure?"

"Thomas, Andre, Niko, and I are heading to the third-floor office. Niko can crack the firewall and send everything to the estate. We'll deal with Carlson."

"But—" Jackson put a hand on his partner's arm shaking his head.

Sebastian ignored the disappointment on his men's faces. "Let's go. Keep it sharp."

Thomas shrugged at Seamus and Jackson on his way to get Ian geared for the assault.

****

Sweat trailed salt down Cordelia's temple. Three times she thought she'd burn to a crisp and three times her eyes refocused on the room around her. Each time, Elsa's liquid, sagacious eyes locked with hers.

Others come.

Somehow from a deep reservoir, tears spilled down her cheeks. She couldn't take the hope. Better to resign herself to the inescapable agony than dredge up belief. It had only been a few hours, but Cordelia felt the exhaustion of days piling on her shoulders. *No more, Elsa. I can't stand it.*

Others close. Soon!

Cordelia looked at the creature, the only witness to her suffering. Elsa's hand signed something over and over. The creature shuffled across the cage to lift a corner of her tidy pile of blankets. The floppy-eared bunny in her clutch, Elsa brought out a slender length of wire. *Tool. Key.* The creature looked at Cordelia.

Cordelia realized Elsa could escape. Who knew how long the intelligent thing had been hiding the key? She wanted out. Unable to see around her, Cordelia sent Elsa a question. *Are we alone?*

Elsa tucked the length of wire into the bunny's ribbon. *One man. Woman no. Others close.*

Elsa sent an image of red. Cordelia caught the flash and it caused her heart to sing. It had to be Seamus MacColgan. Help had come; that meant Sebastian. Tears flowed again.

"Two more rounds to go." Rihard moved to check her vitals. "I'm surprised you're alive. Not many have survived the third round. Of course, we're moving too fast. I would increase your morphine, but it won't help."

Cordelia roused up the energy to speak. "Just a minute, please."

Rihard's face caved a little. "Ah, I can do that. I'll call Dr. Carlson in a few minutes. You just breathe slow and evenly. I'll give you a quick shot of Dilaudid. It'll ease the pain for a bit. Might make you a bit queasy, but that's no matter." He pointed to her stomach. "Nothing left in it to come up."

Cordelia didn't want the drugs, but when the cool wave of relief hit her, she almost fainted with relief.

Elsa moved to the lock on her cage. With her deft fingers, she shaped the wire into a crude pick. The sentient creature twiddled with the lock, and in moments the cage door popped open a half inch. *Be still.*

Cordelia didn't move. She held her breath. The flash of the concussion charge shook Cordelia's frame and knocked Rihard off of his feet. At the same time Seamus and Anthony stepped through the door, Elsa stepped out of her cage. The two men stood wide-eyed for a breath, then Cordelia's vision shifted. Seamus's body seemed to expand, taking up more space. His clothes ripped away and he reared up, no longer a man.

Elsa stepped back and wagged her finger at him. The creature Seamus deflated a little until a bullet grazed his shoulder. Glad to have somebody worth tearing up, Seamus leaped past Cordelia and Elsa.

Cordelia couldn't see behind her, but she could hear a sickening tear followed by a gurgle sounding Rihard's end.

Anthony moved to Cordelia, wary of Elsa. "Can you walk?"

"No idea," she croaked.

Ian stepped into the lab. "Blimey!" The sight of Elsa whooshed the breath out of him.

The cause of this awe stood serenely near Cordelia clutching her bunny. Ian recovered when he saw Cordelia strapped into the frame. "Tony, leave her a minute till I get a look at what's what." He stepped behind Cordelia. "Cordelia, can you tell me what they're doing?"

Cordelia needed to moisten her mouth. "Water first?"

Anthony pulled a bottle from a pack and looked past her to Ian. "Can she?"

"Careful, just a little right off. I see Dilaudid here. Cordelia, did they give you this?"

Cordelia nodded as Anthony dribbled some water into her mouth. It felt blissful. "Yes, the IV is a combination of things including morphine." More water and the ashes began to wash away from her throat. She could hear movement behind her and a growl.

Anthony shook his head. "You stay shifted in case we're interrupted." As if in response to his comment, Cordelia heard another brief explosion and some popping gunfire. Anthony saw her look of fear. "Don't worry, we've got this place locked down. There are two men outside of the door and two more down the hall. We're getting you out of here."

Tears threatened again. Cordelia shook them off with a gasp.

Ian felt around her neck. "There's an injection port here. I can remove the tubing, but the port will have to stay until we get you out of here. Do you think you can walk?"

"I've been strapped here for hours. I've no idea. Just get me out of this goddamned thing."

Ian took a breath. "Hang on for a minute. This is going to hurt."

Cordelia cried out while the worm of tubing slithered out of her spine.

"Sorry. Tony, I think we can cut her out. Seamus can you steady her?" Before the hulking, crimson-haired shape could move forward, Elsa slid between Cordelia and Anthony. She looked at Anthony, sized him up, and handed him her bunny with a stern look. He didn't know what to do so he took the bunny and tucked it into the pack the water bottle had emerged from.

Elsa carry. Bunny be safe.

Cordelia couldn't laugh. "This is Elsa. She'll carry me if I need it, but you have to keep her bunny safe."

"I'll be damned," Ian swore. "She's magnificent."

Elsa likes red.

"I think she prefers Seamus."

Seamus made a chirruping sound.

"Christ," Anthony swore. "Can we get this circus moving?"

"Get me out of this." The dulling effects of the Dilaudid started to wear off and Cordelia's limbs began to smolder.

Anthony pulled a serrated knife from his belt and made short work of the strap around her head. She struggled, but managed to keep it up.

The serious Bostonian gave a meaningful look at Elsa and moved the blade to Cordelia's shoulders. Elsa placed her mammoth leathered hands on each of Cordelia's arms. Anthony sliced while Elsa held Cordelia up with little effort. The strap at her waist and ankles gave way. Cordelia slid like a marionette cut from its strings into Elsa's powerful grasp.

"Okay, Seamus, you lead the way since you're bulletproof. I'll lead Elsa and, Ian, you bring up the rear with Mdivani's men," Anthony ordered.

Seamus nodded and headed out the door. Anthony assumed Elsa understood. Working with the unusual seemed to prepare him for the impossible. Cordelia felt impotent as an army of nerves began to twitch with blood flow. Elsa hefted Cordelia as gently as she held her bunny and followed Anthony as he slipped through the door. Ian patted Cordelia's shoulder then followed Elsa.

One arm around Elsa's shoulder and the rest of her dangling, Cordelia tried to see through the haze of smoke. A fire alarm started screaming and emergency strobes blinked on and off. She could barely make out Seamus's hulk ahead of them. Two rough-looking fellows with assault pistols led the way without reaction to the seven-foot brute of claw and tooth. Cordelia wondered if they had seen something similar before.

Chaos continued to spread through the compound. The staff tried to flee. Guards fought to secure the building. The charges Seamus set on the way down to the lab exploded at regular intervals creating rubble and smoke. Electric connections sparked. The people Seamus came upon screamed and ran. Their armed escorts fired off a couple of dispassionate rounds, but most people turned tail quickly leaving the group to move at a steady pace toward ground level.

Unable to stand the feeling of helplessness any longer, Cordelia insisted on walking.

Elsa carry? Faster.

I need to walk, Elsa. Cordelia burned with fever but managed a slow walk. Anthony saw the grim look on her face and didn't say a word. He slowed the pace to accommodate her. They hadn't faced much resistance with Seamus in the lead.

Ian walked shoulder to shoulder with Cordelia, cupping her elbow to steady her hitching gate. "Tony, she needs to stop."

Anthony nodded. He turned to the two men at their rear. "Smo si ustavljanje za minuto. Bom povedal drugi." *We're stopping for a minute. I'll tell the others.* He slid up the corridor to cover Seamus.

"Cordelia, I can give you a shot of the Dilaudid, but Elsa will need to carry you." Ian offered.

She shook her head. "I need to keep my head clear. I'll manage."

He felt her head. "You're running a fever. If we're right and the gene sequencing delivery used a virus, your body's fighting it off."

She looked at him. "My body could kill it?"

He said, "I don't know. We interrupted the insertion, but I've no idea what that means, in the long run."

Cordelia looked to where Seamus and Anthony disappeared. "I could still change."

Ian shook his head. "It's not likely. After your help, we took another look at the research. I'll explain once we get out of here."

Trouble.

Cordelia stiffened. "Elsa says trouble's coming."

Ian pushed Cordelia into Elsa. He stood as the two men at the rear fired several rounds into the smoke. Several guards rushed them from behind. The two Slovenian gypsies fell and Ian took a bullet in the shoulder, but managed to get off a couple of shots. Seamus leaped out of nowhere, flying over them as Anthony covered him with controlled fire. Cordelia dropped to Ian's side and pushed her hands onto the wound.

"In my bag, a med kit." His face paled.

Cordelia fumbled in his pack. Another guard caught her by her hair, yanking her backward. Elsa's arm reached out of the smoke with leonine grace. She threw the guard back into the fray. A few guards approached from the front. Anthony and Seamus fought back to back making their way closer to where Ian lay.

With herculean effort, Cordelia took Ian's gun. "Elsa, protect him." She moved in front of Ian and Elsa. "Pumpkin on a post," she muttered. Two of the attackers dropped.

Anthony creeped up the wall beside her. "You're a natural. Can you walk? Because I think Elsa will have to carry Ian."

She nodded. *Fuck.*

"Good, Seamus will take the rear while you and I clear a path. You can do this."

“Damn straight,” she hissed through clenched teeth. Ignoring the pain and twitches, she focused on the obstacles in front of her.

“Okay, we’re firing Ruger P90s. We have twenty-five-round magazines. If you hear a click you’re empty.” He draped Ian’s clip belt across her body. “Drop the clip like this.” He squeezed the clip release. “Pull a new one and slide it in.” He shoved the magazine back in with a clip. “Got it?”

“Yep.” She let him take the lead and lurched up the corridor one leaden step at a time. She ignored the screaming nerves in her legs, instead honing her focus on the space just beyond Anthony. Elsa moved behind her carrying Ian and Seamus brought up the rear.

CHAPTER THIRTY-ONE

Sebastian followed Andre through the complex. Thomas brought up the rear with Niko. Tension roiled in the pit of his stomach. The thought of Cordelia caused his knuckles to crackle with the threat of shifting. His own pain with its chain reaction loomed freshly in his mind. *Cordelia suffering, possibly dead.* He couldn't think about it. She had to be strong enough.

Sounds of the other team's incursion floated up the stairwell as Andre continued to enter codes into keypads leading them closer to their target. Small charges began blowing at regular intervals. The lights were extinguished, and the intermittent flash of emergency strobes lit the way.

Andre put his hand up. "This is where things get dicey. The hallway is guarded. Two men in Kevlar, armed with nine-millimeter carbine modified Glock twenty-sixes. I don't know if they're loading armor-piercing rounds."

Thomas whistled. "Bugger." He thought a moment. "Andre, you and Niko hang back. Sebastian, I have a drill in my pack. We could take them out through the door."

"Only if they're positioned perfectly." He closed his eyes. "Feeling fast today?"

Thomas sighed. "No problem. You drop the door; I'll double up."

Niko leaned in. "If you can drop the door, I can take one."

Sebastian tapped Niko's armored vest. "If they're piercing rounds this won't do you a bit of good."

"I won't miss."

Sebastian nodded. "On three the door will come down; start firing before it hits the floor."

Andre faded back at Thomas's signal. Niko and Thomas took positions to either side of Sebastian. Slinging his weapon, Sebastian braced his feet in a wide stance. He lifted his hand. One. Two. He thrust his foot into the middle of the door. The slab flew forward, at the same time Thomas and Niko took aim, firing through the dust. The guards, agog at the collapse of the heavy door, took a minute to regroup. Niko hit his target in the shoulder. The guard dropped to his knees, gun dangling. A second shot to the head ended him.

Thomas hit his target in the leg, but the guard managed to keep his weapon and return fire. A bullet whizzed past Sebastian, who rushed the hallway. A second round nicked Thomas in the ear. "That's bloody it." He dropped the guard with his second shot. The hallway fell silent except for the sounds of skirmishes from the lower floors. Thomas turned to motion Andre up and saw the young man holding his arm. "You're hit." He strode over to take a closer look.

With a glance, Niko moved up to cover Sebastian.

"It's not bad. Just hurts." Andre gritted his teeth.

"Yeah well, you've been shot. That's how it works." Thomas suppressed a grin. He moved the man's hand. "Not bad, through and through." He pulled a pressure bandage from one of his pouches and wrapped the wound. Andre grunted a bit. "You'll live. Let's move."

They entered the hallway following Sebastian and Niko. Sebastian looked at Andre.

"At the end of the hall." He pointed with his good arm.

Sebastian nodded, and the trio made their way to Vivienne Carlson's office.

Unlocked, they opened the door without effort. Sebastian entered, leading with his weapon. The others stopped short of him.

Vivienne sat composed at her desk—-no guards, no apparent weapons visible. She smiled. "Welcome."

Sebastian held back a snarl. "Dr. Carlson."

She tipped her head. Raising her hands to show them empty, she rose to step around the desk. Rather than approach closer, she leaned back and folded her arms. "I've been waiting for you."

"Here I am." Sebastian narrowed his eyes.

She smiled again. "My curiosity is piqued. Did you find the woman?"

A growl rose deep in Sebastian's throat.

Thomas moved forward a step. "What've you done?"

Vivienne gave him a brief glance. "Merely made some needed improvements."

Thomas raised his weapon, but Sebastian's hand held him.

"You control your dogs." The approval in her tone ground Sebastian's teeth.

"Better than you do." He nodded toward Andre without breaking eye contact.

Vivienne blanched just a little, then composed her face. "Andre moja draga, bomo pustil to mimo." *My darling, we'll let this pass.*

Andre's face hardened. "No, we won't."

She gazed at her foundling. "Ah, vsi mladiči zapustijo gnezdo." *All fledglings leave the nest.*

"How wishfully she looks on all she's leaving, now no longer hers." He lifted his chin.

She tsked. "Back to Blake?"

"Ti ni me prekinil." *You failed to break me.*

"I don't often fail." She looked at him with a touch of pride.

Sebastian stepped between them. "It's becoming a habit."

She approached him. "Oh no, you're my crowning achievement. Proof the mortal grossness of man can be surpassed. Remember your question, who decides?" She reached out to touch him. "I decided when I first saw you. Look at you. Powerful, healthy, all aging processes slowed. A brave new world."

"You're sounding a lot like Hans Kahler, or should I say Arthur Carlson?"

Her eyes narrowed, twisting her features. "Never. He was a doddering fool looking for answers in pseudoscience. Where he stumbled, I've flown on wings. Look at my work, you're perfect."

Sebastian contained his inner storm building to a tempest. "You didn't fly. You blundered, Vivienne. You tripped over your grandfather's last experiment."

Confusion filled her eyes, then denial, the belief in her own superiority secure.

"In the '60s, your grandfather worked with MI6 and the CIA. He developed a vaccine against bio-weapons. A vaccine that would improve the immune system and prevent infection. Sound familiar? A group of field agents volunteered as test subjects. No one suffered any permanent effects, but the results were inconclusive."

"Your fairy tale means nothing to me." She straightened her spine.

He strolled to the window to look out at the carnage flowing out of the building. Smoke billowed out along with people. He turned to look at her. "It took some time, and he burned to death in a fire before the proof of his work became evident." He knew the trail of bodies she'd left behind her. "In Afghanistan, his immunization against biotoxins proved invaluable." He watched her fit pieces of the puzzle together. Pieces she never thought related gained meaning.

"That mission suffered a one hundred percent casualty rate," she said. Sebastian could see her holding onto the last shred of doubt.

Thomas moved forward. "Not exactly. You see we didn't figure it out until you sent your new project against Sebastian, but once we had the DNA samples it all fell into place."

Vivienne looked at Thomas. "You were on that mission."

Thomas nodded, but Sebastian spoke it out loud. "Yes, we were. We watched our friends die. Some of them right then and others, well, they took a little longer. Thomas and I, we lived. We didn't know why, but we've figured it out. My father received Arthur Carlson's vaccine. We all survived the biotoxin exposure with zero effects. Your grandfather's research saved our lives."

Vivienne grabbed onto the edge of the desk. "You carried the antibody and the dormant bacteria. That's what enabled the gene sequencing. His vaccine interacted with my DNA vectors."

Sebastian controlled the building rage.

Vivienne drew herself up. "Don't you see, Sebastian. We've done it. We've solved humanity's debility. It isn't eugenics. It's real science. Breakthrough science. We can improve the human race." She looked triumphant.

"Only one problem, Vivienne. You don't know what you've created." Sebastian let his wrath simmer near the surface. "You haven't improved humanity. You've eliminated it."

"Just look at you, Sebastian. You're superb. Together we can change the world." Her eyes glowed with admiration and desire. He watched her vision manifesting before her eyes.

"You've changed me, Vivienne. That's true, but your influence on the world ends here."

"Think about what you're saying. Think about who you are. You're destined to be more. I knew the minute I met you."

Sebastian's vision blurred crimson. He felt his irises shifting. The pith of his rage boiled on the surface of his brain. His words felt awkward as the structure of his jaw elongated. "You have no idea what I am."

Thomas gestured the other two men back. Sebastian registered his friend's grim approval as he grew to fill the space of the room.

Vivienne shrank back in horror as he expanded his shifting form—hands lengthening to claws, legs growing into powerful haunches his skull taking on the aquiline lines of vicious jaws. The jet onyx of his hair spread from scalp to limbs. Remnants of clothing shredded to the floor. Chest and ribs spread to support the heavy musculature of a beast. Neither man nor animal, Sebastian loomed above seven feet. His heavy breathing reverberated through the room. Stripped of the man, naked of form and soul, he stood transfigured. Beyond the humiliation, he stood full figure, engorged testicles and cock exposed. He towered over her diminutive form.

Vivienne's keen fear was sharp in his nose. Unable to speak, his eyes transmitted her failure. He drilled into her the truth of what she'd done. He looked at her with the same disdain and scorn with which she viewed her grandfather. He waited until the realization bloomed.

"Sebastian," she scrambled. "I can fix this. We can go back. I would never have this happen to you."

He lifted his lips in a loud snarl.

She paused at the sight of his scimitar canine, then began to babble. "We can test the DNA. We can work with Ian."

Sebastian felt no grace for her. He thought of his friends, both dead and changed. He thought of Cordelia. *Dead or alive.* He wondered which would be better. The thought burst the dam on his rage.

Vivienne saw it in his eyes. As she moved back behind the desk she reached her hand to him. "Sebastian—"

Leaping forward with a thunderous roar, he stretched his powerful arm. Extending scimitar claws from the ends of his fingers, he separated her head from her body with one graceful swipe.

CHAPTER THIRTY-TWO

Sebastian's chest heaved with rage. Looking at Vivienne Carlson's head brought no relief of the bitter anger inside of him. He moved his ebony-pelted bulk away from his butchery.

"Sebastian," Thomas said quietly. "We need to clear out."

Niko pulled some clothing from his pack. "I thought you'd need these."

Glancing at the offering, the creature closed his onyx eyes. He drew deep hissing breaths into and out of his lungs. Quieting his mind, he allowed his fury to soften. Contracting and pulling in on himself, he diminished in size. By degrees, the savage faded, returning dominion to the man.

Niko carefully moved forward and extended the garb.

Taking them gingerly, Sebastian said, "Hvala, moj prijatelj." *Thanks my friend.*

"Prijatelja spoznaš v nesreči," the gypsy said grinning. *A friend is known in adversity like gold is known in fire.*

Sebastian chuckled, rolling his eyes. Pulling the pants on, he looked to Andre. "You okay?"

"There is no restraint from the greatest of all restraints on imaginative living," Andre said, his voice weak.

"William Blake." Thomas chortled.

Drawing the shirt over his head, Sebastian grimaced. "A bit too romantic for a monstrosity."

Andre cleared his throat. "No, you misunderstand. What you become can't be contained by reason or rationale. It's existence beyond the imaginable."

Niko stepped back to clap him on the shoulder. "And that, nephew, is the point. The blessing in this is Sebastian is a better man than this consummation of science without conscience."

Sebastian snorted. "All human beings are commingled with good and evil. You give me too much credit."

"Vsak je svoje srečе kovač." Niko returned. *Every man is the smith of his own fortune.*

"Blimey, enough proverbs. Let's get out of here," Thomas said. "We're going to have Interpol all over us." He looked at the carnage. "What're we going to do with her?"

Sebastian didn't glance back. "Burn the place down."

****

Cordelia sat in the open back of one of the Rovers watching the flux of people and smoke drift out of the building. Confusion reigned as the police arrived backed up by military personnel. Seamus shifted back prior to their exit from the wreckage. Dressed in a black shirt and khakis, he stood speaking to the police commander near their vehicles. Officers and military units tried to round up the lab staff that tumbled out of the gaping doors. People coughed from smoke inhalation and raved about monsters.

Ian lay on a gurney at the rear of a van parked next to the Rover where Cordelia sat. Anthony directed the two Slovenian medics hovering over both Ian and her. He tried to insist Cordelia lay on a gurney as well but retreated at the dark, hollow look she'd given him. A medic handed her a steaming cup of chocolate, thick and richly bitter. Each time she took a sip, she closed her eyes to the sensuousness.

Ian chuckled. "Enjoying that?"

"Mmmm." She tugged a bit at the IV in her arm. The awareness of the tubing sent shivers through her as she fought memories. Ian had insisted and Anthony backed him up. She didn't win that one. Another point she lost was morphine. After the adrenaline rush getting out of the lab, she couldn't stand from the aftershocks and twinges of nerves. Ian instructed the medics to set her up with a morphine pump. She agreed with reluctance, but she pushed it once when a tremor in her hands caused her to drop the first mug. She scanned the crowd once more.

"He's fine," Ian said. "Thomas checked in. They're taking a last sweep of Carlson's office to be sure we have everything before we turn this over to the police."

Cordelia nodded. "I know." She squinted through the smoke.

Others are good. I like chocolate.

Elsa, ensconced out of sight in the van behind Ian, drank her own cup of chocolate. Ian refused to let the authorities get a glimpse of the creature.

Cordelia responded. "I like the chocolate too. They're good men."

Not man. Others. Man in white coat good.

Cordelia understood Elsa made a distinction between Seamus and Ian. "Yes, Ian is a very good man."

Others come.

Cordelia sat up and stared toward the door. She saw him. The smoke couldn't hide his fluid movement. Her breath shortened and she drilled her thoughts at him. She willed him to come. He'd experienced her pain. The feelings of gravity she'd felt in his kitchen had become vast, the moon drawn to earth's pull. Police approached him. Seamus made his way toward the group. She pushed a tangible thread drifting across the void reaching out to Sebastian.

The men, including Thomas and two men Cordelia didn't recognize, stood in a conference while she ground her teeth.

"Breathe, Cordelia, you need to breathe." Ian's words jerked her back into her body. The monitor set up to the pulse cuff on her finger skittered and beeped.

She drew in a taste of oxygen and sighed it out. Her pulse slowed. "Got it. Breathing."

"Cordelia—" Ian started, but she put her hand up.

"I got it. I'm okay." She watched the caucus waiting for Thomas and Sebastian to break away. *Goddamn it.*

Seamus broke off first talking on his phone and headed their way.

"Finally," Anthony said. He started giving orders in Slovenian. Another van pulled up and the medics readied Ian's gurney.

Cordelia felt dazed. She hadn't spoken to Sebastian. He hadn't even looked her way.

Seamus reached them. "We're clearing out. The Slovenian government is on their way to do some damage control and we have to get you and Elsa out of here."

"Isn't Sebastian coming?" Cordelia realized she sounded sunken. As if hearing his name, he turned to meet her eyes. Relief flooded her. He would come put his hands on her shoulders, comfort her, and get her out of here. Electricity passed between them. The hairs on her arms crackled to attention. She held her breath.

Sebastian held her gaze for a moment then turned away to confer with a new group of officials.

The breath left her body. She heard Anthony giving orders. Seamus took her elbow and led her into the passenger seat of the Rover making room for the equipment attached to her. Things moved around her in slow motion.

"Cordelia?" Seamus sat in the driver's seat. He asked her a question.

She pulled the rags of her soul together. "Sorry, what?"

"You asked about Lorena."

Cordelia looked at him then realized she'd whispered Lorena's name. He'll fuck it up. "Yeah, I did."

"Sebastian didn't think I should tell you, but you want to know, right?"

"Right." Sebastian's thoughts didn't interest her any longer. Anthony mentioned bulletproof. Cordelia hoped.

Seamus didn't soften his words. "She didn't make it."

Cordelia dropped her head into her hands. The sobbing didn't stop until Seamus pulled onto the tarmac at the airstrip. He'd had sense enough not to say a word for the entire drive. She looked around to see Ian being loaded onto the same jet she had flown on into England. *When? Only days ago?* She felt years older. She scanned the field.

"Sebastian and Thomas are arranging Elsa's transportation. Ian wants her at the estate. They'll need some extra time and the cover of dark to get her out of the country," Seamus told her. "We'll meet her in England."

"That's good. She'll like the estate." She let him hold her elbow. She felt wobbly, either from the drugs, the pain, or the other, it didn't matter. "Seamus?"

"Yeah?"

"I'd like to go home."

Seamus nodded. He saw Sebastian at the compound. "I know, England first. Get cleaned up and shipshape, and then I'll get you home."

She nodded. "I would love a shower."

"Already arranged." Seamus helped her into the jet.

He sat her near Ian and left to get his equipment and pack.

"We'll get you into the lab at the estate and run a full panel of tests. Most of your injuries are from the car crash, but we'll patch you up." He smiled at her from his gurney. "Lindsay's already planned a fabulous meal and a hot bath for us when we arrive."

Cordelia sighed. "You gotta love that man."

Ian smiled. "I do, believe me, I do."

CHAPTER THIRTY-THREE

Cordelia sat in a wheelchair in Global Sureties' London hangar watching Sebastian's people unload the plane. Wrapped in a blanket and still attached to an IV drip, she waited for the ambulance Ian ordered to take her to the estate. Elsa squatted next to her. Cordelia could feel her interest in the process.

Elsa fly.

The simian's excitement shone in Cordelia's mind yellow and orange. *You did. You'll like the estate. There's a huge garden.* Cordelia felt an unusual tickle in her thoughts.

Animals too.

Cordelia got the impression Elsa had combed through her memories. Cordelia's initial excitement was tempered by concern. *This is why people worry I'm reading their minds.*

Cordelia is angry with Elsa?

"Shit," she said aloud. *No, absolutely not. This is new for me. I'll need to get used to it. You understand?*

Like Elsa will get used to the barn.

Cordelia nodded. *Exactly.* She started shivering.

Cordelia is not well.

"You're right," the woman said out loud. A low throb grew in her head and her stomach roiled. "Elsa, can you find Ian? You remember Ian?"

The smiling white coat.

Her increased shivering eliminated the brief amazement she felt at Elsa's grasp on things. *Please.*

For a large creature, Elsa moved quickly. Before her vision started to blur Cordelia had a moment of tickling sensation—Elsa feeling out with her mind to find Ian.

Cordelia's body tremors deepened and while it took only a couple of minutes, the agony of waiting felt longer. Elsa returned leading a worried Ian by the hand.

"Cordelia?" Ian asked, taking her pulse. "Can you hear me?"

She managed a weak nod. Teeth chattering, Cordelia struggled to talk. "Don't feel too good."

Ian placed his hand on her forehead. "Your fever's spiked." He dug into his medical bag. "I'm going to administer an antibiotic and an additional antipyretic." Ian injected the medication into the IV port. He looked around frantic. Waving one of the Global Sureties men down, he shouted, "Taylor! Find Sebastian and Thomas. We've got to get Cordelia to a hospital, and find out where my bloody ambulance is!"

Taylor sprinted off.

"Cordelia, you have to hold on. I'm going to get you help." He grasped her hand.

The ambulance came to a stop at the hangar doors and two paramedics stepped out. Ian yelled, "Emergency, you barmy gits!"

Cordelia's vision started to tunnel. Before going completely black, she saw Sebastian racing the EMTs in her direction.

****

The ICU monitor glowed next to the bed. Heart rate, arterial pressure, and oxygen levels jogged up and down creating a mountain range of Cordelia's vital signs. The waxing light of predawn peeped through the heavy drapes drawn across the windows facing the garden. Leaning in the doorway, Sebastian thought about the last time he'd been in this room with Cordelia. He heaved a sigh.

His exhale roused the older woman dozing in the chair next to the bed. She stretched her arms and shifted her comfortable bulk. Lucia Fiore rubbed her eyes and then pinned him with her gaze. "Your exhaustion isn't going to improve her condition." Her tone mixed admonishment and concern.

Sebastian puffed his breath out. "Never been able to sleep much when someone on my team is down."

"Team, huh?" Lucia grunted softly. "Okay, if that's how you're calling it. Your brother said her fever is down. He might try to bring her out today." She reached out to stroke Cordelia's hand. "You know, I sat like this with her mother." She looked around. "Course, this place is much nicer than Vancouver General. Food's better too."

"Where's Mr. Fiore?" Sebastian asked.

Lucia leaned back and reached her arms overhead. "He's sleeping. This is hard for him. Too many memories fanning his fear."

"I'm sorry," he offered, knowing it meant nothing.

"Oh shoosh." Lucia waved her hand at him. "You've nothing to do with this. The way I figure, you took care of the woman responsible."

"Good morning, love." Lindsay stepped into the suite followed by Reynolds bearing a tray of tea. He nodded to Sebastian. "Morning. We've brought Lucia some breakfast."

The older woman heaved her weight out of the chair. She reached up to pat Sebastian's shoulder as she passed. "I've got a good feeling."

He didn't reply. Shifting his gaze from Cordelia to the monitors, he could only smell the medication Ian used to induce her coma. The absence of her scent pricked him. The sounds of dishes and cups drifted behind him.

"Don't be stingy with the cream, young man," Lucia said.

"No, ma'am," Reynolds responded.

Sebastian turned to see Lindsay sit across the little table from Lucia. Reynolds, unflappable as always, served with aplomb.

"Some tomatoes, Lucia?" Lindsay asked.

Lucia smeared a piece of toast with jam. "Oh yes, you know I worried about the food here, but it's delicious."

Lindsay chuckled. "Thank you, I consider it a great compliment coming from you." Lindsay looked up at Sebastian. "Join us, old chap?"

"Not hungry, Linds. Thanks." Sebastian started to leave.

"Sebastian." Lucia's voice stopped him. "Sleep and food. I'm telling you, I've got a good feeling."

Continuing on his way, he didn't look back. He heard Lucia tell Lindsay, "That man is bound up tighter than a fourteen-year-old's testicles."

The sound of Lindsay choking didn't help Sebastian suppress his own chuckle. *Cordelia's nonna isn't short on pluck.*

****

Cordelia walked with care through the gardens. She managed to escape both her father and grandmother. Ian and Lindsay had gone to London to arrange for supplies to be delivered to the estate lab. She had no clue where Seamus or Anthony had disappeared, but it didn't matter. Her sanity teetered on a narrow edge. A week in a medically induced coma aside, three days awake surrounded by hovering well wishers and an extremely anxious physician had her ready to scream.

She begged a nap and decamped through her French doors to the gardens at the first moment of solitude. She drew in a deep breath of soggy air. The overcast gloom didn't bother her a bit. Her joints felt loose and achy, but the increased blood flow to her limbs improved her disposition. Her surprise to see her family upon opening her eyes increased to shock when she discovered the Coles revealed the entire truth to them. *No secrets left now.*

Sebastian had been the only conspicuous absence. Her grandmother assured her the impassive Englishman had spent many sleepless nights watching Cordelia unconscious. *Not sure what I'm supposed to think about that.* She broke off a twig of rosemary and brushed it under her nose. The fever and the coma left her brain feeling stuffed with cotton. Not only couldn't she sense the hum that had grown familiar the last few weeks, but she couldn't detect anything or anyone outside of her normal physical senses.

Ian assured her it would clear over time. For the first time she could remember she was like everyone else. It irritated her to no end. *I didn't realize how much I used my talent.* She felt blinded somehow. It set her on edge. Additionally, she dealt with sorrow at the loss of Lorena. So many people dead because of Vivienne Carlson. Growing tired, she turned back and took a pause on a bench overlooking a koi pond. *I hope it doesn't start raining.* Leaning back a bit, she folded her arms across her belly and shut her eyes.

"Ian's looking all over for you." Sebastian's voice broke her moment of quiet. "And your grandmother is rampaging through the house. Even Reynolds is keeping his head down."

She forced her eyes to remain closed. "If I could've made a break for the airport, I would've. As it is, this is as far as I got."

"You know, you just woke up from a coma." His dry tone pricked her frustration.

"Give the man a prize." She opened her eyes. "You can tell them I'm fine and I'll be back after I've sat a bit."

His eyebrow rose a hair. "You mean when you've gathered enough strength to get back."

Goddamn that eyebrow. "I'm surprised you're even here," she snapped.

"I knew where you were," he said, shrugging. He made no move to leave.

Cordelia leaned on an elbow. "You're going to stand there and watch me?"

"I'm going to wait until you've rested and make sure you don't crash and burn on the way back to the house." He moved to lean against an ash tree. "I've got time."

"Time for me now, but not the last three days." She shook her head. *Childish, Cordelia, hitting low.*

Sebastian didn't respond right away. "I've been thinking about what to say."

Well fuck, now I have to be civil? "And?" she asked, keeping her voice neutral.

"You throw me off balance, Cordelia." He locked eyes with her. "You have since the moment I laid eyes on you." He paced back and forth. "I can't keep my people safe if I'm not thinking straight. When I'm around you, I don't feel …"

"You don't feel what?" she asked.

"In control," he said flatly. "Look what happened." He pointed to her.

She sat quiet for a moment, too many thoughts bouncing around in her woozy brain. Cordelia stood up. "You have an overdeveloped sense of heroics." She advanced on him jabbing her finger for effect. "I'm alive because you and your team acted quickly. Vivienne Carlson is the only person responsible for what happened to me and I can't deal with her because you already have." Close enough to poke him, she did, hard in the chest. "You've pushed me away claiming to be a monster. You hide from me claiming not to have the right words and you think isolating me will restore your self-possession. You're an idiot." She turned on her heel and marched toward the house. She shouted in no particular direction, "Control is an illusion. We have choices and reactions. You hope I'll buy your 'I can't be a soldier with you' bullshit?" She threw her hands up in the air. "You want to hear bullshit? I told Vivienne Carlson you'd never come for her and you know what? I was wrong; you did."

She heard him walking behind her. He said, "You understand I had to? For my men, for Lorena, and even for you?"

Within sight of her patio, she whirled around. "Oh for fuck's sake, of course I understand. I'm not a child. I didn't need you to come crashing in to rescue me. I did need you for just a minute outside of the lab. Just a minute to show me you knew what I'd suffered. I'd have taken a goddamned pat on the back! But you cut me out, sent me off without a word all for your precious control." She snorted at the stunned look on his face. "Here's a shocker: you were never in control. You've been running after Vivienne Carlson since Afghanistan. Now? Now you're just hiding." She took a breath. "Sebastian, my head hurts. I ache all over and when it's all said and done I've no idea what's going to happen to me. I do know one thing: I'm not in control and I don't need to be."

"Cordelia—" he said, but she cut him off.

"I'm going home, Sebastian. I'm going to get back to my life and if you ever decide you're okay with off balance, you know where to find me. For now, bugger off." She whipped around on the patio and caught her toe on a stone. Pitching forward, she fell to her hands and knees. "Goddamn it!"

Sebastian moved in a blur to help her up, but she pushed his hands away. "Don't."

Ian burst out of her room. "Bloody hell, Cordelia, you've given me a heart attack." He took her arms and helped her up. "Shite, Sebastian, you couldn't help?"

Cordelia snorted and glanced at Ian's brother to see him turn silently and walk away.

CHAPTER THIRTY-FOUR

Two weeks after her arrival at the Cole estate, Cordelia stood at Swaffham Airfield for the last time. Seamus leaned against the car, his arms folded with disapproval. "Are you certain this is what you should be doing?"

With a regretful turn of her lips, Cordelia reached out and patted his arm. "Seamus, I have a life to figure out."

Enzo held his hand out to Seamus. "Thanks, my boy."

Cordelia thought Seamus's eyes glistened as he shook her father's hand. "Any time, Mr. Fiore."

Her father took his bag and approached the jet. Letting one of the flight crew take his bag, he climbed the stairs to the cabin. "Hurry up, Mama," he called back.

Lucia Fiore stood next to Cordelia. She clasped the redhead in a tight hug. Her head barely at Seamus's chest, her arms couldn't close on his bulk. "You come and see me, Seamus. I'll make you a feast."

"Yes, ma'am, I will." He hugged the old woman and placed his chin on top of her head.

Cordelia's grandmother made her way to the plane and allowed the crewman to help her into the cabin.

An ebony sedan raced to a stop behind Seamus's forest-green Mercedes. Rachna flew out of the passenger side. Ian, a hair's breadth behind her, leaped from the driver's seat. The beautiful woman's face creased with worry, and her eyes threatened tears. "Cordelia, you can't go like this." Rachna clasped Cordelia's hands. "Nothing's happening the way I thought it would. I thought he'd come to his senses."

Ian stood behind Rachna, his face painted with frustration. "That would require he have sense to begin with."

"I'm okay. I have to get back to Vancouver." Cordelia removed one of her hands from Rachna's tight grip and put it on Ian's shoulder. "We'll be in touch." She turned to hug Rachna.

Rachna gave her a squeeze. "I'll call once a week."

Cordelia closed her eyes, a trick she learned as a child. She worried it might not work given her foggy brain. She let a trickle of thought touch her friend. Smiling, Cordelia leaned close to whisper in her ear. "Liam. Liam's a good name for a boy."

Rachna gasped, releasing Cordelia in her surprise.

Ian gave instructions. "You have Dr. Preston's number in Vancouver. He's a trusted colleague and I've sent him your file. He'll send me copies of your tests and blood work."

"Yes, yes. Lindsay already added appointments to my calendar. I'm fine. You said so yourself." Cordelia smiled.

He hugged her. "My brother's a blooming idiot."

"I'm not arguing."

She signaled Seamus, who grabbed the two leather satchels Lindsay had given her. He helped her pack the things purchased to replace those lost in the accident. With Seamus leading the way, Cordelia strode toward the Gulfstream. One of the crew took her bags. Seamus turned to face Cordelia. She saw in his face the things he wanted to say but couldn't. She nodded her understanding. *Comrades in arms.*

Seamus hugged her with crushing force and with one last look left her to board the plane.

Cordelia couldn't look back for fear of losing her resolve. She made her way up the stairs and ducked into the cabin. Dropping her shoulder bag on the floor, she sank into a plush seat near a window.

"I'll be glad to get back to the shop," her father said.

She felt the tears building up in her eyes and steeled herself to look at the airfield.

"You need a good hearty meal and a night in your own bed," her grandmother advised. "And I miss my kitchen."

Rachna and Ian stood side by side watching the plane as it began to taxi toward the runway. Seamus got into his car and pulled off in the opposite direction. The rich, green English countryside slid past as the plane taxied into position. The small private runway paralleled the road.

"You know, cara mia, all men have their faults," her grandmother said. "Even your father."

Enzo clucked. "Hey!"

Nonna pointed her finger at her granddaughter. "Listen. It's the way God made them. Brought up from the clay, what can you expect?"

"There's nothing about God in what happened to Sebastian."

Nonna shook her head. "Everything contains a spark of the divine. Sebastian's papa given a vaccine that would save Sebastian's life, not once, but twice. You have a gift that saved his life. That doesn't just happen, bebe. It's design."

Cordelia leaned across the aisle and kissed her nonna on the forehead. "Someone should sue the engineer."

"Damn right," her father agreed, settling back into his seat. "I hate takeoffs."

Roads always surprised her. She never knew which way they would take her. She craned her head to look further along the paved lane. In the brief moments it took the pilot to run up the engines to full throttle for takeoff, Cordelia saw him.

Sebastian stepped out of the car, one foot propped on the doorsill, hands on the frame. Her breath caught. Without warning the plane leaped forward and Sebastian disappeared, left behind in the swirling vortices curling off of the wings.

She leaned back into her seat and closed her dry eyes. Reaching out with her mind through the growing space, she focused her second sight on his presence to feel nothing. She opened her eyes with a sigh and watched the clouds as the plane carried her home.

Upon her return, Cordelia received a large manila envelope. Her cousin Adrianna delivered it after picking up the mail. "You gonna open it?"

"Sure." She slid her finger through the flap. "Holy shit." She stared at the paperwork in her hands.

Adrianna picked up a piece of paper that had slid to the floor. "This is a check. For a lot of money."

"Ms. Fiore, we are pleased to inform you the auctions you facilitated were completed prior to the seizure of Senator Jeffery Matthews' assets. Enclosed to complete your contract is your fee. Fifteen percent of the final sale prices as negotiated," Cordelia read aloud.

"This is seven hundred and fifty thousand dollars, Cordelia." Adrianna repeated the number in a whisper and then asked, "What're you going to do with all of this money?"

Cordelia thought a minute, suspicious of Sebastian's involvement in her windfall. "I'm going to get a dog."

Her cousin grinned at her. "You're insane."

After Adrianna left, Cordelia felt more upbeat. Buoyed by the fact she didn't have to work for a while, she unpacked her bags. She thought of Sebastian standing outside of the airfield watching her plane depart. *He couldn't have come five minutes sooner?* "You know what?" She spoke to her empty apartment. "He needs to figure it out and I'm not moping around." *Why is there a hollow feeling under your ribs?* her imp asked.

Ignoring her emails and phone messages, Cordelia opened a bottle of Toad's Hallow Merlot. Her grandmother had sent dinner up, somehow knowing Cordelia preferred solitude. It took some time to adjust to being home, but she ate a little, drank a lot, and collapsed into her bed.

She woke up in the morning with the feeling she dreamt it all. She caught sight of her shoulder in the mirror and the scars skipping haphazardly across the surface of her shoulder blade anchored her in reality. *No dream.* She brushed her fingers across the raised scar at the base of her neck while washing her hair and the weight of what happened pressed down on her.

After an Internet search, Cordelia made a few calls and drove two hours to Aldergrove. Love, at first sight. The wrinkled, roly-poly ball of fat and fur curled in her lap the entire ride home.

Enzo threw his hands up when he saw her carrying the puppy into the bookshop. "He's going to chew up the place!"

Her nonna cooed and crooned while ruffling the puppy's floppy ears. "Oh, what a face! I'm going to pinch those cheeks every day."

Cordelia had a kennel with cushions and a fleece blanket at the ready. She supplied the apartment with chew toys and a variety of squeaky toys and named the little bulldog Busto, short for sturdy in Italian. Busto ended up sleeping on the bed with her. She liked the company, even if the snoring rumbled.

Busto made himself a permanent feature in the shop. Whenever Cordelia left to run errands or to meet with Adrianna, Busto followed Enzo around the store. Nonna took to carrying a little bag full of tidbits from the kitchen. Busto discovered a little wag of his tail and a well-timed woof received a treat and a rub. The bulldog soon became a favorite with the university crowd. The steady stream of college students in the shop for books or coffee began to carry dog biscuits in hopes of sharing an easy chair with the wobbly brute while reading or drinking their coffee.

Busto couldn't run with her, but Cordelia enjoyed having him grumble in the corner over a new bone while she occasionally consulted from home. The apartment didn't feel quite as empty. Sometimes she caught herself checking her cell phone or looking at the land line in anticipation. *Who's not moping?* the imp in her head mocked.

As her head cleared, her psychic powers increased. She discovered a way to put up a screen preventing the constant overflow of people. If she didn't stay focused, she could easily slip into someone's mind and see with clarity. Often she would get a physical tingling in her fingers before something happened. *You're just imagining he's going to call,* her dark imp chided.

After dropping Busto off at the shop with Enzo before opening, Cordelia headed out for a long run with a plan to hit Jericho Beach. She almost felt back to full health and she itched to run outside. Starting off at the shop, she headed north out Westbrook Crescent and began the ten-mile run along North Marine Drive. She kept an even pace, strong and fleet as she covered the distance until she could break out onto the sand.

A bank of early morning fog clung to the trees along Burrard Inlet. Cordelia ran along the beach leaving swirling tendrils of mist in her wake. Turning up the volume on her iPod, the chords of AWOLNATION swept her along and powered her forward. The heat of exertion radiated from her center and spread out in waves, leaving her mind blank of everything besides the music and the movement.

As she swept back up the beach, the sun struggled to break through the fog. Cordelia slowed her pace to a walk and began her cool down before turning around for home. David Gray's music poured over her as she watched some gulls diving into the shallow surf for breakfast. She stretched her arms out, reaching for the sky as she released the last bits of tension. Lifting her foot onto a trunk of driftwood to tighten her laces, something tugged at the edge of her mind. She straightened and opened up her awareness to the energy around her and stiffened.

Without a second's pause, Cordelia turned and headed further east up the beach into a thick swath of fog toward the park. She pulled her earbuds out and left the chords dangling around her neck, pushing the tinny sounds of Dana Glover into the mix of surf, gulls, and silent fog. Slowing, she made out a looming shadow walking on the beach toward her. She clenched her fist into her stomach in an attempt to hold herself together. She closed her eyes and reached out with her mind. The tall shadow emerged from a gap in the fog and stopped a few feet from her. *Nope.*

Anthony Jackson took shape out of the mist. "Good run?"

"Yeah, I needed it." Snippets of his thoughts had reached her before his words did.

It must've showed on her face because he tapped his head. He asked, "It's stronger now?"

She nodded. "What happened?"

"We don't know. He stopped at the estate for a few days after visiting Thomas and Rachna. He booked a ticket for Vancouver. We thought …"

Cordelia unclenched her fists and pressed the heels of her hands into her eyes. *Just because he was coming here, nothing's changed.*

“This is bad. He’s not here.” Anthony touched her shoulder.

She looked up at him. “No.”

He put a finger up and flipped out his phone. “Lonzo, he’s not here. Uh huh, I’ve got her.”

“Let me guess, England?”

“Yeah.” He nodded.

“I’m taking my dog.”

Anthony threw his hands up.

Continued in ***The Esau Convergence***

###

www.ingramcontent.com/pod-product-compliance
Lightning Source LLC
Chambersburg PA
CBHW022036240626
47154CB00007B/2429

* 9 7 8 1 9 4 0 4 2 1 0 0 1 *